BOOK 3

BATTLE DRAGONS

CITY OF SECRETS

BOOK 3

BATTLE DRAGONS

CITY OF SECRETS

ALEX LONDON

SCHOLASTIC PRESS
NEW YORK

Library of Congress Cataloging-in-Publication Data available

ISBN 978-1-338-71669-6

1 2022

First edition, March 2023

Printed in the U.S.A.   23

Book design by Maeve Norton

FOR MADDIE, GROWING FASTER
THAN A BABY WYVERN

"THERE'S NO SAFE WAY TO LOSE
A DRAGON RODEO."

THE MOON HUNG OVER GLASSBLOWER'S Gulch like a polished meat hook, and the stars flecked around it like shimmering bloodstains . . . or something.

Abel wasn't much for metaphors.

Or was that a simile? The difference had something to do with if you used the words "like" and "as," he thought, but he couldn't quite remember which was which.

He wasn't much for the rules of literature and grammar and all that, and he'd never been great at focusing in school . . . or focusing anywhere else, really. Abel got distracted easily, especially when he was stressed out.

And he was currently very stressed out.

The school counselor had said it was a kind of attention disorder and anxiety condition—and also somehow related to puberty, which he didn't really want to talk to the school counselor about. But it didn't matter, because they weren't his school counselor anymore. He didn't have a school counselor anymore.

The school in the remote desert town of Glassblower's Gulch didn't have one. Or school supplies. Or even qualified teachers. His parents had tried to reassure him it might be good to have a change, though it seemed like they were trying to convince themselves of that too. None of them had actually chosen to move to Glassblower's Gulch. They'd been forced to move there by the government, so in that way, it wasn't a move but an exile, and it was kind of Abel's fault they'd had to move, because he'd raided an experimental dragon laboratory and he'd battled against the dragon-riding kins *and* the secret police and then he also—

Oops.

He was doing the thing again, getting distracted by his own thoughts.

He remembered enough grammar to know that was a run-on sentence in his brain, and he knew enough about himself to know that now was not the time for running on sentences. Now was the time for running like his life depended on it.

Because it did.

He was currently standing on the smooth glass desert above Glassblower's Gulch, looking down the throat of a very angry dragon.

That's why he was stressed.

It was a reasonable response.

The dragon's scales and skin were almost clear. Abel could see its jagged skeleton underneath, and its mouth made a sound like bones breaking. When it roared, it spat a single sharp spike from its throat, one as long as Abel's arm and sharper than the meat-hook moon hanging in the sky.

Meat-hook moon? Was that a metaphor? he wondered as he dove out of the way. The spike embedded itself six inches deep in the solid-glass ground. Cracks spiderwebbed the surface around it.

Cracked desert glass wasn't a spiderweb, and a ten-ton wild dragon wasn't a spider, even though Abel certainly felt like a fly caught in its trap.

Like a fly! That's a simile! I got it!

"Focus, Abel!" he told himself as he rolled across the ground, still thinking about metaphors and similes and his own impending doom. Until his foot bumped into another spike from an earlier attack that he'd just barely dodged.

The crowd cheered.

This was the dragon rodeo, a brutal sport. Either the human won and captured the dragon or the dragon won and flew off with the human. But neither of them could go down without a fight.

Abel definitely wouldn't.

As the Bone Reaper charged at him, its crackling roar signaled another spike was on the way. Abel kicked the one he'd bumped free from the ground and hefted it like a spear.

With all his strength—which, to be honest, wasn't much; he wished he'd done some of those at-home workouts he used to mock his older brother for—he hurled the spike straight into the dragon's wide-open mouth. The Bone Reaper recoiled, coughing.

Sorry, pal, Abel thought. *I hate to hurt you, but I'd hate to die even more.*

The crowd cheered again.

They'd come for human-versus-dragon drama. Abel knew he had to put on a show, give them action and tension and sudden reversals. He had to sell his performance tonight.

Then, against all his competitive instincts and the basic human desire not to throw yourself into a dragon's claws, he had to lose.

The Bone Reaper snapped at him. He fell backward, waving his arms for relief, as the rules allowed him to do.

On cue, three colorfully dressed Dragon Distraction Divas sprinted from the safety of their dugout. They flapped their silk costume wings at the dragon, twirling and dancing in a glittery display that was supposed to calm and distract the enraged rodeo dragon and slow the fight down.

A dragon rodeo wasn't meant to end quickly. It had to *drag on*, as the saying went, so that people had time to place bets and change bets and buy more overpriced snacks from the concession stands. Also, there was nothing else to do at night in Glassblower's Gulch, so the sheriff liked it when the rodeos went long. It kept folks from getting into other sorts of mischief.

As for the Divas, dragon distracting was a risky job. Dressing up like a half human, half dragon and dancing in the middle of someone else's rodeo wrangle took guts as well as makeup. The Divas always got big cheers from the audience. They also got their pictures on playing cards after they retired or were eaten, both of which tended to happen early in their careers. The Divas were all young, because dragon distracting wasn't a job someone could grow old doing.

The three Divas dancing for the Bone Reaper right now were working hard. The center one spun pirouettes in a neon gown beneath a giant mirrored helmet of bedazzled dragon horns. The Divas on either side did their best twirls and pliés, though they looked more terrified than graceful. One kept tripping over their own costume tail. The puzzled dragon cocked its huge head at them.

Just like Abel, this *was* the Bone Reaper's first rodeo.

Abel used his opponent's moment of confusion to scramble to his feet again.

He looked at the crowd spread out across the colorful glass slope above the arena, trying to find his parents' faces—or anyone friendly at all—but it was too big an audience. The only face he could see clearly was the sheriff's, with her short shock of green hair and her dark green uniform. She had her arms folded across her chest, like she was bored of this match and wanted it to be over and done with.

Abel knew she wanted *him* over and done with too. He saw one of her deputies across the way pull a yellow glass perfume spray bottle from his utility belt, hiding it from sight in his big, hairy hands. He must have thought no one was watching him, distracted as they were by the Divas.

The deputy spritzed the air with a burst of bright orange perfume, which quickly disappeared in the breeze.

"Here we go," Abel whispered to himself. He turned to face the Bone Reaper again. The Divas retreated to safety. The center Diva caught his eye and winked for luck.

The huge skeletal dragon lowered its head and sniffed, sucking in the faintest whiff of the perfume. Its eyes widened, and it scratched three sizzling-hot grooves in the glass with one swipe of its claw.

The dragon roared and rushed him. Abel crouched, signaling that he was going to try to dodge or jump onto its back—moves the dragon would surely expect. He had to let it get close enough to smell him.

He hoped that'd be enough. He hoped the dragon would understand. He hoped to lose the rodeo without getting eaten.

Abel had a lot riding on hope.

Sweat ran down his forehead, stinging his eyes. He brushed the hair off his face, ignored the roaring crowd, and focused on the roaring dragon. He readied himself to leap and to go as limp as an unplugged charging cable the moment the dragon swatted him away.

Hey! he cheered himself. *That's a simile! I've figured it out!*

His relief was short-lived, because he also figured his odds of survival were about one in three. Then again, he was even worse at math than he was at grammar.

As the dragon lunged, Abel jumped and saw the big front claw rising to knock him out of the air.

He squeezed his eyes shut, bracing for the brutal impact. He wondered how he always managed to get into trouble with dragons no matter where he went, even a place as dull as Glassblower's Gulch. He wasn't supposed to go *near* a dragon here, let alone get smashed into pudding by a wild one in a midnight rodeo.

He should be safe in bed, or at least have a safer way to do what he was attempting right now. But as he'd learned during his short time in this town on the edge of civilization, there's no safe way to lose a dragon rodeo.

PART ONE

"YOU HOARD TROUBLE LIKE A
DRAGON HOARDS TREASURE."

1

ABEL HAD ARRIVED IN GLASSBLOWER'S Gulch a few weeks earlier. His family traveled together for the first time in as long as Abel could remember. An unspoken rule of the overnight flight was, apparently, that his older brother, Silas, and his older sister, Lina, wouldn't speak to each other. Abel and his parents acted as go-betweens until they realized how silly that was and that they did not want to be involved in teenager drama, and they left Silas and Lina alone.

Abel settled onto one of the soft reclining chairs by a window and watched episodes of the animated *Dr. Drago: VDV (Vigilante Dragon Veterinarian)* series on his phone until he fell asleep. He occasionally woke up to look out at the Cloudflayer's wings beating their way through the air, but after they left the gleaming sky-scrapers and bustling dragon traffic of Drakopolis, there was nothing to see but the endless expanse of the Glass Flats all the way to the mountains on the horizon. At least once the sun set, the glare wasn't so blinding, and he could stare out at the stars.

Silas spent the entire flight sitting bolt upright doing some kind of meditation thing he must have learned at the Dragon Rider Academy, though Abel suspected he'd actually been asleep. There was drool inchworming its way down his chin.

Lina ate and slept and read fantasy novels about teenagers in a world that had no dragons—just romances and high school and sometimes murder—and then she slept some more. Which was about the same thing their parents did, just with fewer sighs. Lina did not want to move to Glassblower's Gulch, and she made sure the whole family knew it.

It was nice that they were the only passengers in the travel compartment on the back of this Cloudflayer, a long-wing transport dragon. There was a separate freight compartment, but the passenger cabin had been chartered just for Abel's family, paid for by the City Council of Drakopolis itself.

Officially, they were all moving together to support Silas, who, at only nineteen years old, would be the youngest lieutenant deputy sheriff ever appointed. It was a promotion from an undercover Dragon's Eye agent pretending to be a Dragon Rider Academy cadet, which was his former job, until Abel's trouble with the kins complicated things.

Unofficially, the family was being exiled to a remote town at the edge of nowhere. Each of them had, in their own ways, been involved in massive criminal activities with a variety of dragon-battling kins. The choice was either to go together into exile in Glassblower's Gulch or to go separately to Windlee Prison for the rest of their lives.

So family exile it was.

The whole thing had been Abel's fault for racing and battling dragons against all three major kins in the city—the Red Talons, the Thunder Wings, and the Sky Knights—and then releasing hundreds of genetically altered mutant dragons into the wild. He stayed pretty quiet on the flight. He wasn't eager to remind his family that he existed.

But his whole family got reminded real quick the moment they climbed down from the dragon's huge wing onto the landing platform in the blazing morning light of Glassblower's Gulch.

"Nice to meet you folks. I'm Sheriff Bina Skint, and I won't put up with any trouble in my town!" The sheriff stepped up to greet them, locking her gaze straight on Abel and scowling. She had mirrored wraparound sunglasses hiding her eyes, so all Abel could see was his own puny reflection in the glaring light off the glass around them.

"We don't abide kin activity here in Glassblower's Gulch," Sheriff Skint warned. "And no one touches a dragon without my express say-so, got it?"

Abel swallowed hard, prepared to answer, when Silas spoke for him.

"Yes, Sheriff," his older brother said. "I'll keep my family in line; you can be sure of it."

The sheriff broke off her glare at Abel to look her newest lieutenant deputy up and down, which gave Abel a chance to get a good look at *her*.

She had a weathered face and short green hair with blond spikes in it. Her uniform was dark green and wrapped with a black utility belt that held a stun gun and zip ties and all sorts of fearsome-looking law enforcement tools. Over it she wore a long gray coat with patches on the sleeves that had the Dragon's Eye emblem: a humanoid dragon with an eyeball for a head wielding a curved sword. On her chest she wore a silver badge shaped like a star held in a claw. It said SHERIFF in raised gold letters.

Sheriff Skint sucked her teeth at Abel's brother. "You're Silas, huh?"

"Yes, Sheriff," Silas said, his voice dropping deeper than usual in an effort to sound more adult. Abel and Lina shared a quick eye roll at their big brother's expense, which Silas noticed. "It'll be my honor to safeguard the peace in your city from—"

"Some city," Lina muttered.

Silas glared at her. "From *anyone* who would cause trouble," he said.

"Well, that's nice," the sheriff replied, obviously patronizing Silas in a way he pretended not to notice. That's how Silas was, so puffed up with pride he was like a balloon blown too full. Even the tiniest prick would pop him. "I think you city salamanders will find our town rather quiet compared to Drakopolis. We don't have all the amenities you may be used to, but we don't have all the problems neither."

"What's 'amenities'?" Abel whispered.

"They're like perks," Lina said back, not bothering to whisper. "Movies and restaurants and indoor plumbing."

The sheriff swung her attention to Lina. "Oh, I think you'll find our plumbing quite adequate," she snarled. "Lina, is it?"

Lina nodded, and the sheriff spat onto the colorful cracked desert glass at her feet. It sizzled in the heat.

"Lina," she repeated with a breathy sigh. She knew exactly who Lina was. "You'll get to know our plumbing well during your time here. I know you were a dragon thief back in Drakopolis, and I wouldn't want you to be tempted into your old life of crime in our little town. So I've taken the liberty of getting you a job where you'll be far from any temptations: working in the sewage department. Hard to steal a dragon when you're up to your waist in muck, thirty feet underground."

Lina started to object. She even took a step forward, fists

balled, before their dad coughed and pulled her back. They couldn't make enemies with the sheriff. She wasn't just Silas's new boss; she was the law out here, and the entire family had to stay out of trouble. Punishment for any one of them would be punishment for all of them. That was one of the terms of their exile. For good or bad, they were all in this together.

Of course, as a family, they always had been, whether they acted like it or not. *It's us against the world*, Abel thought. *Not just me.*

Lina looked at her sneakers and seethed quietly.

The sheriff smiled, satisfied. "You'll see how our town works soon enough," she told them. "Everyone's got a job, and if everyone does theirs, we all get along just fine. We even have some fun, in our own ways."

Behind them, a dozen or so people scrambled to unload the cargo carrier on the Cloudflayer's back, hauling off all sorts of crates and supplies. Then a dozen *different* people hustled to load different crates and supplies back into the containers that had just been emptied. It looked like sweaty, bone-busting work, the kind that was done by dragons back home, not by people.

This is home now, Abel reminded himself.

The huge long-wing Cloudflayer laid her belly on the warm glass ground, absorbing the heat with a contented grin on her giant gray face. Her scales were glossy pale blues, grays, and whites, with three bright red octagonal streaks on either side, like bloody gashes in a puffy cloud.

In spite of their terrifying name and twenty-five-ton size, Cloudflayers were gentle dragons, or as gentle as long-wings got. They could still breathe a pillar of fire onto a moving target from a mile in the air and crush a dozen humans in one set of claws if they chose, but they usually didn't choose to. Other than flying long distances, they were famously lazy dragons.

This one was already asleep.

A few brightly colored cockatrices scurried around the landing platform, their long, spiked tails swishing. Their feathery wings flapped them in awkward little hops away from the landing area. It occurred to Abel that he'd never seen a live cockatrice in person. They were usually plucked and roasted and hanging upside down in restaurant windows. The rooster-headed dragons were bigger than he'd pictured them, and meaner too. They shrieked and slashed at each other until the huge transport dragon opened one eye and roared at them. Then they scurried off the landing platform, leaving a few bright feathers behind.

"Don't touch their feathers," Lina whispered to Abel. "Cockatrice feathers are poisonous until they've been dried out or boiled."

Abel nodded. The poison in a fresh cockatrice feather could turn your skin to glass and, if you didn't get treatment in the hospital fast, your internal organs too. Working in a cockatrice processing plant was one of the most dangerous jobs you could get in Drakopolis, but at least there they were kept in cages. The ones here wandered freely. In Drakopolis, a cockatrice wandering the streets would get devoured by a dragon in seconds, but other than the Cloudflayer they rode in on, Abel didn't see other dragons anywhere.

Was this a town . . . without dragons?

"We are the main supplier of glass and raw sand for Drakopolis," Sheriff Skint told them. "We send shipments to the city once a week. And once a week we get supplies. Can't grow much here except sand for concrete and glass for buildings, but the city can't get enough of either. The money the city pays us, pays for everything we import, even water." She looked Abel up and down. "So keep your showers short."

What is that supposed to mean? Abel wondered, trying to smell himself without being noticed. Did he stink, or was the sheriff just one of those people who automatically disliked kids?

"Silas, if you'll come with me, we'll get you all set up with your uniform and your new partner," the sheriff said. "The rest of you can make your way down into the gulch, where you'll find your new home." She handed Abel's dad a piece of paper with the address. "No phone service out here, so we do things the old-fashioned way."

"No phone service!" Lina groaned. Abel had planned to stay in touch with his best friends, Topher and Roa, back in the city. And he'd been texting with Arvin, the heir of the Red Talons kin, too, whom he'd only recently met in their last caper but had immediately grown fond of. Abel enjoyed having a powerful friend like that, especially after what they'd been through with the mutant dragons they'd freed. Now he'd be cut off from all three of his friends. Even Silas looked upset about his social life vanishing, but he did his best to hide it.

"What's wrong with you?" the sheriff asked him. "You look like you need to eat some prunes."

"Nothing, Sheriff." Silas fixed his face. His trying-not-to-look-disappointed face looked a lot like a constipated face. The sheriff was observant. Abel would have to be careful with her. Some adults didn't notice anything kids did, because they didn't think it was important. But some adults noticed *everything* kids did, because they enjoyed punishing them. Abel was pretty sure he knew which kind of adult the sheriff was.

"Don't worry, kids," Sheriff Skint laughed at them. "There's so much work to do, you'll be too tired to play on your phones anyway. Glassblower's Gulch isn't like the city, where dragons do everything. Out here, people do for themselves. So, you'll want to get to your new home and clean up. You better get walking."

She nodded at them again, then led Silas away. He cast one look back at his family and trotted after the sheriff over the shimmering hot glass.

Abel's dad clapped his hands and put on a big smile.

"Well," he said. "These bags won't carry themselves. Luckily, I've got two strong kids with me!"

Abel and Lina shared a look. They'd been brother and sister for Abel's whole life, but they'd also been partners in crime and enemies in battle, dueled dragons for rival kins, and betrayed those kins to protect each other. They'd even saved Silas's life once or twice, despite him trying to arrest them at the time. They'd been through a lot together in the skies above Drakopolis, but now they were stuck here, grounded in Glassblower's Gulch.

They didn't know it yet, but things could get a lot worse.

A GULCH, AS ABEL PRESENTLY learned, is a narrow ravine with steep sides, usually cut into the ground by flowing water. Glassblower's Gulch was definitely narrow, and definitely deep, but it had been cut into the great glass desert not by water but by thousands of years of flowing sand. It was dry as a dragon's bones, a few of which Abel could see suspended inside the colorful canyon walls.

The town itself was carved into the sides of the ravine, above the mines and workshops at the bottom. There were houses and buildings stacked on top of each other, with ramps and steps and bridges linking them every which way. The rooftops of one house formed the front yard of the ones above it, and the deeper you went down the gulch, the cooler and darker it got. The sun set at the bottom of Glassblower's Gulch hours before it did at the top. There were solar-powered lanterns hanging everywhere. They made sounds like wind chimes when the desert breeze blew through. It was lovely, in an eerie kind of way.

Abel's parents were either thrilled or acting like they were thrilled, because they rushed through the new apartment marveling at the amount of closet space and pointing out how it was so much bigger than the one they'd lived in back in Drakopolis. It was about halfway down the gulch's south side and had a front courtyard with steps going up and down. They shared the courtyard with two neighboring families, which was still unlike their city apartment, where the only outdoor space they had was the public park that they shared with thousands of their neighbors.

Off the round entry room to this apartment, there was a sunken living room and a big kitchen with brand-new appliances. The counters and tables were all carved directly from the colorful, smooth canyon glass, which made the whole place shimmer under its LED lights. You could get lost staring into the patterns in the walls, which were covered here and there by thick hanging rugs woven with geometric patterns.

"It's all very stylish," Abel's father noted. "I didn't expect that."

"Yeah, it's fashion week year-round here," Lina grunted. She made her way to the narrow spiral staircase cut into the kitchen. It led up to the second floor, where there was a narrow hallway also decorated with hanging rugs. A door to a huge master bedroom loomed at the end of the hall, lined by three other doors to the other bedrooms.

Lina rushed to claim hers, letting Abel pick from the remaining two. Silas would just have to accept whichever room was left, which Abel and Lina agreed without speaking would be the smallest and closest to their mom and dad's.

"Whoa," Abel said when he stepped into the one he'd chosen.

It was bigger than his old room, and, like everything else here, it was carved directly from the colorful glass. An extra-large platform bed stood at the center, surrounded by shelves and a dresser and more thick rugs on the floor and walls. It also had its own bathroom—and a balcony out over the courtyard. He could stand on it and look along the gulch, or across to the neighbors, or even down, down, down, to the glassworks and sand mines and work-shops at the bottom.

Without dragons flying everywhere and criminal gangsters ruling the neighborhoods, he figured people didn't mind having their bedrooms open to the air like this.

Maybe small-town living won't be so bad, he thought. *Even if I have no friends.*

"Abel!" his mother called up the steps. "You have a visitor!"

How could he have a visitor already?

Abel peered over the edge of the balcony into the courtyard and saw a kid about his age standing at the front door. He couldn't see their face beneath the big, floppy hat they wore, but they had a bouquet of flowers in their hand.

"Flowers?" Abel wondered aloud. The kid suddenly looked up at him, shielding their eyes from the sun. Abel first noticed that the flowers weren't real; they were made of colorful blown glass. Secondly, he saw that the kid's face and clothes were smeared with ash. They waved up at him with their free hand.

"Welcome to 2G!" they shouted, which took Abel a second to decode. Glassblower's Gulch. Two *G*s. Everyplace had its slang, he figured. He'd have to learn this place's. He wondered if he'd sound weird to the kids here, with his Drakopolis slang. Did they say "savvy" here when they meant "yes"? Did they know that being "thick as scales" was an insult but "wings wide" was encouragement? Did they play DrakoTek?

Abel didn't like being the new kid.

"I'm Kayda," the kid in the courtyard announced.

"Abel!" Abel shouted down.

"I know!" the kid shouted up. "I came here to see you!"

"Oh, right! Hi!" Abel shouted down.

"Why don't you go down there instead of shouting?" Abel's mom shouted from the stairs.

"Oh yeah!" Abel shouted back. "Sorry, Mom!" He scuttled down the stairs to meet this mysterious kid who'd shown up with a bouquet of glass flowers.

THE MOMENT ABEL STEPPED INTO the glaring sun-
light of the courtyard, the kid stuck the bouquet out toward him
and said, "These are for your parents."

Abel took them slowly. They made little tinkling sounds as they
rubbed against each other. "Why didn't you just give them to Mom
when she answered the door?"

"Because I was told to ask for you," the kid said with absolute
seriousness. "I made those. Well, the stems and seven of the
petals."

Abel looked down at the flowers again. The stems were long, thin
tubes of pulled glass, and the petals were each individually bent
and shaped, then fused onto the stems. They looked amazingly real,
but in more vibrant and varied colors than nature grew flowers.

"My moms are glassblowers at the Decorative Arts hotshop
down at the bottom. I'm their apprentice. My pronouns are she/her.
My favorite dragon is a Rose Thorn wyvern. My favorite color is all
of them. And I'm twelve but I know all about boys, so don't get
weird with me or I'll feed you to a Rose Thorn wyvern. I'm supposed
to show you around town, so put those flowers inside. Tell your
moms or whatever parent you've got that you're going out. Oh, and
grab a canteen, because you're gonna get thirsty and I do not abide
whining boys."

Somehow, Kayda said all that in one breath.

"Um, okay," Abel said, also in one breath, which was far less impressive.

He dropped the glass flowers off with his mom and dad and followed the soot-covered girl through the courtyard and up the steps that led back to the ridge over Glassblower's Gulch.

"We'll start at the top and work our way down," Kayda said. "That's the best way to get a tour, in my opinion, and since I am your tour guide, my opinion is the only one that matters to you right now. Also, you have to do what I say while we're together, because I don't want to get in trouble and we've all been warned that you, Abel, are trouble. I don't believe everything everyone says all the time, and I admit you don't look like trouble, but neither does a Bone Reaper. You ever see a Bone Reaper? They look just like piles of dried-out white bones until you get close and they sit up huge and terrible, with sun-bright yellow eyes and translucent skin, and they snap you up whole, spitting out your flesh and blood and only crunching on your bones. It's gruesome but impressive. You don't look gruesome or impressive, no offense. So is it true, what they say about you and the kins? Also, sorry to be rude—I forgot to ask. What are your pronouns and your favorite color and your favorite dragon?"

Again, she'd said all that in one go, and Abel was left reeling. Kayda spoke the way his brain worked when he was nervous, all jumbled and fast. He never really managed to turn his jumbled thoughts into words when they ran together like that, but it seemed like Kayda couldn't *stop* from turning all her thoughts into words. It made him wonder if she was anxious right now. He guessed *he'd* be anxious if he'd been asked to give a tour to a notorious criminal in exile from the big city.

The thought made him feel a little proud. He liked the idea that he was notorious.

"Um," he started, trying to remember what she'd asked him. "Right. Yeah, so my pronouns are he/him. My favorite color is, I guess . . . I dunno? Orange?"

"Is that a question?" Kayda asked.

"What?"

"You said 'orange' like it was a question," Kayda told him. She took the steps up two at a time. Abel had gotten in pretty good shape racing illegal dragons, but he found he was out of breath after two flights of the steep stairs into town. Kayda kept having to wait for him. The girl had boundless energy. Abel was quickly finding the bounds of his.

"Like you don't know what your favorite color is," she continued. "Are you an indecisive person? My mama says you can't be indecisive in the hotshop because glass shatters if you let it get too cool and that life's just like a hotshop that way. Better to *decide* and *create* than *abide* and *wait*. That's what she says anyway. 'Abide' and 'wait' mean basically the same thing, but she likes to make up sayings, and I don't want to go around correcting people all the time. Seems like a waste of energy and also it annoys people and I'm trying not to annoy people, you know? People say I can be annoying, and no one wants to be annoying, right? So I'm, like, *working on it*, as they say, though it doesn't feel like work. Work is something you do with your hands, in my opinion. It's not sitting around thinking and feeling. My mimi says that's a misconception but I dunno what she means by that. Oh yeah, so, orange?"

"Right. Orange." Abel had really lost the thread of the conversation now, so he went back to the last thing he remembered her asking. "My favorite dragon is a Sunrise Reaper," he told her.

"Oh, like the one your sister stole that you fought the Red Talons with?" Kayda said.

Abel stopped midway up a steep section of stairs. The sun blazed straight down. Kayda was a silhouette above him. "How did you know about *that*?"

"Everyone here knows everything," she said. When Abel didn't start moving again, she shook her head and came back to talk quietly to him. "The pilots of the freight dragons that come every week tell the unloaders what the latest news is from Drakopolis. Plus, we have our own town newsletter. Plus, a few folks get internet from the factory offices. All that comes together into gossip and that gossip spreads faster than anything. We call it the 2G internet. You could sneeze on these steps right here and someone across the gulch and a thousand feet below us would hear about it before I could say, 'Bless your breath.' No secrets in the 2G, Abel. This town's got no dragons and no secrets. Well, except one, but—"

She stopped talking suddenly, clamped her mouth shut.

"But what?" Abel asked.

"Nothing," she said. And she didn't say anything else.

"You started to tell me something," Abel said. "You said there are no dragons and no secrets in Glassblower's Gulch, except one. What's the one? Did you mean one secret or one dragon?"

Kayda's mouth didn't open. She shook her head, then resumed her upward climb.

"I didn't mean absolutely no dragons," she called back to him. "The sheriff has a Hog dragon, and Deputy Manchi rides a Reaper. And there's the Cloudflayer that comes every week with deliveries and pickups. We're not, like, *ignorant* out here, if that's what you think."

"I didn't say that," Abel protested, rushing to catch up. He noticed she hadn't really answered his question, though. Kayda was a blabbermouth about everything except one thing—and now he wanted to know what it was.

Secrets are a lot like dragons, he figured. *Having one can make you powerful, but it can also swallow you whole.*

THE VIEW FROM THE TOP of Glassblower's Gulch was breathtaking. Or it would have been, if Abel had any breath left to take.

As it was, he had to stop and put his head between his knees and gasp for air to recover from the hike.

There were no houses near the top of the gulch, just storage buildings and a supply depot for the sheriff's department. Abel also noticed—once he could see straight again—a huge ring of fencing opposite some bleachers. As far as he could tell, the bleachers looked out at nothing but more glass desert.

On this side of the gulch sat the landing area, where his family had arrived, and the big solar energy panels that powered the town. They weren't fenced at all, which made Abel curious.

"Why is that fencing over there?" he asked Kayda.

"That's a security question," Kayda said. "Did I not mention I'm a twelve-year-old glassblower's apprentice? I'm not a security expert."

"Um, okay. Sorry." Abel didn't know why she was so touchy about it. He guessed the fence and the town's secret were connected. In Abel's experience, nervous people with secrets and mysterious security fencing meant only one thing: dragons.

"No need to apologize." Kayda smiled at him. "Curiosity is the only abundant natural resource we have in Glassblower's Gulch."

She lowered her voice to a whisper. "Just be careful with it. It's flammable."

"Curiosity is flammable?"

"It is in Glassblower's Gulch," she replied gravely. Then she pasted her smile back on and spoke loud enough for anyone nearby to hear, though Abel didn't see anyone nearby at all. "Let's get on with this town tour, shall we? This is the top of the gulch. No reason to come up here unless you're sent to help with the weekly deliveries, which you won't be because . . ." She looked him up and down and bit her lip.

"I'm too scrawny?" Abel finished her thought.

"I didn't say that," she muttered, then quickly pointed him toward a zigzagging ramp cut into the ground. "We'll go this way."

The ramp was intersected by dozens of bridges across the gulch, staircases that led to other ramps strung with lights and cables and laundry lines. They filled the air at all angles. That sort of system of bridges and wires and clothes flapping in the wind would've been impossible in a town with a lot of flying dragons.

All along the walls of the gulch were doors cut into the thick colorful glass and hand-printed signs for all sorts of businesses, from coffee shops and noodle bars to tailors and rug stores.

"What's with all the rugs?" Abel asked. Back in Drakopolis, people had rugs, of course, but they didn't usually have so many of them and they didn't hang them on their walls.

"We live in a gulch in the desert, Abel," Kayda said, like it was the dumbest question she'd ever heard. She checked the antique watch she wore on her wrist. "In about seven hours, when the sun starts to drop, it's gonna get cold. Like, really, *really* cold. If you hadn't noticed, everything here is glass, metal, and concrete. The rugs are to keep your apartment from turning into an ice cube tray. They're insulation."

"Great," Abel groaned. How could people live in a place where the days were brutally hot and the nights were brutally cold? Then again, people here probably wondered how anyone could live in a city like Drakopolis, where you could forget nature existed if you wanted to.

"This is the shopping district." Kayda continued the tour. "It's basically the same on either side of the gulch. When you get down to the middle section, where you live, that's where all the apartments are, though the other side of the gulch isn't as nice as your side. The sheriff must've wanted to keep your family happy, giving you a spot like that. Or just to keep an eye on you, because *she* lives on that side too. My moms and I live down lower on the *other* side, just above our shop. Have you ever been to a hotshop before?"

Abel shook his head. He knew that handblown glass was made in places called hotshops, and that it was sweaty, dirty, difficult work, but that's all he knew. Back in Drakopolis, glass was made in big factories with huge Infernal dragons blasting tons of sand and machines pouring it into molds. There wasn't a lot that was handmade by people. When they got to Kayda's family hotshop, Abel saw why. Making glass by hand was *a lot* of work.

There was a line of ovens along one wall, and one of Kayda's moms was feeding fuel into it to keep the fire burning blue-hot. Dragons could've done that effortlessly, but she was sweating with the labor. Kayda's other mom had picked up a bunch of colored sand on the end of a long tube. She held it through a hole in the opening to one of the ovens, also dripping with sweat. After a little while, she pulled a burning blob of glass out on the end of the pole, swung it onto the edge of a table, and blew through one end of the tube. Kayda's other mom used a big metal tool to shape the balloon of hot glass before it got too cool.

Then it went back into the oven for another round of heating and softening.

"One nice vase can take hours of work," Kayda explained. "And they can shatter anytime if they get too hot or too cold too fast. Or just for no obvious reason at all. It's an uncertain art, but isn't it beautiful when it works?"

"Kind of like friendship," Abel mused. He was feeling philosophical and missing his old friends. He hadn't been able to see them in person before his family was exiled. Had their friendship cooled too fast? Would his exile shatter it?

Kayda pursed her lips, thinking about what he'd said. "Deep," she finally replied. Then she pointed to a shelf along the far wall of the shop, where beautiful glass pieces were lined up in rows. "Check these out."

There were sculptures and vases and drinking cups and perfume bottles. There were platters and lamps and paperweights. The way the light caught them, they looked alive. Each had its own flaws and bubbles and imperfections. No machine-made glass could ever look like that, like a human mind and a human hand had bent their purpose together to create each object from sand and heat.

They looked expensive.

Abel stepped closer to the shelf and found the price tags.

They *were* expensive. Even a salt-and-pepper shaker set cost more money than his mom had earned in a week back at her factory job in Drakopolis.

"Handmade stuff takes a long time," Kayda said to him. "So it has to cost more too. Mostly, they sell their stuff to rich people back in Drakopolis. Not a lot of people here can afford them."

Abel nodded and resisted the urge to touch any of it. He was pretty sure he'd break something, and he was old enough to know that whatever he broke, he was going to have to pay for—one way or another.

He looked past the shelf and saw a narrow door carved into the thick wall next to the ovens. The door was cracked open, and steam poured out of the gap. Abel could see the glimmer of a pile of broken glass in all different colors, and on top of the pile rested a curled shape about the size of his pet pangolin, Percy.

"You have a pet?" Abel asked. He loved pangolins.

"What?" Kayda said. She quickly shut the door. "No, that's just the storeroom for broken shards. I'd keep out. Wouldn't want to cut your feet." She leaned toward him in a dramatic fake whisper. "My moms break *a lot* of stuff."

"You can't make anything worthwhile if you aren't willing to risk some breakage along the way," a voice behind him said. Abel turned to see the women who had been blowing glass now standing side by side, sweaty in their thick aprons. They smiled at him and their daughter.

"That's Mama and Mimi," Kayda told him.

"I'm Althea," Kayda's mama said with a little laugh, bowing her head in greeting. "And this is Kimber."

Kayda's mimi wiped some soot from her face and also nodded. "It'd be awkward for the boy to call us Mama and Mimi, don't you think?"

"Right, right, sure," Kayda said. She turned to Abel. "I don't have a lot of friends my age, so I wasn't sure of the etiquette for introducing you to my parents. Sorry if that was awkward. It was not my intention to make you uncomfortable. I know you have your own mom and dad and I wasn't trying to trick you into replacing your parents with mine. It's really the trouble with language, I think. How your mom is your mom and my moms are my moms and us calling the other one's mom 'Mom' would be weird but it'd also be weird not to call our own moms 'Mom.' Though having two moms, they had to come up with different mom names for themselves, which is weird because I don't actually call either of them quote-unquote 'Mom,' but maybe if we came up with a system to—"

"Kay-Kay," Althea cut her daughter off with a smile and a nickname. "Deep breath."

Kayda took a deep breath, then narrowed her eyes at Abel. "You ever call me Kay-Kay, you die, savvy?"

"Savvy," Abel gulped.

"Welcome to Glassblower's Gulch," Kimber said. "There aren't a lot of kids here, and none Kayda's age, so we're all very excited to meet you, Abel. We'll have to get together with your folks soon."

"I'm sure my parents would love that," Abel said, careful not to commit to anything. He didn't want to be unfriendly; he'd just learned to be wary of strangers.

In Drakopolis, where the kins ruled, just being polite to the wrong person from the wrong kin could get you and your family fed to a drake. A family in a Red Talons building couldn't have a family from a Sky Knights neighborhood over for dinner, even if none of them were actually in either kin. A Sky Knight couldn't have a coffee with a Thunder Wing, even if they'd been friends since first grade, and none of the kins could even admit to knowing someone from the Wind Breakers. They were the most hated of all the kins, and also the most mysterious. Add to all that the Dragon's Eye, who had secret police and spies and informants everywhere. It made even a simple dinner invitation as complicated as the plot of a soap opera.

"Well, we'll be sure to pop by and invite them ourselves," Althea told him. "So, what do you think of our town?"

"It's nothing like where I'm from," Abel said. "It's not even lunchtime, and we've walked the whole thing. In Drakopolis, you couldn't even walk my neighborhood before lunch."

"I imagine it's quite a change," Kimber told him. "But don't worry. It's a good place to live, quiet and safe. As long as you stay out of trouble."

Abel didn't like how the last bit came out like a warning. Did people here already think he and his family were troublemakers?

Of course, they weren't wrong. Every one of them, including his parents, had made some sort of trouble in Drakopolis. Still, in a town without dragons or kins, he wondered what kind of trouble he could possibly get into.

That was when trouble walked through the door, with his big brother trailing close behind.

5

SHERIFF'S DEPUTY MANCHI LOOKED LIKE a
boulder stuffed into a uniform. His arms and neck were thick,
each tattooed with colorful scenes of warriors slaying dragons.
Abel's attention went into full focus, like it did when he was
riding a dragon. He took in the huge man quickly. There were
symbols hidden in the deputy's tattoos: Some of the dragons
wore chains with kin symbols on them, while the warriors had
armor and helmets emblazoned with the Dragon's Eye emblem.
Abel didn't know what the symbols meant, but he figured it was
nothing good.

Deputy Manchi's head was shaved bald, but he had a thick black
mustache. His heavy eyebrows peeked out above mirrored sunglasses. He scanned the shop as he entered, his body casting a
shadow across the colorful glass.

Silas wore the same uniform but looked scrawny beside the bigger man. A pebble next to a boulder. His name was stitched on a
patch on his chest opposite his badge, just like Deputy Manchi's,
but his uniform hung loose. Abel had never thought of his big
brother as a weakling before. Silas was a lot of things, but he spent
enough time lifting weights that he was definitely not weak. Still,
beside the bruiser he'd been partnered with, he looked as fragile as
the glass on the shop's shelves.

He didn't even acknowledge Abel when he came in.

"We have reports of suspicious activity here," Deputy Manchi said, ignoring Abel and Kayda.

"Excuse me?" Kimber stepped forward, fearless. "We do nothing illegal here."

Abel saw Kayda glance at the door next to the ovens and bulge her eyes at her mimi. Althea gave her head a quick shake. The deputies hadn't noticed, but Abel sure had. Whatever was in that room, they did *not* want these officers of the law to find it.

"We'll see." Deputy Manchi pursed his lips. He strolled around the store like it was his own living room, picking up the glass pieces and feeling their weight in his hand, then setting them down roughly. It was obvious by his attitude that he didn't fear paying for anything he might accidentally break. His attitude suggested, in fact, that he might break something on purpose.

"All those pieces are for sale if you're interested," Althea said when he picked up a glass candelabra that was made to look like seven dragons intertwined with each other, their mouths shooting up to hold the candles. The glass was swirling with colors so that whenever Abel's eye fixed on one spot, the colors just outside his focus seemed to twist. It was one of the most beautiful things Abel had ever seen.

Deputy Manchi dropped it.

"Oops," he said flatly.

Kayda and Abel dove at the same moment, heads smacking into each other as they tried to catch it before it hit the ground. Their heads bounced with a *crack*, and the candelabra hit the hard floor with a *crash*.

"That was days of work!" Kimber cried out.

"Send an invoice to the sheriff's office," Deputy Manchi snarled.

Abel recognized his swagger. It was just like the kinners back home. This deputy might wear a badge and have the law on his side, but Abel had already sized him up. He was a goon.

So what was *Silas* doing here with this goon?

Abel cast a look to his brother, whose eyes were hidden behind his own mirrored sunglasses, but whose face looked tense with disapproval.

"We're here on law-enforcement business," Silas said, like just by saying it, he could make it true. "The more you cooperate, the easier this will be."

Kayda's moms looked at each other nervously.

"It's my partner's first day in town," Manchi said. "So he doesn't know how things work here yet. I brought him by to teach him."

"Can't he learn someplace else?" Althea pleaded.

"Now, now," the deputy scolded them like he was talking to small children. "Why put off till tomorrow what you're gonna have to do today anyway?"

Abel didn't fully understand what was happening. The deputy strolled over to a water meter on the wall near a big metal sink and studied it, nodding.

"As I thought," he told them. "You're over your water limit. Don't you know there's a fee for water overages?"

"We are not over our—" Kimber objected, but Althea stopped her.

Manchi raised an eyebrow at her as he turned on the faucet, letting the water whoosh out as the meter rose.

"We'll pay whatever fee you think fair," Althea said meekly.

"What's going on?" Abel whispered to Kayda where they knelt beside each other on the floor, surrounded by the shattered shards of the candelabra.

"Shh. Nothing," Kayda whispered back.

"What's in that room?" Abel tried.

Kayda just shook her head.

No one moved as Deputy Manchi approached the two women and loomed over them. The water still whooshed from the faucet and slapped into the sink.

"Any fee I think fair?" he said, staring them down. Menacing them.

The women nodded. Silas shifted his feet uncomfortably. He didn't understand what was happening any more than Abel did, but he wore a badge and uniform and had to stand there and trust his partner.

Abel was not in a badge or a uniform. Abel didn't *have* to do anything.

"You're the one wasting their water," he declared. "We're all watching you do it."

"Quiet," Kayda snapped, elbowing Abel hard in the side.

Deputy Manchi's gaze fell on Abel with the force of a dragon landing on a waterbed. Abel's insides sloshed under that gaze. The deputy's boots crunched on the broken glass as he moved to stand over him.

"Now, I know you think you're some hotshot dragon rider back in the big ol' city," Deputy Manchi drawled. "But do you see any dragons in this town, kid?"

"No," Abel answered.

"Wrong," the deputy barked. "*We* are the dragons in this town." He made a gesture to Silas, who looked uncomfortable being included in whatever his partner was about to do. "You wanna try climbing on my back? See if you can tame me?"

Abel thought of a few insults he could toss at the sheriff's deputy, something about needing a shovel for all the dung.

"I'm sure my brother didn't mean anything," Silas suggested, cutting off any wisecracks Abel had been considering.

"Oh, I think he meant *something*." The deputy squatted down to Abel's level.

Abel straightened his spine and lifted his head to meet the man's eyes, trying to look confident. When you tamed a dragon, you had to show confidence or else it would incinerate you where you stood. Men with power were the same way.

Abel locked his eyes on the huge deputy and said flatly, "We all saw you turn their water on. If anyone's wasting water, it's you."

"You all saw it?" Deputy Manchi smiled. Then he looked from Abel to Kayda. She tensed. "What did *you* see?"

"I . . . Well . . . Perception is a tricky thing," Kayda started. "Like, how do I know what I call green is the same color as what you call green? Maybe what you call green is what I think of as blue."

"What is she talking about?" Manchi asked her moms.

"Please, leave her out of this," Althea said.

"Of course." Deputy Manchi softened his voice. "Once she answers my question. Who left the water running?"

Kayda swallowed hard. The air smelled like hot glass and sweat. Abel felt a trickle race down his back, though whether it was sweat or molten glass, he couldn't have said. Both would've been equally uncomfortable at that moment.

"No one!" Kimber shouted, crossing the shop in defiance and shutting the water off. "No one left it running! It's not running at all now, right?"

Deputy Manchi chewed his lip, then turned to Abel's brother. "Well, Deputy Silas, it being your first day, why don't I leave this one up to you, *savvy*?"

"Um . . ." Silas said.

"Savvy?" the other deputy repeated ominously. "Savvy" was usually kinner slang. It was not something that a Dragon's Eye agent back in Drakopolis would ever have said, at least not while wearing their uniform. It seemed to Abel that in a town without dragons or kins, the sheriff's deputies were filling both those roles for themselves.

Would Silas, who loved rules and laws and whatever he thought of as justice, play along?

Silas cleared his throat, ran a nervous hand over his undercut hair, and then gave Abel a look that clearly said, *Keep your mouth shut.*

"If their water meter is over the ration limit," he announced, "then they should pay the fee."

"That's the law," Manchi agreed. "But in light of your little brother's *objections*, maybe we can let this one go, huh?"

Silas looked confused. Abel was confused too. Why was the deputy suddenly letting Kayda's family off the hook?

Abel quickly realized he wasn't.

"Of course, we're not here for water violations," the deputy said. "We're here because of the cockatrice bones."

"The what?" Abel wondered aloud, though no one else spoke.

"Your neighbors reported piles of cockatrice bones behind your shop," Deputy Manchi said to them. "More than a family of three could possibly account for, even if you ate dragonet stew for every meal."

"Those things run wild all over town," Kimber said. "Who knows what they get into?"

"Or what gets into them?" Manchi said.

"What are you implying?" Althea asked.

Deputy Manchi shrugged. "I might just look around, yeah?" He started to pace the shop, studying the floor and the shelves. As he walked, he spoke to Silas.

"Deputy Silas, what's the penalty for owning an unauthorized dragon in Glassblower's Gulch?"

"I haven't studied all the local laws yet," Silas said, "but I believe the penalty is forfeiture of property and immediate arrest."

Deputy Manchi smiled. "That means I can take your house, your shop, and lock all three of you up," he said.

"Only if they're harboring an illegal dragon," Silas pointed out.

"Of course," said Deputy Manchi, slowly meandering toward the closed door to the storage room. Kayda had taken up standing in front of it, and Abel had a pretty good idea why. Her eyes looked wild, desperate.

The deputy brushed her aside with one hand and pushed the door open.

A blast of steam erupted from the room. Abel thought it was some kind of breath weapon from a hidden dragon, but the steam cleared and the deputy was unharmed. He stepped inside, and Abel peered past him at the heap of broken glass.

There was nothing on top of it. The deputy looked around the room a moment, then came back out, kicking glass shards in front of him.

"Must've been a misunderstanding from the neighbors," he said.

Abel saw Kayda's expression turn from terror to confusion. She had *expected* the deputy to find something in there. Was her family hiding a dragon? And if they were . . . where was it now?

Kayda's moms sprang into immediate action.

"Thank you for your thorough investigation, Deputy Manchi," Kimber said while Althea packed a crate up with some of the nicest pieces of glassware from the most expensive shelf in their shop—a red vase, some crystal candlesticks, a yellow perfume spray bottle. "As you can see, we are just simple artisans who would never dream of wasting your valuable time with lawlessness." Althea handed the crate to the deputy.

"Oh, I couldn't accept this," Deputy Manchi said.

"Please, consider it a gift," said Althea, "on account of your generosity with our water meter. And for all the good work you do for the community." It was obvious from her tone she meant the opposite of what she was saying.

"Well, if you insist," said Deputy Manchi, whose own tone made it obvious he'd take it and more if he wanted to.

"Um," Silas started to question his partner, but Manchi gave him the sort of look Silas had just given Abel, a *shut-your-mouth* look.

Silas nodded and followed his partner out of the store.

Abel, Kayda, and her moms stood in sweaty silence for a long time after the sheriff's deputies left the shop.

Finally, Abel couldn't bear the quiet anymore. "Did the police just rob you?!" he asked.

"Welcome to Glassblower's Gulch," said Kayda. "You really shouldn't have complained."

"But—" Abel started to object. He looked around. "Do you actually have a dragon?"

"Dragons are illegal for citizens in Glassblower's Gulch," Kayda told him, like she was reciting a line she'd memorized from a book.

"Then whose is that?" Abel asked, pointing at the red-hot, spike-covered baby Rose Thorn wyvern that had just stuck its nose out of the glassblower's oven.

It blinked once at him, then hopped down to the floor, where its claws sizzled against the concrete. Steam rose from its rapidly cooling scales.

Just then, Silas came back through the door to give Kayda's family a ticket for their water use. Those were the rules, and if there was one thing Silas loved, it was rules.

6

"**APOLOGIES FOR ANY CONFUSION,**" SILAS said, not looking up from his ticket book while he wrote. "I'm giving you form 904-7-B to submit a claim for the broken candelabra, as well as a formal Water Usage Warning Notice, as per Town Ordinance 173 subsection A-5."

Kimber and Althea had frozen where they stood, but Abel and Kayda immediately turned around, shoulder to shoulder, with their backs to the piping-hot baby wyvern. The two of them formed a wall in front of it. Sweat ran down Abel's neck all the way to the small of his back, and it wasn't because of the heat off the dragon's body, though that wasn't helping any. The moment Silas looked up, he would see a steaming baby wyvern on the floor!

Silas's pen stopped moving. He sniffed and frowned, and Abel's stomach formed a knot as hard as dragon scales. Silas looked up at last.

"Smells like something's burning," he said. His eyes fixed on Abel, but he couldn't see through his little brother, not literally anyway. "Is your back on fire?"

"My back?" Abel asked.

"You've got smoke coming off your back," Silas said, and took a step toward Abel.

"Must be the heat off the ovens," Abel replied quickly. He glanced over his shoulder just as Silas got closer. Abel saw the wyvern's tail slip behind the nearest shelf. He and Kayda parted, revealing empty floor at their backs. There were singe marks from two dragon feet and Abel needed his brother not to notice them. "It's a hotshop, if you didn't notice. Maybe you were too busy harassing these innocent people."

Silas locked his eyes on Abel, like Abel knew he would. Abel puffed up his chest, and Silas puffed his back. Brothers were a lot like dragons. If you challenged one's honor, they might spit fire on you, but if you backed down, they would definitely spit fire on you. Either way, Silas would be so distracted defending his honor, he wouldn't notice the baby wyvern taking wobbly hops behind a shelf of expensive vases. The curves of the glassware shrank and enlarged bits of the wyvern as it snuck past, a huge eye here, a tiny shoulder there.

"Are you criticizing the way I do my job?" Silas demanded of Abel, not noticing anything besides his annoying little brother.

"Criticize Deputy Silas?" Abel replied. "I wouldn't *dare!*"

"Sarcasm is the refuge of a coward," Silas told him. "And it's *Lieutenant* Deputy Silas."

"And a bully hiding behind a badge is still a bully," Abel told him back, then added as sarcastically as he could, "*Lieutenant* Bully."

Silas's fist looked hungry for Abel's face.

"Please, boys!" Kimber stepped forward, opening her arms wide. "There is no need to fight. Everything is fine. We're grateful the deputy has given us the proper paperwork. And, Abel, we're grateful that you paid us this visit, but we have a lot of work still to—"

Her speech was cut short when she bumped a bowl with her hand and sent it to the floor with another loud crash, shattering it. Silas looked to the noise, which gave Althea the chance to open the storage room door again. Kayda shooed the wyvern back into it with a broom.

The door slammed, and Silas looked up at her, holding her broom, breathless.

"I'll sweep it up," she said quickly.

"Hey!" Deputy Manchi's body filled the doorframe again. "What was that crash? What's taking so long?"

"Just a broken bowl," said Silas. "Everything's under control."

"I don't know why you wanted to do that paperwork." Manchi sighed. "But be quick about it. The barbecue place saves the best cuts for us, and I want lunch." Only then did he bother to look at Kayda's moms. "And, you two, watch yourselves. I *will* be back for an inspection."

"Any time," Althea said calmly. "You are always welcome here."

It was obvious she didn't mean it but also obvious she didn't have a choice. The deputy *would* be back.

Silas tore the pages from his ticket book and handed them to Kimber. He glared at Abel and then turned to his partner to leave.

"Y'all take care, now," Deputy Manchi said, spitting on the floor on his way out.

Kayda's family just stood in silence for a long, long time.

Finally, when Abel was sure his brother and the other sheriff's deputy had actually gone, he turned to Kayda. "You have a baby wyvern!" he exclaimed.

"Shhh!" She rushed forward and put her dirty finger on his lips.

"What are you doing with a baby wyvern?" Abel asked through her finger.

"I found the egg a few weeks ago, just lying out in the open at the top of the gulch, like it'd fallen there." She frowned. "It had a small crack in it. Night was coming, and it would get cold. Dragon eggs need heat to survive, so I rescued it and put it in the furnace. It hatched two days later, and we've been hiding it ever since. That was a week ago."

Abel looked at Kayda's moms, their faces etched with worry lines like the patterns on one of their vases.

"We can't keep it here anymore," Kimber said sadly. "It's growing and needs to be trained."

"The deputy will be back," Althea said. "And he'll search more thoroughly."

"We have to hide it where the deputies will never look!" Kayda said. "At least until it can fly away on its own. We can't let the sheriff get her hands on it. She's not—" Kayda stopped herself, took a deep breath, and then told Abel, "She is not kind to dragons."

"Oh," he said.

He felt both moms looking at him sadly. Kayda's expression turned from desperation to expectation.

"Oh," he repeated. This was why they'd sent their daughter to Abel with flowers. He was a famous dragon tamer. Well, an infamous one at least. They wanted his help. It was disappointing to think they'd only been so nice to him because they wanted something. Maybe they'd have been nice anyway, but now he'd never know. Abel found it was harder and harder for him to trust people, but he really didn't want to become the kind of person who didn't trust people, like some paranoid kin boss.

"So, will you take it for us?" Kayda asked.

Abel didn't have a lot of deeply held beliefs in life. He didn't pray often, and he didn't pay attention to politics. But there were three personal commandments he tried to live by: Always say yes to free pizza, always use the bathroom before going out, and never turn down a dragon in need.

"Not *it*," he told Kayda and her parents with a sigh. "*She*. That wyvern is a *she*. And yeah . . . I'll take her for you."

• • •

Abel had never met a baby dragon of any kind before. At school in the city, they practiced basic dragon care on Educational Resource Dragons, which were flightless dragons the size of a bathroom stall and just as stinky. The kids called them NERDs, for *not Educational Resource Dragons*.

As for the dragons he had flown himself, his first, Karak, was a full-grown, ten-ton Sunrise Reaper when they met, and his last, Brazza, was a half-trained, nine-hundred-year-old hellion of unknown breed. He'd never ridden a wyvern, let alone a baby one. In Drakopolis, only the Dragon's Eye and a few criminals rode wyverns. If you ever got close to one, it meant you were in trouble or you were making trouble.

The first step to getting this one out of the shop and hidden somewhere safe was to earn her trust, so Abel stepped to the storage room door. He knocked, just to be polite, and pushed the door open.

"She have a name?" he asked Kayda.

"I've been calling her Omelette," Kayda said. "You know, because of her cracked egg and that saying—you can't make an omelette without breaking a few eggs?"

Abel rolled his eyes. What kind of name was Omelette for a wyvern that would grow to be at least ten tons, spit acid or poison or blue-hot flame, and eat prey that was still alive and struggling on the ground in front of it? Then again, if she didn't like her name, she wouldn't be shy about letting them know. She'd probably eat them all just as soon as she was big enough. For now, at least, she was only the size of a punch bowl.

"Hey, Omelette," Abel called to her. "My name's Abel. It's nice to meet you."

The storage room was dark, and his sneakers crunched on the broken glass that the baby dragon had scattered around for her nest. As far as dragon hoards went, a room full of colorful broken glass wasn't much, but it was a start. It was something to work with.

"Mind if I call you Omi?" he asked. He couldn't in good conscience call a Rose Thorn wyvern Omelette. They were proud and jealous dragons, and he didn't want her to resent her name once she was the size of a three-bedroom apartment. "Hand me something pretty," he called over his shoulder. "Something you don't mind breaking."

Kayda handed him a red-and-gold plate from the nearest shelf. Her mothers sighed.

Abel took the plate and called out to the dragon, "Hey, girl? I brought a present!" He smashed the plate on the floor in front of him, and as the shattering sound echoed around the storage room, a small gold face popped from behind the huge glass pile. The wyvern had silver eyes, and several small spurs of bone running along the sides of her long snout. Her nostrils flared as she sniffed in Abel's direction. Then she crept around the pile, gold wings folded flat against her red back. Even in the dim light, her red scales gleamed.

She shuffled over to Abel in an awkward walk that reminded him of the cockatrices outside. Wyverns were two-legged dragons. Instead of front claws, they had talons on the ends of their wings, which they could flex almost like fingers on a hand.

Omelette flexed hers to mantle her wings over the newly shattered plate. She swept the glass up toward the edge of her next pile, and it looked like she was counting the pieces one by one as she did it.

Do dragons know numbers? Abel wondered. He imagined her helping him with his math homework, an option he'd never before considered. He could definitely use help.

Once she'd secured the new shards in her hoard, she turned back to Abel and studied him warily. He was bigger than she was, for now, so he opened his arms and stretched his neck out, showing his weak spots. If she wanted to leap up and rip his throat out with her fangs, she could. He certainly didn't want her to, but by offering her the chance, he was building trust. Her body relaxed. She sat back on her haunches, settled her wings, and waited.

Abel relaxed his posture too and met her gaze, keeping his eyes as soft and gentle as possible.

Okay, he thought. *She's not afraid of me, and she's not trying to kill me. What now?*

"Everything okay in there?" one of Kayda's moms called through the door.

"Yeah!" Abel called back. "We're just getting to know each other."

"Okay, well, you might want to do it quickly," Kayda said. "Once the deputies end their lunch break, it'll be a lot harder to get her out of here. Now's kind of the best time."

"For us, not for her," Abel said. "She's the one who gets to decide!"

He turned his attention back to her. "Whaddya say, Omi? Want to come home with me?"

The baby dragon swished her tail through the glass and then let out a hiccup, which turned into a burp, which then turned into a loogie, which she then spat on the floor, just like Deputy Manchi had.

It melted a hole in the concrete.

"Okay, so you're an acid spitter, good to know," said Abel.

He really hoped the wyvern wouldn't melt their apartment before he could train her. Then again, the one place he figured the sheriff's office wouldn't search for an illegal wyvern was in one of their own deputy's apartments. Abel would just have to keep the secret right under his brother's nose, which meant keeping her a secret from the rest of his family too.

Why am I always stuck keeping secrets? he asked himself. *And why are they always about dragons?*

Just once he'd have liked to have a secret candy stash, or a secret vault of jewels, or even a secret romance with a secret admirer. Instead, time after time, he found himself with a secret dragon and a long list of dangerous enemies.

The baby dragon was still small enough that he could probably tuck her inside his shirt to walk home, but first he had to convince her to get into his shirt and then to stay there. And also not to melt him.

"You ever left this shop?" he asked her, not sure if she understood words or not. "Want to come with me to see more of the world?"

He knew dragons were smart and that they could understand human language, but he didn't know how much they knew when they were little or even how they learned it. *Am I going to have to read to this dragon?* Abel wondered, and found he kind of liked the idea.

He'd read stories to his last dragon, Brazza, and she'd helped him take on an army and win. In Abel's experience, there was no better way to make a friend than sharing a story. He was already thinking about what he'd read to Omi once he'd hidden her in his bedroom. He'd have to sneak her food from dinner and train her after everyone else was asleep.

He wished Roa were here. They knew everything about the care and feeding of dragons and would have a lot of helpful advice. As it was, Abel was on his own, and he'd have to do his own research. It'd be like homework, except he didn't mind the idea of doing it because there was a point to it. Hard work was fun when it mattered to you, he figured, and he was ready. He would—

Oof!

The wyvern slammed into his chest, interrupting his rush of chaotic thoughts and knocking him through the door into the shop on his backside. His head bounced off the floor with a thump. Omi stood on his chest proudly, like she'd conquered him, then used her claws to rearrange his shirt and curled into a tiny ball right on his stomach. She immediately fell asleep. Her skin had cooled from the oven but was still about as hot as a pizza pocket fresh from the microwave. Abel tried not to wince or cry.

"I guess she decided I'm okay," he told Kayda.

They helped him move the baby wyvern into a box lined with glass from her nest and then they covered her with a cloth and put a set of drinkware on top.

"Better than your T-shirt," Kayda explained.

"A gift for your parents," Althea said.

"And cover if you get searched or questioned on the way home," Kimber added.

"Thank you," Abel told them, like they were doing *him* a favor and not the reverse.

"You'll take good care of her?" Kayda pleaded as he made his way to the door.

"I promise," he said. "You can visit her anytime—"

"No," Kimber interrupted, and put a hand on her daughter's shoulder. "She can't. We can't risk drawing the sheriff's suspicions. Deputy Manchi will be watching."

"But we're friends," Abel said. "Can't she come hang out just like friends do?"

The moms looked at each other. The look said something, something like they didn't *want* their daughter to be friends with Abel. Like they were relieved he'd taken the dragon off their hands and hoped he'd now go away. He felt used.

All they said out loud was: "We'll see."

As he made his way home with the secret dragon and the brand-new glass cups for his mom and dad, he felt like there was still a lot the adults weren't telling him. He really wished grown-ups wouldn't say "we'll see" when what they really meant was "no."

He was the boy with the dragon now, after all. The least they could do was be honest with him.

7

"**THE LEAST YOU CAN DO** is be honest with us!"

As Abel returned to his new home carrying the crated dragon, he found his mom and Lina arguing inside. Mom looked exasperated and Lina nonplussed, which meant the same thing, really, and which kind of summed up his sister and his mother's relationship lately: two similar yet mutually incomprehensible words.

"*Flame and bile*, Mom, I *am* being honest!" Lina yelled, throwing her arms into the air.

"Don't use that kind of language with me, young lady!" their mom yelled back.

"I'm telling you—I didn't *do* anything wrong." Lina was still in her work overalls and thick rubber boots. The smell was powerful, which was a relief, because the smell from the crate in Abel's arms was powerful too.

"You wouldn't have gotten a citation if you weren't doing anything wrong," Abel's mother scolded her, waving a paper ticket in her face. It looked just like the kind Silas had given to Kayda's moms.

"The sheriff has it out for me," Lina said. "One of her deputies was following me all day. The moment I stepped outside for lunch, they gave me a ticket for loitering! What even is that? It literally means standing around doing nothing! How is that a crime?"

For once, Abel was glad his mom and big sister were arguing.

They were so distracted in the kitchen, he could slip right past them and sneak upstairs to conceal his baby wyvern. He was soaked in sweat, even though the temperature outside had started to drop. The dragon inside his crate was giving off a lot of heat. He also thought the crate felt heavier than when he'd first picked it up. He knew dragons grew fast, but he wasn't sure how fast. Maybe his arms were just super weak.

"You know how it is, honey," he heard their father say. Dad was always trying to make peace between Lina and Mom—just as Lina and Mom were always trying to start fights with each other. Probably because they were so similar. Or because Lina was the middle child. Or because she was a teenager and acted like it. Abel tried to act as little like a teenager as he could. That was his way of keeping peace in the family. "A crime is whatever the ones with the badge say it is," Dad continued. "So you need to be extra careful here."

"They still see you as the criminal you were," their mom added gently, which provoked a very ungentle response.

"I was not a criminal!" Lina yelled.

"You did a lot of crimes!" Mom yelled back.

The two of them were like racing dragons, going from the cool ground to the blazing sky with one snap of their wings.

"What I *did* and who I *am* are totally different things," Lina said. "Does scolding me all the time make *you* a scold?"

"Your mother is not a scold," Dad said.

"See?" Lina growled.

"Honey," Dad said. He coughed a little, a lingering effect of the Scaly Lung he'd had. "This town is a chance to start a new life for you."

"I *liked* my old life," Lina whined.

"Well, between the Dragon's Eye wanting you arrested and the Sky Knights wanting you dead, you didn't really have a choice, did you?" their mom said.

"It's not my fault any of that happened!" Lina replied. "It was Abel who—"

Just then, Omi sneezed. The crate shook in Abel's arms, and he froze where he stood.

"Abel? You home?" Abel's mom called.

He heard a sizzling sound and smelled something burning. When he looked down, he saw a hole bubbling open in the side of the crate. A curious little dragon eye peered out of it.

"Yeah, Mom, I'm home!" Abel shouted, and rushed to his room. "I just . . . um . . . I need to go to the bathroom!"

He slammed his door and dropped the crate, peeling off the top and pulling out the glasses. The inside was more crowded because Omelette had indeed grown just during Abel's walk home. Several of the glasses had broken under her weight, not to mention the ones melted by her acidic sneeze. When he scooped her out of the crate, she blinked her large silver eyes at him and licked her lips.

"Hungry?" he asked. She just blinked, so he set her on the bed and mimed picking up food and eating it.

Still, she just stared at him.

"Oh, right," he said, and then he mimed breathing out acid onto something, then diving in with his face and devouring it. He even made little *nom-nom* eating sounds.

Omi squeaked out a tiny sound that Abel decided meant yes.

"Okay, you hide here." He opened his closet door and waved her inside. He dumped the glass shards from her crate onto the floor and let her settle on top of them, trying to avoid cutting himself. It was unfortunate she'd made her nest from broken glass, but then again, she was a dragon. She didn't choose her housing situation based on what was comfortable for humans. She hadn't chosen to be born into a human town at *all*. Making her comfortable was the least Abel could do, even if it came with some risks. "I'll be right back with some food."

Once she'd settled in, he shut the closet door and brought the surviving glasses down to his mom and dad.

"Kayda's parents sent a gift, but they got a little jostled when I dropped the box," he explained.

"Well, isn't that thoughtful of them?" his mom said, looking at the hole in the box quizzically. "I'll have to invite them for dinner sometime."

"Can I get a snack?" Abel asked, opening the fridge. He didn't see anything a wyvern might like. Everything they had was either junk food or vegetables. Wyverns ate meat. He wasn't sure how he'd smuggle meat into his room, even if they had it. He settled on a jar of black bean butter, which he figured at least had protein like meat.

He took the whole jar back to his room.

Omelette recoiled at the smell.

"I'm sorry," he said. "It's all I could find. Maybe dinner will be better?"

She hesitated, then sniffed it again, her golden nostrils flaring. Then she spat on it to make it sizzle. She briefly looked between Abel and the jar of bean butter before devouring the whole thing with a single startling *crunch*—glass and metal lid and all.

Omi followed it up with a burp and went right to sleep.

Abel sat on the end of his bed and stared at her, wondering what he was supposed to do now.

Roa would know. If they were here, they'd have all sorts of plans for feeding and training schedules. Topher would probably design some kind of cool harness and flying rig for her. And Arvin would be able to get any supplies they needed, and probably bribe the sheriff to keep them from getting in trouble. Roa's and Topher's families were as broke as Abel's, but Arvin's mom was one of the richest people in Drakopolis. He was the only son of Jazinda Balk, boss of the Red Talons kin. They were the most feared criminal kin in the city. The fact that she hated Abel complicated his friendship with Arvin but didn't stop it.

Family is complicated, Arvin had told him once. *I want to be my own man.* At the time he'd said it, he was dressed up as a glamorous bejeweled dragon queen for a live performance. The memory made Abel chuckle.

He really missed his friends. Before he left, he'd given each of them one of his favorite T-shirts, hoping they wouldn't forget him. Topher got a *Wing Maidens* T-shirt. Roa, his DrakoTek Elite Silver T-shirt. And Arvin got *Dr. Drago on Ice!* They all smelled like him, and they all said something about his personality. They felt like a part of him he could leave behind.

In the end, though, they were just shirts. Knowing his friends had them did nothing to heal the loneliness he felt.

He wasn't allowed to contact his friends; that was one of the rules of his exile to this town. But his heart leapt when he saw one little bar of reception on his phone. The Dragon's Eye was probably monitoring their calls, but he decided to risk sending a message to the group chat. It had to be in code so the agents couldn't understand it, but it had to be understandable to them.

He lay back on his bed, thinking about what to write.

"Dr. Drago, St. George's Day Special, page four," he said aloud as he typed. It was an issue of the comic he knew they'd all have. On page four, Dr. Drago says, "Friendship is better than a cell phone, because the connection doesn't require batteries. It makes its own electricity."

He hoped they'd look it up. What he was really saying was, *Please don't forget me.*

He stared at his phone, waiting for the little dots to appear that meant someone was typing.

He waited and waited and waited.

No dots.

He looked at his pictures of his friends, remembering all the fun they'd had, all the danger they'd faced. He even had photos of their addresses so that he wouldn't forget where they lived. Maybe he could send them a letter.

How? he wondered. No way the Dragon's Eye would let a letter get through. They wanted Abel and his family cut off, and it looked like they'd succeeded.

His phone buzzed, and he switched to the message screen, already smiling.

The smile vanished when he saw the red error sign: MESSAGE FAILED TO SEND.

His one little bar of signal was gone.

He threw the phone down and groaned.

This was the cruelest part of the punishment he'd gotten for illegal dragon battling. It was the part that made him maddest. He was alone. He had a Rose Thorn wyvern and didn't even have anyone to tell about it.

He lay there for a long time, seething about the injustice of it all. But Abel must have fallen asleep, because the next thing he knew, he was waking up to a life-or-death duel taking place on his bed. And no matter who won, Abel was going to lose.

Somehow, Omi had gotten out of the closet while Abel was asleep. And somehow, Percy, the family's pet pangolin, had gotten into his room. They were both on Abel's bed now, on opposite sides of his body, snarling at each other.

A pangolin is a scaled mammal with a long snout and thick, strong claws. Its body is armored, and it can roll into a defensive ball when it's frightened or when it wants to attack.

Percy rolled into a ball just then as Omi hissed and spat acid at him.

"Omelette, no!" Abel yelled, but the acid sizzled harmlessly on Percy's scales. Pangolins had evolved protection against dragons' breath. A few drops burned holes in Abel's sheets, though. He wasn't sure how he'd explain that to his mom. Silas had been washing his own sheets since he went to the Academy; Abel figured he should start now too.

Percy rolled forward, and Abel pulled his knees out of the way just in time. The armored pangolin ball smashed into Omi and bowled her over. Both creatures crashed to the floor. They were about the same size and immediately began grappling with each other; the spiky wyvern clung and clawed uselessly at Percy's back, wings flapping, while Percy rolled and crashed about, knocking Omi into the nightstand and the bed frame and the wall with thunderous *thunk*s.

"Stop it, stop it, stop it!" Abel warned them both. "Percy, down! Omelette, it's okay! He's a friend!"

"Everything all right up there?" Abel's mother called.

"Yeah!" Abel shouted back. "I'm just . . . uh . . . doing exercise?"

"Are you wrestling?" his mother shouted.

"With . . . um . . . Percy?" Abel replied, and wished it hadn't come out like a question.

"Well, get cleaned up for dinner!" she told him. "Your brother's home!"

Abel dove on top of his pet and his wyvern and yanked them apart. A wing smacked his face and a claw tore his shirt, but they parted. Percy even uncurled enough to hiss at the wyvern, who hissed back.

"You two are family now!" Abel said. "I need you to watch out for each other, not attack!"

The wyvern lowered her wings, relaxed her body. Percy uncurled further.

"I've got enough problems without you trying to eat each other," he added, though Percy was an insectivore, meaning he ate insects. But he had been known to snack on spicy banana chips, unattended dumplings, and even mint chocolate Wyvern Wafers. It wasn't beyond imagining that he'd try to snack on an actual wyvern.

As for Omi, she was probably starving for meat and Percy had plenty on him. So, Abel thought, did he. If the little wyvern got hungry enough, both of them could end up dragon food.

Still, training a dragon was mostly about trust. He had to show Omi he trusted her.

"I've gotta go downstairs for dinner," he said. "Will you be okay up here on your own?"

Omi snorted and walked her little waddling way back to the closet, where she curled on her pile of glass again. Percy snorted at her but followed Abel from the room. Abel closed the door behind him, took a deep breath, and went downstairs to face his family.

• • •

Their dad had just set out dinner, though Lina said she wasn't hungry for his spiced chickpea burgers or cucumber salad or even his homemade chili rolls.

"Working in the sewers all day kind of steals your appetite," she said.

"Stolen, huh? That's ironic," their mom told her, licking a glob of roasted eggplant dip off the wooden stirring spoon.

Clearly, the two hadn't come to much of a peace agreement while Abel had been napping. Lina rolled her eyes.

"Looks delicious to me," Silas said. "Thank you for cooking, Dad."

Silas was still in his green deputy's uniform. Abel tensed at the gleam of his badge. He was harboring an illegal dragon just upstairs, and he didn't know if Percy and the wyvern were going to get into another fight in the middle of dinner. So far, at least, the pangolin stayed close, rubbing against his ankles. He was probably jealous.

"Abel, please take your seat," said their dad. "And, Lina, you don't have to eat, but you do have to sit with us. It's our first dinner in our new home."

"Ugh." Lina groaned but obeyed.

It was a rule in their family that whenever they were all home, they would sit together for dinner, no matter what else was going on in life: extra shifts, exams, or exile to an isolated desert town. Family time was his parents' favorite thing, even family time as fraught as theirs.

"Fraught" was a word Abel had learned from the school counselor back in Drakopolis, when he'd been assigned to see her twice a week. It meant basically "causing or affected by anxiety or stress." He was told to avoid fraught situations so as not to trigger his anxiety while he was still learning coping strategies.

Easier said than done.

He was harboring an illegal wyvern in a town where the sheriff hated him, the deputies were corrupt, and his brother was loyal to the law Abel was currently breaking.

Also he still missed his friends.

Every situation in his life was fraught.

"How was your tour?" Mom asked.

"Well, why don't you ask Silas?" Abel replied, giving Silas a look as hot as a kiln.

Their mom cocked her head, curious.

"Abel met my partner, Deputy Manchi," Silas said. "They didn't quite get along."

"Oh, Abel," his dad sighed. "Please don't start trouble with the sheriff's deputies on the first day."

"*I* didn't do anything," Abel countered. "Silas's partner is a bully and a—"

"And an officer of the law," Silas cut him off. "And you don't know enough about this town to go questioning the sheriff's deputies before you've even unpacked your cartoon underwear."

"My underwear doesn't have cartoons on it!" Abel objected, though he did have three pairs of Dr. Drago boxer shorts.

"Don't stick your nose into police business, Abel," Silas told him.

"Don't stick your nose into my underwear!" Abel told him back. "Creep."

"You really shouldn't get caught up with the wrong sort of people, Abel," Silas warned. "That's kind of how we ended up here in the first place."

"You're *glad* we're here," Abel snapped at him. "You get to be a big shot in Glassblower's Gulch, and you *like* it. I saw how afraid Kayda's parents were. You *liked* terrorizing innocent people."

"I don't like terrorizing people," Silas said.

"You terrorized people?" their mom asked.

Silas looked at his plate. "No, Mom, I didn't," he said. "I did my job. How they felt about it isn't in my control."

"Silas, that sounds like an excuse," their dad said. "Not a denial. If you terrorized people, you really should apologize."

Silas threw his hands in the air. "I didn't terrorize anyone! I am a sheriff's deputy!" He tapped the badge on his chest. "I'm not a criminal like your *other* children!" He glared at Lina and Abel.

"We only ever stole from other criminals," Abel said. "You're the one who robbed civilians today. Just because you wear a badge doesn't mean you can't be a crook."

"If anything, it's more likely," Lina grumbled under her breath.

Silas glared at her, then at Abel. His face twitched. Abel had hit his mark. His brother needed to see himself as the hero, and Abel had just poked a hole in the most important story he told himself about himself.

Silas set his jaw and stood up from the table. "I am not going to sit here like a wyvern warming an egg while you all insult me." Abel froze. *Did Silas know?* "I'm the only reason you aren't all in Windlee Prison right now," he continued. "And what thanks do I get? Abel calls me a bully and a crook, and none of you come to my defense!" He looked from his brother and sister to his parents. "I'm your son too, you know!"

Silas's voice cracked. His eyes were wet. No one answered him.

Silas snorted. "I'm going back to the station." He hesitated, then turned to Abel like he was going to say something else. Instead, he stormed out. The rest of them sat in the heavy silence that followed.

Lina finally broke the tension her big brother had left in his wake. "Well, he feels guilty."

Their mom and dad shook their heads. "You don't poke a dragon in the armpit when it's opened its wings for you," his father told her. It was an old saying. A dragon's armpits were its weakest spot.

That was the thing about family, Abel thought. They often knew you better than you knew yourself—and could poke you in your weakest spots better than anyone. It was a powerful thing to know other people so well, and, like any power, it had to be used responsibly. Every day a family didn't make each other storm out in rage or burst into tears was a mercy. It was like riding a dragon. Even though you *could* use it to burn everything around you to cinders didn't mean you *should*.

"You want to tell us what happened?" Abel's dad asked.

Abel shook his head and stood from the table. "I gotta apologize to Silas." He hated that he had to be the bigger person. He was six years younger than his brother, but angry words were the same as fire or acid, really. Once you spat them out, you couldn't just take them back. They burned whatever they hit. The only thing you could do afterward was to help heal the hurts you'd caused, and Abel had caused some hurt.

Abel ran outside to catch up to Silas.

"Go back inside," Silas snapped at him as he took the stairs up from their house two at a time. He moved fast, heading for the top of the gulch.

"I didn't mean to call you a bully," Abel said.

Silas stopped. He looked down at Abel. "Yes, you did," he told him. Then he sighed and leaned against the wall beside the stairs, his eyes still teary. He knocked the back of his head against the hard glass canyon wall. "Manchi *was* bullying those people, and I didn't stop it. He went there again, you know?"

"He did?"

"Yeah," said Silas. "Tore the place apart looking for signs of an illegal dragon. Didn't find anything."

"That's good, though, isn't it?" said Abel. "That they weren't hiding anything."

Silas shook his head. "It means you were right. We terrorized innocent people."

"I was—" Abel gasped. He wasn't certain that at any point in his thirteen years drawing breath in the world, Silas had ever told him he was right about anything before. Somewhere below, two cockatrices clucked and screeched at each other.

Abel felt a little bad. For once, Silas was being a decent guy, and he was beating himself up over what he'd done . . . except he hadn't been exactly wrong. Kayda's family *was* hiding an illegal dragon. They weren't 100 percent innocent, technically.

"I knew what Deputy Manchi was doing was wrong, and I didn't stop him," Silas said. "I should have. I'm going to Sheriff Skint right now."

"What are you going to tell her?" Abel asked. He knew his brother loved being a cop—and he also knew that reporting something like this on his first day on the job was a big risk. What if she didn't believe him? What if she believed him but didn't care?

"I'm going to tell her what happened," said Silas. "That the girl and her parents were innocent, but Deputy Manchi used his badge to threaten and rob them. And I'm going to request that Manchi and I be suspended until a full investigation can take place." He looked at his little brother sadly. "You might have to testify," he said. "It might be trouble for all of us."

Abel nodded. "I'm used to trouble," he said.

He tried not to think about the wyvern in his room, growing hungrier by the minute.

"I know you are, little brother." Silas laughed and gave Abel a gentle shove. "You hoard trouble like a dragon hoards treasure, don't you?"

"It's not like I *try* to find trouble," Abel said. "I just notice when things aren't fair, and I try to help."

"In Drakopolis, nothing's fair," Silas said.

"But we aren't in Drakopolis anymore," Abel pointed out.

"So maybe we can actually make a difference here," Silas said. "Now go home. Let me handle this. For once, it's a mess I made myself."

Silas turned to go up the canyon stairs, but he only made it about two steps before a shadow dropped from the center of the canyon. A stubby, horned Hog dragon with huge, jagged tusks flapped in place over them. Its belly was armored, and its sparkling brown scales were mostly covered in combat gear and equipment. Even its head was helmeted, like it was prepared for war.

"That's a RAD," Silas whispered.

"I mean, sure, I guess it's cool," Abel agreed, confused by his brother's old slang at a time like this.

"No, R-A-H-D," Silas clarified. "A Rapid Assault Hog Dragon. We used them in Drakopolis for sieges and hostage situations. You do not want to be on the wrong side of one."

"Okay, so what's it doing here?" Abel whispered back. He took a few shuffling steps closer to his brother, whether for protection or to protect him he wasn't quite sure. He just knew when you were staring down the snout of a Rapid Assault Hog Dragon, it was good to have family as close as possible.

The dragon rider shined a horn-mounted spotlight at Silas and Abel, blinding them in its glare.

"Just the boys I was looking for!" Sheriff Skint shouted. A rope ladder dropped in front of them. "Deputy, if you wouldn't mind, I'd like you and your brother to come for a ride."

Silas grabbed the rope ladder. "Try not to let your mouth get us in any *more* trouble," he told Abel as he climbed up.

Abel glanced back down the canyon toward their apartment and wondered what kind of trouble they were now in. As he settled into the passenger saddle on the dragon's back, he really hoped Omi could wait a little longer for dinner before trying to eat the family pet. Or the family.

Lina stood in the doorway, their parents behind her, watching the sheriff's dragon fly away over the top of Glassblower's Gulch.

Abel looked at the moon and stars. So far from the lights of Drakopolis, he could see swirling galaxies in the distance, and brilliant constellations like the Reaper's Hoard and the Claw of the Moon. He'd never been able to make them out from home before because the building lights and advertisements and pollution dulled the night sky. Out past civilization, the sky was so much grander. Abel would've liked to enjoy it more, but something told him the sheriff wasn't taking them for a stargazing flight.

"The station's that way, isn't it?" Silas asked Sheriff Skint over her shoulder.

"Who said we were going to the station?" she replied. Then she turned her Hog dragon sideways, banking over the security fencing toward the broad plain of the glass desert, gliding in for a landing.

That's when Abel saw the bleachers filled with people and bright lights pointing at a large, flat oval, its surface scarred with gouges and scorch marks and bubbles of melted and re-hardened glass.

"Welcome to the dragon rodeo," Sheriff Skint said. "I think you'll both find it very *interesting.*"

At that moment, Abel heard the roar of a dragon—a Candy Cane Reaper—as it was pulled in chains to the center of the oval. Three people waited there for the dragon . . . and they too were in chains.

It was Kayda and her moms.

THE CROWD IN THE BLEACHERS—which must have been everyone in town except for Abel's family—cheered as the Reaper was pulled forward like a pet pangolin on a leash. And just like a pet pangolin, it resisted being led. A sheriff's deputy behind it had to jab its side with a stun spear, forcing it forward. Deputy Manchi, positioned in front, yanked its chain.

The Candy Cane Reaper was a medium-wing dragon with pale pink scales, bright white horns, and wide, white-striped wings. It looked like a candy cane and had a sweet name for such a deadly dragon.

Abel had never seen one outside of his DrakoTek game deck, though he'd lost the only card he'd had of it to Roa last year. Candy Cane Reapers had a breath weapon of "sticky fire." They shot globs of slow-burning goo that stuck to whatever it hit, whether it was the wall of a building, an enemy's armor, or a person's fragile flesh.

The three people chained up in front of it certainly looked fragile when its gleaming yellow eyes settled on them.

"That's Kayda and her family!" Abel cried out, sliding off the sheriff's dragon and hitting the ground with a thump. He looked up at Sheriff Skint. "What's happening to them?"

The sheriff took her time climbing down and stood behind Abel. She rested a heavy hand on each of his shoulders. It was a gesture that would look friendly to anyone watching, but if hands could talk, hers would be whispering threats in his ears.

"This is how we settle disputes in our town," Sheriff Skint said.

"What do you mean?" Abel asked. His voice came out hoarse. Silas stood next to him. He and the sheriff wore the same uniform, but suddenly, it looked far too large for Abel's brother, like he was shrinking in it with every word Sheriff Skint spoke.

"We're on the edge of the wilds here," the sheriff said, "and we have to keep the peace somehow. So we hold the dragon rodeo, as we have since before my great-great-grandmother's great-great-grandmother was sheriff here. It's our oldest tradition. Maybe even older than Drakopolis."

"This isn't right," Silas said as quietly as a mouse sighing.

Still, the sheriff heard him. "You have *an objection*, Deputy?"

"This isn't right," Silas said louder, turning to face his boss, who gripped Abel's shoulders more tightly. She was just barely taller than Abel, and much shorter than Silas, but she was built much more powerfully than either of them. And she shimmered with authority the way heat shimmers off a grill.

"I am not sure you understand what you're saying," the sheriff told him. "These people"—she pointed toward the family cowering in front of the chained Reaper—"are criminals. We are a town of limited resources. Rather than investigating them for eons just to jail them and pay for their upkeep in prison, we give them a fighting chance. They'll be untied, as will the dragon. And then they can attempt to subdue it. If they do, all is forgiven *and* they're given a healthy cash prize. If they do not, well . . . the dragon gets *them* for a prize. This isn't some tame beast from the city breeders either. This is a wild dragon, caught last night as it prowled the edges of our town. You see, when I say we have to keep the peace, I don't just mean with each other."

The sheriff pointed to the distant horizon beyond the bleachers and gulch, out toward the endless expanse of stars over the desert. "There are wild dragons out there who would lay waste to us here if we let them, dragons by the hundreds who threaten all we've built. It would take an army to fight them off, and the death toll would be incalculable. But instead, since this town's first founding, we've had a kind of truce. Citizens of our town versus one of them. If our people win, we take the dragon captive. If they win, they get the people. As long as the rodeo has run, the wild dragons have left us mostly alone. If the rodeo doesn't happen, well . . . they'll attack. The last time some reformer tried to stop it, we lost dozens of good people, carried off to feed wild hatchlings."

"But Kayda's family is innocent!" Abel objected, not exactly truthfully.

"We're humans in a dragons' world," said the sheriff. "None of us are innocent."

That, Abel knew, was entirely true.

Sheriff Skint pulled a whistle from her belt. "And besides, they knew the rules. Someone has to be in the rodeo."

Deputy Manchi finished getting the Candy Cane Reaper in position and released the chain from its neck. Then he turned to Kayda and her family and said something Abel couldn't hear. Kimber must not have liked what she heard, because she spat in the deputy's face. Kayda tried to kick him in the shin. He glared down at the girl and wagged his finger, putting one hand on the stun gun at his belt. Then he undid their chains and signaled the other deputy to scurry from the arena to the stands.

For a long moment, the family stared up at the dragon and the dragon stared down at the family. Abel's heart raced, but he didn't dare so much as breathe lest the slightest noise trigger the violence to begin.

The Reaper snorted and stomped, lowering its head to the humans' level. It opened its mouth to show the flickering flame at the back of its throat. Across the distance that separated them, Abel heard Kayda whimper.

"Someone has to help them," he whispered.

Silas nodded, but neither his feet nor Abel's moved. It was easy to imagine yourself heroic, but it was a lot harder to actually put yourself between an angry dragon and its prey. Fear had a way of overruling feet.

Abel felt the sheriff's grip tighten again, in case he or his feet did eventually find their courage. She whistled three shrill bursts, and Abel saw that his new friend and her parents weren't nearly as helpless as he'd imagined.

Because the moment the third whistle blasted, Kayda did a diving forward roll. At the same time, her moms each dove sideways in opposite directions. When the dragon's ball of flame fired, it sizzled and smoked against empty swirls of desert glass.

Kayda rolled right back to her feet, under the dragon's exposed belly. She scooped up a shard of glass that the dragon's stomping had broken free. Then she used her forward momentum to thrust the glass shard up into the dragon's skin.

A loose shard of glass would have shattered against dragon scales, but the flesh of the underbelly, though still thick and tough, was a lot more vulnerable than any other part of the dragon. That's why battle dragons always wore armor over their bellies—and why remote-controlled ground weapon cards were valuable in DrakoTek.

They could attack from underneath and gave a +3 damage bonus against armored dragons.

This was no card game, though, and Kayda wasn't playing. She was fighting for survival. The thrust of her shard found its mark, driving into the Candy Cane Reaper's thick pink skin.

The dragon roared and leapt into the air, flapping backward away from the girl. The glass shard was still stuck in its flesh. Kayda held on to it and lifted off the ground with the dragon, feet dangling as she rose.

"Savvy!" Althea yelled—kinner slang again. It must have been a signal, because Kayda let go and dropped to the ground in a crouch. Kimber ran across the flat glass to use her daughter's back as a springboard, leaping up and smacking the shard deeper into the dragon's belly in one smooth jump. She landed perfectly on her feet and ran for cover, hand in hand with her daughter. They'd practiced this.

The dragon roared in pain, so loudly and shrilly it made Abel wince.

He didn't want to see this family hurt, but he didn't want them hurting the dragon either.

The crowd cheered the humans' victory, and Abel heard Sheriff Skint let out a laugh behind him. It made the hair on the back of his neck prickle.

"See?" said the sheriff. "Everyone smart prepares for a night like this, and your new friend and her parents are pretty smart. Maybe they'll win?"

"How often do the humans win?" Abel asked.

The sheriff snorted. "Almost never."

Abel pinned his prayers to the "almost," not the "never."

10

THE REAPER FIRED THREE QUICK balls of flame,
which hit the glass like meteors and sizzled slowly. They bubbled
against the surface, melting the colorful glass to white-hot liquid.
Then the dragon took a deep breath and blew a massive jet of air
from its nostrils with such force that the liquid glass shot into the
air. It cooled immediately into thousands of tiny needles, all of them
flying toward Kayda and her family with the speed of the dragon's
snort. The Reaper beat the air with its wings so the tiny shards of
glass scattered, making a dodge impossible.

Althea and Kimber locked arms and enveloped Kayda under their
bodies, using their backs to shield her from the rain of glass. Tiny
pinpricks were cut into their clothes, revealing body armor
underneath.

"We aren't monsters," said Sheriff Skint. "We wouldn't send our
fellow citizens up against a dragon completely unprotected." She
paused and spat on the ground. "Besides, the match would be over
too quickly. That wouldn't be any fun, would it? What would
people bet on?"

"You're the sheriff!" Silas objected. "You're not supposed to do
things like this! And gambling on their lives? That's—that's—"
Silas was at a loss for words.

"Monstrous," said Abel.

The sheriff let go of Abel's shoulders and spun him around to face her. Silas stepped toward him, but Sheriff Skint held up a hand, stopping him without a word.

"I use the profits I make from the gambling at the rodeo to buy supplies for the town," she said. "To import water and to buy rugs that protect against the cold. To bring in raw materials needed to make everything from food to furniture. If you hadn't noticed, this ain't the big city, kids. We can't get anything we want with the touch of an app. Everything's expensive out here on the edge of the world."

"Except life," said Abel.

"Excuse me?" The sheriff scowled.

"You're treating life like it's cheap," Abel said. "But it's the most precious thing anyone has!"

"You haven't yet been here a day, so I'm going to forgive that one," the sheriff said. Then she looked at Silas. "But you need to keep your little brother in line. Honestly, Deputy, I expected trouble from him and your sister, but not from you."

"I'm not trying to cause trouble," said Silas. "I'm just trying to serve justice. And this does not seem like justice."

The sheriff shook her head and clucked like a cockatrice. "Top of your class at the Academy, they told me, and yet you don't understand a thing." Silas frowned. "You don't serve *justice* in that uniform. You serve *the law*, and the law here is what I *say* it is. Got it?"

Abel looked at his big brother, so proud of his deputy's uniform, so eager for his career to thrive—but also, Abel knew, an idealist. Loyal to his family. Far from his own friends and his partner and his life back in the city. He was here because he always put duty first and believed in justice, but now his duty told him to serve something obviously unjust. The contradiction was making Silas's face look like a glitching video game.

Abel, on the other hand, felt no conflict whatsoever. He knew right from wrong. Neither Kayda's family nor the Candy Cane Reaper deserved what was happening to them.

"If the authorities back in Drakopolis knew what you were doing, they'd haul you off to prison," Abel told the sheriff. "We can report you."

Instead of being afraid, Sheriff Skint laughed. "The authorities? Oh, Abel, for an unreformed kinner, you are dangerously naive! How have you survived this long without being eaten? You really think the authorities care what I do to keep the wild dragons from attacking the city?" The sheriff patted Abel's shoulder, patronizingly this time. There wasn't even a threat in the gesture. She was genuinely amused. "Anyway, where do you suppose some of the rodeo money goes? Those same Drakopolis authorities you're talking about!"

"What?" Silas gasped. "No. That's corruption!"

"That," Sheriff Skint said, "is Drakopolis. Everyone's just trying to survive. Even your beloved dragons."

She gestured back at the arena, where the Candy Cane Reaper was circling Kayda and her parents on foot. Its head was low to the ground, eyes narrowed to slits. Its wound had made it wary. Dragons were not reckless monsters of wanton violence. Abel knew they were smart, calculating creatures, and this one would not underestimate its foes again. They'd earned its respect, but that didn't mean it would spare them.

"Come on!" Kayda taunted the dragon. "Wanna try again, you candy-colored cloud cuddler?!"

The dragon growled. Dragons did not like to be mocked. Flame grew in its throat, and Kayda's moms adjusted their footing to attack.

In his own dragon rider training, Abel had learned about something called the OODA loop, which was a technique for making quick decisions in a combat flying situation. It was an acronym, where each letter stood for an entire word. O-O-D-A: observe, orient, decide, act.

With every situation, you observed what was happening, oriented yourself in the battle, decided what to do, and acted on that decision. You kept running through that OODA loop until the battle was over or you'd been fried alive.

Abel saw now that, for all their preparation, neither Kayda nor her parents were skilled dragon battlers. They had a plan, and they were sticking to it, preparing another dodge and attack. They'd already decided their next action, skipping the *oo* and going right to the *da*.

The problem was, the Reaper wasn't going to fall for the same trick twice. Kayda and her moms didn't observe its massive, spiked tail slowly curling around to the side, or orient themselves in response. If they tried the same diving roll they'd used the first time, the dragon's tail would swing around and slash all three of them down in one brutal sweep. Then it'd be easy for the dragon to incinerate them.

In the stands, Abel saw Deputy Manchi handing glass coins to someone and getting a scrap of paper back. He was placing a bet on the battle, and it definitely wasn't a bet in Kimber, Althea, and Kayda's favor. He'd gotten them into this trouble, robbed them, and now he was profiting off their destruction too!

The injustice was infuriating, and Abel felt helpless against it.

He thought about the Rose Thorn wyvern back in his room. If Omi grew up fast and he could train her, he could challenge this lousy sheriff and teach her a lesson.

And then what? He was one little kid with one little dragon, who wasn't going to grow any faster just because Abel wanted her to. Even if she did, and even if he could train her, he couldn't take on the sheriff and her RAHD. There was no way to help Kayda and her moms right now.

I'm catastrophizing again, he told himself. But then he realized, as the crowd roared and the Reaper spat fire, that it wasn't *catastrophizing* if you were witnessing a real-life catastrophe. Kayda's family was really about to get burned to cinders if someone didn't help them.

Abel looked at his brother.

Silas was a trained dragon rider himself, an experienced agent of the Dragon's Eye. He'd run his own OODA loop and made the same observation Abel had. He was already shaking his head and muttering, "They're not gonna make it."

"You think you'd do better, Deputy?" Sheriff Skint asked him.

Silas was a lot of things, but humble was not one of them. "Of course," he said.

Instantly, Sheriff Skint pulled out her whistle and blasted it three more times. The crowd hushed. The dragon hesitated, and Kayda's whole family looked back in the sheriff's direction.

That was the first moment Kayda saw Abel, and she cocked her head at him, puzzled.

"You'll get your chance," Skint told Silas. "Right now." Then she yelled out toward the arena, "Substitution!"

"What?" Silas exclaimed.

"What?" Abel groaned.

"You're so concerned with protecting this family from the law, despite your partner's report that they're criminals," said the sheriff. "So why don't you take their place? If you choose to."

Silas shifted on his feet, took a deep breath, and nodded. "I will," he said.

Sheriff Skint blew her whistle one more time, and that's when the Divas came out.

11

THE DEADLY BATTLE BETWEEN THE family and the ferocious sky serpent transformed into a silly sideshow.

As soon as the Dragon Distraction Divas scurried onto the field, the Candy Cane Reaper reared back on its hind legs and grunted, confused.

There were three Divas, each dressed in bright colors, wearing huge silk wings and made up to look like brilliant half human, half dragons. They came out dancing. One, dressed to look like a Jewel dragon, twirled a long sparkler, while the other two did flapping leaps in front of it, like two wyverns at the Dragon Ballet . . . until they pretended to trip over each other, tangling their hands like claws and pretending to battle with a series of growls and snarls.

The crowd laughed.

Kayda's family looked on, stunned that their duel had been stopped.

"Well?" the sheriff said to Silas. "The Divas can't stay out there forever. That dragon's going to try to flay them alive too. If you want to serve and protect this so-called innocent family, now's your chance. Get in there."

Silas swallowed hard, then stepped toward the arena.

"Silas!" Abel cried out. "Let me help!"

Silas held a hand up. "No," he said firmly. "This is my job. Just . . . keep yourself out of it, okay? Whatever happens. Look out for Mom and Dad. Keep Lina from going back to her old ways."

"I—" Abel didn't know what to say. His brother was doing something risky and selfless—and it was kind of Abel's fault. Abel wasn't even getting scolded for it! He was, for that brief moment, in awe of his big brother. "I will," he choked out through almost tears.

"Swear on a secret," his brother said.

"I swear," Abel told him. "I swear on . . . uh . . . well, I think you're just about the bravest guy I know."

Silas smiled. They weren't the sort of brothers who said nice things about each other, at least not *to* each other.

"Now you swear on a secret that you'll come back safely!" Abel said.

Silas looked at the Candy Cane Reaper and then at Abel. His eyes were damp. He chewed his bottom lip. "I won't make a promise I can't keep," he said. "If anything happens, get a message to my old Dragon's Eye partner in the city, will you?" he asked. "Tell Kai I tried."

"You'll tell him yourself!" Abel pleaded.

"I really hope so, Abel," Silas sighed. "But it's not up to me."

Just then, the Candy Cane Reaper lost patience with the Divas. It fired three blazing balls of sticky flame, which they all dodged with acrobatic tumbles.

"This is all very touching, Deputy," Sheriff Skint said. "But if you're gonna help those people, do it now."

"Ep ep," Silas grunted in his military way. He gave his boss a formal dragon-claw salute, which she definitely didn't deserve, then threw another to Abel, which he definitely didn't want. It felt like a goodbye.

Abel watched helplessly as Silas ran toward Kayda and her parents, tapping them out. They had a quick discussion, maybe an argument, but then scuttled from the arena to the relative safety of the stands. Silas turned to face the dragon alone, watching as the Divas skipped away toward their dragon-proof shelter.

One of them tripped. The crowd gasped as the Candy Cane Reaper leapt for them, twelve tons of wild dragon crashing down over a fragile, brightly costumed human. But just as the dragon's massive claw came down on the Diva, Silas slide-tackled them out of the way, pushing them aside and positioning himself between two of the dragon's claws.

He popped to his feet before the Reaper could crush him, then climbed the huge claws like they were a kid's playground equipment. Soon Silas stood on the back of the dragon's foot, taunting it with an astonishingly loud and totally unexpected sound.

"PLLLLLLLLLFFFFT!"

The crowd froze. The dragon froze. Even Silas froze.

"Was that a fart noise?" Sheriff Skint wondered aloud.

"I don't think they teach *that* in military school," Abel said.

Dragons, of course, were proud creatures. They could abide pain and bloodshed and even being harnessed and put to work, but they would *not* abide disrespect. Silas's sound was the height of disrespect.

The dragon roared and spat a ball of fire straight down at Abel's brother . . . who was still standing on its foot.

Silas leapt away while the dragon screeched and whimpered and whined, hopping around the arena as its own fireball sizzled on its foot.

This gave the last Diva time to get to their shelter—and gave Silas time to position himself to mount the dragon as it hopped past. It didn't even notice him climb the spikes on its tail.

"Your brother is good. I'm glad I hired him," Sheriff Skint said, like she hadn't been the one who'd forced him into the arena in the first place. Abel started to wonder if this whole thing was a test for Silas. Perhaps it had nothing to do with Abel or Kayda or her family. If that were the case, it made him like the sheriff even less. It was one thing to mess with Abel. He didn't mind being treated like trouble, because, in fact, he was. But all Silas ever did was obey orders and try to uphold the law. To use that against him for some kind of dangerous test was just cruel.

Abel glared sideways at the sheriff and gave his brother a compliment he'd never have said to Silas's face. "He's the best dragon rider I've ever met."

"Better than you?" the sheriff asked.

Abel didn't answer. He just shrugged. In truth, Abel thought both he and Lina were better dragon riders than Silas, but Sheriff Skint didn't get to pit the siblings against each other. Whatever their differences, they were family from snout to tail.

The Reaper had noticed Silas on its back by now. It thrashed its tail wildly to get him off, bucking and rolling and beating its wings. But Silas held on, using the dragon's white and pink spikes for handholds, even as hot steam erupted from the seams between the scales the angrier the wild dragon got.

The crowd cheered when Silas reached the top of the dragon's neck and gripped its horns, standing tall on the top of its head. Then they gasped when the dragon did a sharp nod, tossing Silas off his feet. He dangled over the side of the Reaper's face, holding the horn by one hand. Silas swung himself up again and locked his legs at the base of the dragon's skull like he was ready to ride.

Maybe all those push-ups he does aren't just for showing off, Abel thought. For the first time in his life, he considered exercising even when a gym teacher wasn't forcing him to.

Silas had a firm seat on the dragon now. No matter how much it swung its head and bucked its body, it couldn't shake him off. Abel remembered the time he'd mounted his first dragon. Karak was a Sunrise Reaper, a giant mass of black scales and glowing rage. Abel had nearly been burned and thrown and crushed and eaten, but in time, he and Karak became a team, as close as a human and a dragon could be.

It'd been hard to let Karak go, but Abel had set him free. Then, to his surprise, he'd been forced to tame another dragon only a few months later, a wild mutt named Brazza, who was the fastest dragon Drakopolis had ever seen and also one of the moodiest. Not only had she nearly killed Abel the first time he rode her, she destroyed a department store, a parking garage, and a few city blocks. In time, they'd become something more than a dragon and rider, though. They'd become friends. It'd been even harder to let her go free, but he did it then too. He hoped these dragons were somewhere out in the distant wilds, thinking of him from time to time.

Even the most fearsome dragon could be tamed.

Dragons demanded respect, but they gave it too—*if* a human was willing to earn it and could survive the process. Just because they looked like mortal enemies right now didn't mean Silas couldn't tame this Reaper and win.

"Come on, Silas, hang in there," Abel muttered.

Silas struggled to stay on the thrashing Reaper. The sheriff chortled a little. If Silas won, she got to keep her deputy and a powerful dragon for training. If he lost, she got to prove a point and get rid of a deputy who'd dared to question her. Either way, *she* won.

Except you've made an enemy of me, Abel thought grimly. *And I always vanquish my enemies.*

It was a cool thought to have, especially as he imagined Omi fully grown, dressed in neon armor, spraying acid on Sheriff Skint and her deputies from the sky. It would've felt even cooler if he hadn't let out an accidental yelp at that very moment.

The Candy Cane Reaper did an aerial backward dive, landing flat on its back. It was trying to crush Silas underneath its massive weight!

Abel wanted to throw up when the crowd cheered the dragon's body slam. They didn't care if the human won or lost. Silas wasn't even a person to them, with his own family, his own hopes and loves and wild dreams. He was just their entertainment. They just wanted violence.

What kind of a town is this? Abel wondered. *Maybe the dragon is the least monstrous creature here.*

He held his breath as the Reaper rolled onto its feet and lowered its head to the dust and cracked glass, where Silas's crushed body should've been.

But it wasn't there.

Abel exhaled, wondering where his brother had gone, when he saw Silas clinging to the spikes on the dragon's candy-colored side. His shirt was torn open, his shoulder bloody, but he crept hand over hand back toward the Reaper's neck. Abel could even make out a cocky smirk on his brother's face as he climbed, like he'd outsmarted the dragon.

This was one thing Abel knew about dragons, though. The moment you *thought* you'd outsmarted them was when they devoured you.

The Candy Cane Reaper's nostrils flared. It sniffed the night air. Reapers were great hunters, which was why they were among the best battlers. They enjoyed the hunt and were better at it than short-wings, a lot of whom didn't even have breath weapons. Long-wings, meanwhile, just burned everything they saw from high altitude and devoured whatever was left in the ruins.

Reapers got up close to their prey, and they had an excellent sense of smell.

"Silas, watch out!" Abel yelled as loud as he could, but it was too late.

Without even turning its head, the Reaper snapped its tail down, knocking Silas loose with a sound like a whip splitting the air. Silas fell, limp, into its waiting claw.

The dragon roared at the crowd, sweeping its yellow-eyed glare over them and silencing their cheers. Then it locked eyes with the sheriff, nodding once. She nodded back. Abel's blood chilled in his veins.

The Reaper screeched and launched itself into the air, snapping its wings wide and swirling once over Glassblower's Gulch, before flying away into the glass desert beyond. Silas hung insensate in its claw.

In the stands, Abel saw Kayda bury her head in Kimber's dress and weep while Althea rubbed her back and fought off her own tears. None of them looked in Abel's direction.

Abel didn't know if his big brother was dead or alive. Some Reapers were quick killers, but others hoarded their prey to devour days, months, or even years later. Scientists once found the skeleton of an ancient Lace Wing dragon surrounded by over a hundred human skeletons, all clothed. They hadn't been eaten. They'd been *collected.* Abel didn't know what kind of hoarder the Candy Cane Reaper was, but no living dragons kept humans alive that long. The Lace Wing was extinct. It didn't even have a DrakoTek card. If Silas wasn't dead yet, that was no promise he wouldn't be soon.

A whimper escaped Abel's throat, and Sheriff Skint nodded.

"You'll go home now, Abel," she said coldly.

"What do I tell my parents?" he asked, stiffening his voice despite the tears in his eyes.

"Whatever you want," said Sheriff Skint. "That's not my problem."

Abel clenched his fists, just like Silas when he got mad. She noticed.

"I hope tonight taught you a valuable lesson," she chided him.

"It did," Abel told her through gritted teeth. "It taught me a lot."

She met Abel's eyes, and he didn't look away. "Good. We deal with things our way out here. Don't imagine for a second another junior deputy of mine will risk their life when it's your turn in the rodeo."

"Lieutenant," Abel snarled at her.

"Excuse me?"

"Silas was a *lieutenant* deputy, not a 'junior' deputy. And he earned that rank."

Sheriff Skint's eyes wrinkled with her smile. "That he did," she said. Then she strolled away whistling, leaving Abel to a long and lonely walk home.

He was tempted to jump on the sheriff while her back was turned—to pummel her into sausage, grind her bones, and feed them to a wyvern. But he was just a scrawny kid and she was the law of this town.

This was a fight he couldn't win.

Not yet. Not alone.

Bad things were happening in Glassblower's Gulch, and it was gonna take more than one kid with a baby wyvern to set them right. He needed his friends Roa and Topher and Arvin. Together, they'd brought down scarier thugs than Sheriff Skint. His texts wouldn't go through, but he had to get a message to them somehow. He had to find a way to rescue his big brother. Or at least to avenge him.

He knew now what he'd train Omi to do.

But first he had to tell his mom and dad their oldest son was gone, maybe forever.

PART TWO

"STEALING DRAGONS IS THE
FUN PART."

12

BREAKFAST WAS A GLUM GATHERING in Abel's house the next morning. Silence sat over the table, like a dragon crouched on its hoard.

His parents sipped coffee with puffy eyes from crying all night. Lina was sullen and angry, her thoughts sizzling below her skin like flame building in a dragon's throat. Last night, when Abel told them the news about Silas, she had wanted to charge over to the rodeo and fight the sheriff herself.

"I'll fight this whole town if I have to!" she said. She'd never shown this kind of loyalty to Silas before, Abel thought sadly. It was too bad his big brother wasn't around to see it.

Their parents held Lina back.

"We're not losing another child, not tonight!" their dad had yelled, which shook Abel as much as it did Lina. Their dad was not a yeller.

Abel, for his part, was distracted from his own grief by the plan he was forming and the baby wyvern he still had hidden upstairs.

His family couldn't know. He wouldn't make them a part of his crimes. What had happened to Silas was already his fault. Kayda and her parents would never have been in that rodeo if it weren't for Abel. He had to make it right, by himself. That's what it meant to be responsible. You fix your mistakes, and if they can't be fixed, you do your best to make amends.

Amends or revenge? he asked himself. *Or are they both the same when it comes to dragon justice?*

No matter what, if he got caught with the wyvern, he couldn't risk his family getting thrown into the rodeo too. No way they'd survive. Just as his parents didn't want to lose their children, Abel didn't want to lose his family. He felt responsible for them, which was a weird feeling. Kids shouldn't have to protect their parents, but in a town like Glassblower's Gulch, "shoulds" didn't count for much.

Lina was the first to break the breakfast silence. "Why should I have to work in this stinking town's stinking sewers after they all cheered for Silas's death?" she snapped.

"Hey! None of that!" Their mom pointed at her. "We don't know that he's dead."

"Abel said he got carried away in the claws of a Candy Cane Reaper!" Lina pounded the table. "I know that breed. They are not as sweet as candy."

"And they didn't *all* cheer," Abel muttered. He remembered Kayda burying her face in her moms' arms. Not everyone was happy at the dragon rodeo.

"You will go to work and do your job," their mom told Lina firmly. "We can't risk any more trouble."

"So we're supposed to just do nothing?" she pouted.

"No," said their dad. "I'll write to the City Council of Drakopolis about what's going on here. I'll write to Silas's commanders from the Academy and the Dragon's Eye."

"Why would they care?" Lina scoffed.

"Because your brother is a heroic Dragon's Eye officer who has been grossly mistreated," their mother said.

Lina snorted. "I've been grossly mistreated *by* the Dragon's Eye, and you didn't write any letters for me."

"Lina, you *did* steal dragons, didn't you?" their mom said.

Lina grunted and took a big bite of her breakfast bun. "If you think writing letters is gonna help, knock yourself out. I'll make other plans."

She caught Abel's eye, but he looked away.

"Eat your breakfast," their dad told her. "You too," he said to Abel, though his plate was already empty.

Not that he'd eaten anything. Abel had no appetite. He swiped whatever food he could to give to Omi, though he had noticed new cockatrice bones in his closet when he'd gotten home. She must have snuck out to hunt the poisonous little morsels. At least he knew she wasn't starving.

Abel's new school was even bleaker than his house.

Kayda didn't come anywhere near him, which was hard, given how small the gulch's school was. She could barely even meet his eyes across the room in the morning. All the grades sat together and listened to one of the school's three teachers talk on and on about the history of Glassblower's Gulch and the basic principles of aerodynamic pyro-fluidity, whatever that meant. The lessons were either for little kids or college students, though Abel couldn't tell which. They were definitely not of interest to a single one of the kids there.

Bored as they all were, no one would talk to Abel.

In this town, the best chance of avoiding the wrong side of the dragon rodeo was to avoid earning the sheriff's attention. Word had gotten around that the sheriff thought Abel was trouble, and no one wanted trouble with her. He was best avoided.

The only good part of his day was at bedtime, when he closed the door to his room and read to Omi and Percy.

The pangolin stayed curled on the bed, snoozing to the tone of Abel's voice, but Omi listened intently, perched in his closet, with her head popping out between his shirts. He'd started trying to read her his favorite novel about the Dragon Queen, but she'd lost interest pretty quickly. It took three days to figure out what she did like: DrakoTek player guides.

Omi didn't seem to care much for stories, but she *loved* listening to Abel read out the rules of DrakoTek and the point values for different dragons and equipment. She sat up straight and cooed happily when he listed the numbers for basic wyvern card modifications.

"Okay, so you like numbers," he said, though when he tried to read his math homework to her, she lost interest just as quickly as he did. "But you don't like homework," he observed. "We're not so different, are we?"

The gold-faced wyvern grunted. Abel didn't know if she was agreeing or disagreeing. She yawned—setting him off yawning—and curled up to sleep.

Omi grew several inches in that one night.

The days went on like that all week. Arguments over breakfast followed by silences that were even worse. Their dad's growing anger as his letters back to Drakopolis went unanswered, and then off to school, where Abel learned little and made no friends.

He tried to give Kayda a secret update about Omi's growth and her taste in reading material, but she just shook her head at him and scurried away, muttering, "I'm not supposed to talk to you. I'm sorry . . ."

The only people who *didn't* avoid him at school, unfortunately, were the teachers. Each of the three instructors called on him every chance they could, whether they had a question for the first graders or a question not even a professor of Dragonistics could answer. They just liked to see him squirm, Abel figured, especially because he was so distracted. Half the time, he didn't even hear their questions.

"What are the three overall classifications of dragon species?" a teacher asked. "Abel?"

"Huh?" Abel replied. He'd been staring out the window, trying to think about a way to train Omi to do what he needed.

He wanted to make her a messenger. If he couldn't send a text to his friends back home, maybe he could send a dragon.

"'Huh' is not a recognized classification of dragon," the teacher sneered. The rest of the kids laughed, and then a little boy in the front row who didn't even have all his teeth yet answered.

"Long-wing, medium-wing, and short-wing," the kid said.

"Thank you, Nicki." The teacher turned his gaze back on Abel. "Now that you're paying attention, perhaps you can tell me how many dragon breeds there are within each classification?"

"I . . . um . . . What?" Abel stumbled. "But there are thousands! No one knows that!"

"Oh." The teacher shrugged. "I just assumed an experienced dragon rider from the big city's most dangerous kin would know a little something about dragons. Perhaps the rumors about you are *greatly* exaggerated."

Even the second graders laughed that time.

The Wind Breakers were hardly the city's most dangerous kin. They never hurt anyone on purpose. That was more the Red Talons' and the Thunder Wings' thing. Even the Sky Knights hurt people when it suited them. The Wind Breakers just caused chaos. They showed the absurdity of the system by disrupting it with pranks and stunts and stuff, but never violence.

He didn't think his teachers would appreciate his argument about the different kins, so he kept his mouth shut. He tried to stay out of trouble.

When no adults were around on his walk up the side of the gulch to go home, the older kids shoved him and tripped him, and taunted him with names like "dragon meat" and "lizard-licking slug breath."

"All kinner scum deserve to rot in Windlee Prison," one of the littlest kids with a mean streak taunted him.

"You're gonna get got just like your brother," an even littler kid with an even meaner streak added.

Back home, his father fretted over his letters to Drakopolis, as if the right combination of words to the right government official could bring his oldest son back from a dragon's jaws. His mother moved around the apartment in a daze, bursting into tears at random moments, looking at Lina and Abel and sighing.

Silas, in his act of bravery and selflessness, had broken their family.

No, Abel thought, *Silas didn't do that. Sheriff Skint did. And I am going to make her pay.*

First, he had to get a message to his friends. He had to train this baby wyvern to carry it. But how? He really wished he had some kind of dragon-training guidebook.

Omi kept slipping out from his balcony and returning with cockatrice bones. One night, she had cake frosting on her snout. On a third, she arrived back at the balcony breathless and shaking as the sheriff's Rapid Assault Hog Dragon flapped overhead, a searchlight scanning the neighborhood.

"I have to start training you for real," he told her before sitting down to read some more DrakoTek instructions. "I need to teach you some skills."

Omi let out a little chirping sound.

"Other than DrakoTek," he added.

Omi blinked and waited. She was listening.

Abel started to think his plan might work, though he was afraid he'd already waited too long. He still had so much to teach his wyvern. And for all he knew, Silas was dragon dung by now.

The whole thing made his stomach sick.

13

"**THE WHOLE THING MAKES MY** stomach sick," Lina told him that Friday night as she flopped onto the bed in his room without knocking. She'd taken her second shower of the day, using *his* shower water ration, and still she thought she could smell the sewers on herself.

"It smells like old meat and stomach acid wherever I go," she groaned. Abel glanced at his closet door. He couldn't tell her that the smell wasn't her. It was the baby dragon in his closet.

"I don't smell anything," he said, looking up from the DrakoTek cards he'd laid out on his bed while Omi napped.

"*You* wouldn't," said Lina. "You smell like a mushroom growing in a swamp wyvern's armpit."

His heart raced at the mention of any wyvern-related smells, even though he knew his sister was just messing with him.

"I do not," he objected, before subtly smelling himself. *Do I?* "Anyway, if I stink, it's because you keep taking my shower ration!"

"You weren't going to use it," she said.

"What if I was?" Abel asked.

"Oh?" Lina raised an eyebrow and smirked. "Someone here you're trying to impress? That girl Kayda, maybe?"

"No." Abel swallowed. "Definitely not."

"Is it one of the boys I saw you running with on the edge of the gulch?"

"Not a chance," Abel said again. "And I wasn't running with them. They were chasing me."

His sister sat up, concerned. She dropped her teasing. "Are you being bullied?"

"Nothing I can't handle," he told her, and he meant it. The little bullies didn't bother him. It was the big bullies—Sheriff Skint and Deputy Manchi—that he was worried about.

"I still can't believe they ration shower water here." Lina flopped back down, lightening the mood as she scooped up one of Abel's *DrakoSport* magazines. She flipped through the pages, stopping to look at any Blazeball Aerialists she thought were cute.

Quickly bored, she tossed it back onto his bed. "This place is the *worst*," she groaned. "I can't believe Silas sacrificed himself for these people."

"You were ready to sacrifice yourself for the Sky Knights kin," said Abel.

"But they fought for a good cause," Lina said. "The liberation of the masses."

"You still sound like a revolutionary," Abel pointed out. "Even out here in Glassblower's Gulch."

"I'm a revolutionary wherever it is people need a revolution," Lina replied.

"Even though the Sky Knights kicked you out?"

"Even *more* so," Lina said. "I got so caught up in serving them, I forgot I was supposed to be serving the people of Drakopolis."

"You sound exactly like Silas," Abel told her.

"Normally, I'd call that an insult," Lina said. Then she smiled at him. "But I don't think you meant it as one."

Abel shook his head. "These people need a revolution too."

"These people?" Lina scoffed. "I'm not sure they're worth it."

"Silas thought they were," Abel said.

"Silas was a fool-headed dung bucket."

"No, he's not!" Abel snapped at her. "He's tougher and braver than we ever give him credit for. And for all we know, he's still alive."

Lina's face twitched. She got very still and side-eyed Abel. "Since when do you defend Silas?" She tilted her head. "And is that . . . *guilt* I hear in your voice?"

Abel froze. *Abel, you wingless water weasel, what did you do?* he scolded himself.

He should've just kept quiet. His sister knew him too well. He couldn't keep secrets from her.

"There's more to this than you've told Mom and Dad, isn't there?" she asked, lowering her voice. "You're plotting something. Listen, Abel, I've been a criminal a lot longer than you have. If you're up to your elbows in a dragon's jaws, you *want* me helping you to get out."

"I don't like that metaphor," Abel said, feeling a little puff of pride. He was pretty sure "up to your elbows in a dragon's jaws" *was* a metaphor. It meant trouble. He glanced at his homework on the room's desk, untouched. Maybe if he tried to do it, it wouldn't go so badly. Doing homework was like cleaning up your dragon's dung: It got harder the longer you put off doing it.

"Hey! Focus!" Lina snapped her fingers in his face. "You're doing that stressed-out distracted thing." She lowered her voice again. "So what's your plan?"

Abel took a deep breath and spilled out what he was thinking. "I want to find out where that dragon took Silas, and I want to take down Sheriff Skint, and I think I can do both at the same time, *if* I can get my friends back in Drakopolis to help me."

"That's an objective, not a plan," Lina said.

"The plan is to cheat at the dragon rodeo," Abel said.

"That sounds dangerous."

"It will be," said Abel.

"And you think it'll work?"

"I hope it will," said Abel.

"Hope's not a plan either," Lina replied.

Abel shrugged.

Lina sighed. "I swear, having brothers should be treated as a medical condition."

"I mean, I have a plan too," he explained. "I have to get a secret message back to the Red Talons in Drakopolis."

"You mean to your friend Arvin?" Lina asked. "The Red Talon boss's son?"

"I do," said Abel.

"The same Red Talons who want to feed you to a wyvern?"

"Well . . ." Abel sighed and crossed to his closet door. "That brings me to the other thing I need to tell you about my plan."

With that, he swung the closet door open, to reveal his acid-spitting red-and-gold baby Rose Thorn wyvern.

She'd grown another foot and a half. Omi was just big enough for Abel to ride now, if he could figure out how.

"Her name's Omelette," he said. "Wanna help me train her?"

14

THEY HAD TO WAIT FOR Mom and Dad to go to sleep before Lina crept down the hall to Abel's room again. He was up and ready, dressed in his patchwork leather dragon rider's jacket and the thickest pair of jeans he had. He didn't have a helmet in Glassblower's Gulch, or a saddle rig, or any other riding equipment.

"It's fine," Lina assured him. "This is how the ancient riders did it. None of that fancy big-city dragon-riding stuff. Just you and the beast and the open sky."

"She's not a beast," Abel said. "She's a baby. I call her Omi."

Lina nodded. "That's much better than Omelette."

"I know, right?" Abel shook his head, then turned his head toward Percy, who was clinging to his back, tiny eyes locked on the closet door. "You two really need to get along. She's kind of your roommate."

Percy hissed, which was not a sound Abel thought pangolins could make. It wasn't a happy sound either.

He peeled Percy off, setting the little creature on his pillow. The pangolin curled into a tight ball, ready to bowl Omi over at the slightest provocation. Then Abel opened the closet door to find the wyvern crouched over the last remnants of a cockatrice. The unfortunate dragonet's tough tail and poisonous feathers were all that remained.

"Again?" Abel sighed. He hadn't seen her slip out or come back with her prey.

Omi looked up wide-eyed and innocent. Then she burped and spat out one more poisonous feather, which settled on Abel's sneaker.

"Watch it!" he yelped, afraid it might touch his skin. Omi bobbed her head and extended one dainty claw. She gently dragged the pinion back to her hoard of broken glass and poisonous feathers, then blinked up at him again, all apologies.

"She's a baby?" Lina asked.

Omi was now nearly as long as the closet, and when she stood up to her full height, her head popped over the hanger bar. She wasn't going to fit much longer. She'd already eaten half the wild cockatrices in town. Someone was sure to notice soon.

The young wyvern padded out of the closet and looked around the room. Her silver eyes took it all in.

Suddenly, with an astonishing leap, she jumped onto the bed and landed just in front of Percy. He curled into a tighter ball at the same instant Abel yelled, "Omi, no!"

But she didn't attack, and neither did Percy. Instead, she used her snout to roll him gently forward. Then she stopped and looked at him, waiting. He peeked out from his ball.

The dragon and the pangolin stared at each other. Percy let out one quiet squeak, then rolled himself up again.

Omi nudged him once more, this time harder, so he rolled off the bed and across the floor, hitting the dresser with a soft *thump*.

He uncurled, shook himself off, and scurried to the bed, clambering right back up the sheets.

"What are they doing?" Lina asked.

With another squeak, Percy curled up in front of Omi's feet. This time, Omi kicked him!

"Omi!" Abel scolded as Percy caught air, zipped across the room, and crashed into the wall with a less-soft *thunk!*

When he hit the floor again, he uncurled, ran in a circle, and scurried back to do it again.

"Wait?" Abel said. "You're . . . *playing*?"

The wyvern and the pangolin stopped their game and looked at him, cocking their heads in unison like *duh?* Then they went right back to their game.

Scurry, roll, thunk! Scurry, roll, thunk! Scurry, roll, thunk!

Abel and Lina watched in total wonder until they heard their mom's voice call down the hall: "Abel, are you wrestling again? It's after midnight!"

They all froze, staring at the door. They heard her feet padding down the hall.

"Abel?" she called.

He rushed over and shoved his head through the crack, using his body to block her view.

"What are you doing?" she asked. "Are you okay?"

"Yeah, Mom, I'm fine," he said, not sure how to explain the noise or his obvious panic. He thought through every excuse he'd ever heard his older siblings offer for their own weird teenage behavior over the years—then remembered one Lina had used with their dad that always worked. He modified it for his own use and offered Mom an earnest but vague "You know, just . . . boy stuff?"

She stopped in her tracks, and her eyebrows shot up. Her cheeks flushed a little, though he had no idea why, and then she nodded. "Of course," she said. "Well . . . it's late. And, um . . . maybe . . . um, get some sleep? You and your father can talk in the morning."

"Um . . . okay?" Abel said, wondering if he was in trouble or why he should need to talk to his father in the morning. But he was thrilled the excuse had worked, like a secret password to a sealed vault. He smiled. "Thanks, Mom."

She smiled and added a quick "good night" before scurrying back to her own room in a way that reminded him of Percy.

He closed the door again and shrugged at Lina, the pangolin, and the wyvern, who all exhaled at the same time. "Parents are weird," he said. "Now, playtime's over. Let's get to work."

• • •

Percy watched from the bed as they led Omi onto Abel's balcony. At night, everyone in Glassblower's Gulch closed their shutters because it got so cold. The wind howled through the ravine. It created the perfect cover for their training, though all three of them were shivering on the balcony. Steam rose off Omi's scales where the cold night air met the hot dragon's body. Abel was actually excited to climb on and warm up.

"You know wyverns are ferocious killing machines, right?" Lina said. "The reason the Dragon's Eye uses them is because they're dangerous for humans *and* other dragons. Training one to carry a secret message seems like a waste of their natural talents."

"I know," said Abel, remembering the time he'd chased down Silas's wyvern on the back of Karak, his Sunrise Reaper. Abel had nearly been poisoned, dropped out of the sky, and eaten, all in the same heartbeat, and the Sunrise Reaper was one of the most ferocious dragons that existed. "That's why they won't suspect Omi of being a messenger. Also no one will get in her way *before* she delivers her message."

"You know." Lina smirked. "That's clever, little bro. I guess a lot less mail would get stolen in Drakopolis if they delivered it on wyverns instead of purple-nosed short-wings."

"Yeah, but kids love those purple mail dragons," Abel said. "Remember when Silas dreamed about being a mailman so he could ride one?"

"Mail carrier," Lina corrected him. "Don't be sexist. And yeah, he had the little uniform and everything. He loved playing Government Worker."

"Still does," Abel said. They both chuckled at the memory, but it was a sad kind of laugh thinking about Silas now, wondering if he was dead or alive.

Dead.

My brother might be dead, Abel thought. He wanted to be planning a rescue right now, but he feared he was only planning revenge.

Either way, he wasn't going to fail.

"Okay, Omi, ready to try flying with a rider?" he asked. He bowed respectfully to her before stepping up to climb onto the base of her neck.

In one fluid, graceful motion, the young wyvern stepped to the side, dodging Abel's leg. He mounted only the empty air . . . and fell onto his side with a *thunk* of his own.

Omi bent her neck around to roll him across the balcony, just like Percy.

"That's gonna bruise," he groaned.

"This is why I stole grown-up dragons," Lina noted. "Training dragons is work. Stealing dragons is the fun part."

Abel nodded from the ground, gazing up at Omi's eager face. She was waiting for him to curl up into a ball like Percy so she could roll him again.

"Well, she's the only dragon we've got, so I've got to train her," he said. "I don't have any other plan."

"You ever heard of the KISS principle?" Lina asked.

"Like, kissing?" Abel wrinkled his nose. "Yes, I've heard of kissing."

Did she want him to kiss his dragon?

"No, not kissing," Lina said. "K-I-S-S. It's an acronym, like WW3D for 'What would Dr. Drago do?' or OODA."

"I know!" Abel boasted. "Kin Intervention Safety Specialist. We had one at my school. Remember? He tried to kill you when you were still a Sky Knight."

"I remember," said Lina. "That's the official acronym. But we have a different meaning for it in the criminal world."

"I didn't know the criminal underworld had so many vocabulary lessons," said Abel.

"The world's made of language, Abel," she said. "Why should the underworld be any different?"

"So what's the criminal meaning of KISS?" he asked.

"It stands for 'keep it simple, scoundrel,'" Lina told him. "It's the first thing I learned as a dragon thief. Complicated plans have a lot more places to fail than simple ones. So, a scoundrel who wants to survive. Keeps. It. Simple."

"But dragons are complicated," Abel said.

"People are complicated," said Lina. "Dragons really aren't. Anyway, you should probably trust me on this. I've been taming and stealing dragons since before your voice cracked."

"My voice doesn't crack!" Abel's voice cracked.

Lina chuckled and made her voice extra deep. "Of course not," she joked, then talked normally. "So are you going to listen to my training plan or what?"

"I will," said Abel. "As long as there isn't any kissing," he added.

He wriggled out from under Omi, who had been bouncing slightly on her feet at the banter between brother and sister, like it was some kind of game she didn't fully understand but enjoyed nonetheless.

Abel was definitely going to have bruises from her enthusiasm. Even a baby dragon's good moods could hurt you. He was frightened of what might happen if she got into a bad one.

"First step," Lina said, "mount up!"

It sounded easy enough, but as any dragon rider knows, the first step onto a dragon's back is the hardest one. Done wrong, it can also be your last.

15

IT TOOK EIGHTEEN AND THREE-QUARTERS more tries for him to climb onto Omi's back without her jumping away completely, him getting tossed off and rolled like a ball, or both of them tangling in each other's limbs and falling over.

And then there was the unfortunate incident where Abel grabbed the wrong spot and Omi flipped him over her head and spat acid at him. Thankfully, Abel jumped in time. The spray went harmlessly between his legs, boiling a part of the floor behind him.

But he'd finally gotten it.

Lina was asleep on the bed, with Percy snoring in the crook of her elbow. Abel had to steer Omi by her horns back into the room. They both stood over his sleeping sister. Omi poked her with her snout, and Lina nearly jumped out of her skin.

"Don't sneak up on me like that!" she grunted.

"I'm on a half-ton baby wyvern," Abel replied. "I wasn't exactly *sneaking*. Anyway, I'm on. What now?"

"Well, a messenger needs to fly to a specific place, drop off a message, and return, right?"

Abel nodded.

"So, start by flying her around to places, dropping things off, and returning," Lina said. "First with you on her back to steer, and then without."

"This is going to take a while, isn't it?" he asked. The sun had begun to rise on the horizon.

"You didn't think you'd train a baby dragon to do a complicated task on behalf of a strange human in one night, did you?" Lina asked.

"Of course not!" Abel snapped back a little too quickly. Because . . . like . . . yeah, he totally had. How much time did he really have if Silas was still alive? Of course, if Silas was already dead, he had all the time in the world.

Stop it, he told himself. *Focus on what you need to do now, not some maybes in the future.*

"This isn't like a game of DrakoTek," Lina told him. "You don't just figure out the right card to play and slam it down. It's a process that takes patience, hard work, and repetition. It can even be boring. I couldn't steal my first flying, fire-breathing dragon until I'd stolen at least a hundred Educational Resource Dragons."

"You stole ERDs?" Abel gasped. "Like from schools?"

Lina nodded. "I'm not proud of everything I did for the Sky Knights, okay?" she said. "But I did learn a lot. And selling those dragons kept our medical clinics for the poor open, so I'd say it was worth it."

"Defensive much?" Abel asked.

Lina rolled her eyes. "I think you'd know by now that there are no good guys in Drakopolis, just good causes."

"I like to think there can be both," he said.

Lina smiled at him. "There's a reason I'm helping you, isn't there, little brother? You're the good guy." She wasn't even being sarcastic. Abel smiled back at her. It felt good not to have any secrets between them. The only thing between them now was the wyvern Abel was supposed to fly.

"Okay, get to it," Lina said. "Before the town wakes up."

"Savvy," Abel confirmed. He leaned his body to guide Omi onto the balcony again. She followed the pressure of his legs on her shoulders more easily than any dragon he'd ever ridden. As he nudged her to take off, she bent her legs, snapped her wings, and leapt into the sky without the slightest hesitation.

She's gonna be the easiest dragon I've ever flown, he thought. *She probably won't even try to kill me.*

He was right, up to a point. Omi didn't *try* to kill him, but that didn't mean she wouldn't do it by accident along the way.

• • •

They stayed close to the side of the gulch's steep walls, flapping past shuttered windows and keeping to the shadows, away from the hanging lights over the stairways and bridges.

Omi was straining a little by the time they reached the top and burst into the open night air above the Glass Flats. She'd never carried a rider before, even one as scrawny as Abel, and the extra weight was making her work hard.

You gotta work harder to be harder, Silas always said. Abel was certain his big brother had stolen the line from one of the fitness videos he liked to watch.

The thought of Silas pretending to invent macho quotes while doing pull-ups on the bathroom doorframe squeezed a fist around Abel's heart. He missed his brother. The things that used to annoy him about Silas now just reminded him of what he'd lost. Why was it so hard to appreciate the people you loved until after they were gone?

Ew, he thought. *Did I just admit I love my big brother?*

Of course you do, dung hoarder, he answered himself. *And you better focus if you're going to save him. Or avenge him.*

Abel pulled his attention back to the task at hand.

His idea for tonight was to fly Omi to the landing zone above the gulch, have her drop off a random piece of garbage he was carrying (in this case, the lid to an empty pickle jar), then come home.

Next, he'd see if she'd fly back herself and pick it up. If she failed, no one would think much about random trash near the landing site. And if she succeeded, he could jump to more difficult tasks, like showing her specific addresses on his phone and having her go to them.

The problem was, while he'd been lost in his thoughts about Silas, Omi had flown way out over the glass desert, into the dark and the cold. Now she'd decided to play a game with the wild desert monitors, child-sized lizards who lived in burrow holes in the glass.

She dove for the first monitor she saw. Its long snout and whip-fast tongue snatched at lightning bugs and dragonflies.

Omi sliced right above the lizard, using one of her powerful feet to scoop it from its hole. Then she did a full loop-de-loop with it in her claws. She ended by dropping the lizard, to see if she could get it back in its hole, like shooting a basket.

Except (a) Abel wasn't in a harness—and he had no warning she was going to fly upside down. And (b) desert monitors spat fire.

Omi's first attempt at monitor scooping nearly cost him his life. He dangled off her back, shrieking like a teakettle. Then, when she missed her shot and the lizard spat blue-hot flame back at her, it singed the leg of Abel's pants.

"Omi!" he cried out. "Don't try that again!"

Of course, she immediately tried that again. This time, Abel was prepared to hold on for dear life, but he still caught a jet of flame over the back of his jacket. It sizzled but didn't ignite. He had no idea how he'd explain the burn marks on his clothes to his parents.

Again, Omi had missed returning the lizard to its hole. Now there were two monitor lizards on the ground, hissing and aiming jets of fire in Omi's direction, which she was having a great time dodging. Abel was having less of a great time hanging on and trying not to get incinerated.

"At least warn me next time!" he yelled.

She did not.

Omi dove; Abel screamed in helpless terror. She grabbed and flipped; he screamed some more, while the lizard in the wyvern's claws shot fire in a huge circle, tracing her loop in the air.

When she successfully dunked this one into its burrow hole, she celebrated by flying straight up toward the waning moon. Abel hung from her horns, legs kicking uselessly at the open air above her back.

"AHHH!" he yelled, to which she responded with a squealing chittering sound that he felt pretty sure was the dragon equivalent of a whoop.

"CHEE-CHEE-CHEE!"

When she leveled off, now hundreds of feet in the air, Abel regained his grip and locked his legs around her shoulders, catching his breath. Omi weaved back and forth to catch the desert breezes, gliding and flapping, gliding and flapping. She seemed to be enjoying herself, and it wasn't terribly dangerous for either of them, so Abel used the time to come up with a new strategy for training her.

He'd mastered a proud and violent dragon, a moody and reckless dragon, but he had never tried to ride a straight-up playful dragon before.

If he was going to live, he'd have to turn her training into a game. And it had better be a good one or she'd make her own fun . . . and Abel might not survive it.

"Let's try something," he said, just hoping she understood him. He pulled out a paint marker from his pocket and steered Omi down for a landing.

She watched him, head cocked, as he scurried off her back and tiptoed between monitor burrows. Holding his breath, he squatted beside one, daring a quick glance over the lip of the hole at the wide-eyed creature inside. It hissed at him and shot out a jet of flame that he had to dive onto his backside to escape. He checked to make sure he still had eyebrows.

Omi snorted.

Then he got back onto his knees and approached the edge again, this time not daring a look in. Abel wrote a big number 1 on the smooth glass next to the hole. Satisfied, he scuttled quietly to another hole, desperately trying not to disturb the creature inside as he wrote the number 4. Then another hole, another number, out of order.

For the next five minutes, he scampered between burrows, writing big numbers next to as many as he could without getting lit on fire.

Omi watched him in confused silence until he climbed back on.

"Prrprt?" she said, which he assumed was the dragon equivalent of "huh?" But he just laughed and patted her neck as he coaxed her into the air again.

"I bet you can't bop the lizards in just the order I tell you to," he announced. "Let's try numbers three, seven, one, and four."

The game was a test of her memory as much as her ability to recognize numbers. If she was going to fly to his friends' houses without him on her back, she'd need to be able to remember their addresses. But it was also meant to be a dare. Dragons were proud by nature, and if he suggested she *couldn't* do something, he was pretty sure she'd do anything to prove him wrong.

Omi looked down the length of her neck at him. For a moment, he feared she didn't understand, even after all those nights reading to her. Then he felt the ripple of her muscles shifting beneath her scales. Her jaw bent slightly in a draconic smirk.

She'd understood him. She just thought she was cleverer than him.

Abel held on tight as she snapped her wings closed and dove, corkscrewing through the air so fast he nearly blacked out from the g-forces. She sliced over the desert floor and, with rapid side-to-side swings, used her claws and even her snout to bop the heads of the lizards in the holes he'd labeled 3, 7, 1, and 4. Then she did it again: 4, 1, 7, 3.

"Show-off," Abel laughed. He pulled the pickle jar lid from his pocket. "Now I bet you can't drop this in the landing zone."

She folded a wing and used the claw at the end to snatch the lid from him, then raced back for the platform, doing corkscrew turns the whole time. Abel couldn't help screaming as he hugged tight to her twirling neck.

"AHHH! AHHH! AHHHH! AHHHH!" His voice was snatched away by the wind with each spin.

When they reached the landing zone, Omi launched the can lid and pulled straight up at the same time, like a combat wyvern firing a missile at an explosives factory.

Abel looked back dizzyingly over his shoulder to see the lid skip across the desert floor and embed itself in the hard ground just at the edge of the landing pad.

"CHEE-CHEE-CHEE!" Omi chirped, gloating.

She not only liked a challenge; she liked to win.

Good thing, because so did Abel.

"I'm coming for you, Sheriff Skint," he whispered to himself, feeling a swell of pride. Though the pride had guilt riding on its back. Was it wrong to feel good after what happened to Silas? Was it okay to feel joy, even when you knew someone you loved was suffering?

The sun was starting to peek over the horizon, and the air was warming fast.

He leaned to the side to steer Omi home before the town awoke and folks started opening their shutters. They'd have to do the whole training routine again the next night, but Abel felt like he had a partner he could work with.

Though Omi still took another swipe at a monitor lizard on the way home and it nearly burned Abel's eyebrows off.

They landed outside his bedroom, just before sunrise. Abel snuck through the window and woke Lina up.

"You're wrong," he told her.

"Huh?" She sat up bleary-eyed in his bed.

Abel was exhausted himself, but too excited to sleep. "Training dragons is way more fun than stealing them."

16

ABEL AND OMI SPENT MOST of Saturday sleeping. When night came, they were ready to train again. He tried to send her back to the landing zone to retrieve the lid.

She flew off alone and came back forty minutes later without the jar lid, but gripping a very agitated monitor lizard that nearly set his room ablaze and tried to eat Percy.

He begged Omi to take it away and put it back in the wild.

She obeyed, but this time came back with a cockatrice, which shed poisonous feathers all over his room. Abel had to pick them up wearing heavy rubber dish gloves.

Finally, after four trips, Omi returned with the lid. But she refused to leave again without him on her back.

"Fine," he said, though he was secretly glad she wanted him to ride. Still, she wasn't turning into much of a messenger dragon.

"She'll get it," Lina assured him. "Just keep rewarding her when she does well and try to ignore when she does poorly."

"Hard to ignore when she nearly melts my bedroom," he said.

"If it were easy, everyone would train dragons," said Lina.

"Maybe it's hard because people shouldn't be training dragons at all," Abel suggested.

She shrugged. "You got a different plan?"

He shook his head and climbed onto Omi's back. She was already bigger than the night before. He wasn't going to be able to hide her in his closet for much longer, but if they worked hard, he wouldn't need to. She'd be ready and the next phase of his plan could begin.

He flew the wyvern once through the gulch, making a game out of weaving between bridges and string lights and laundry lines, keeping to the shadows as much as possible.

At one point, they had to hide behind some crates when Deputy Manchi flew over on patrol. Manchi rode a Cobalt Reaper, a medium-wing with deep, dark blue scales. It even spat blue-hot flame. The Reaper was decked out in armor and lights and electrified defensive wire, and it had a full load of smoke bombs and flash-bangs strapped to its belly.

Why would a sheriff's deputy in this sleepy town fly around on a dragon dressed for war? Abel wondered.

Unless that was all it was. Dress-up. People dressed up for all kinds of reasons. To entertain each other or to distract dragons. To feel more like themselves or to feel a little like someone else. To control how others saw them or to share their inside truth on the outside.

But they also dressed up to show what they cared about, or where they belonged, or what their job was, or who their friends were, or who their friends *weren't*. Like kin colors or uniforms, clothes were a kind of communication. What Manchi and his dragon's gear were saying was: *Be afraid.*

"Well, I won't be," Abel whispered out loud as he watched them fly away. "*You* should be afraid of *me*."

He squeezed his legs together to tell Omi to take off again. She turned her head to look at him, then gazed back in the direction the deputy had flown, narrowing her eyes. She bent her legs, ready to launch.

Abel realized what she was thinking a moment too late.

"Wait!" he pleaded. "This isn't a game!"

But she was off, flying fast to catch up with the Cobalt Reaper. The moment it sensed something approaching in the air behind them, the Reaper turned its head. So did Deputy Manchi.

Omi dove straight down, pulling short with a sickening lurch. In a moment, she was dangling on the underside of a bridge that crossed the gulch. As Abel dangled off her back, he really wished she wasn't so fond of being upside down.

"This isn't hide-and-seek," he hissed at her. She responded with a series of quiet clicks. Abel decided it meant something like, *Oh yes, it absolutely is, you tiny little tube of meat paste.*

After an endless instant, Omi let go of the bridge and swung herself upright, slamming Abel into her hard back. Then she flapped after Manchi's dragon all over again. Every time the Reaper looked, she dove for the shadows, or dropped to some balcony where unsuspecting citizens snored just on the other side of closed shutters. She was having a blast, but none of this was making her a better messenger dragon.

Or was it?

Once she got to Drakopolis, she would need to be sneaky. There were patrols that hunted for wild and unlicensed dragons; plus there were the dragon thieves and snatchers, who'd love to snag a young wyvern for battling. And then there were the Dragon's Eye agents, who would be watching Abel's friends, making sure he didn't violate the terms of his exile by contacting them. Omi would need all the stealth skills she could muster, and what better way to learn than this?

Not that Abel had a choice in the matter. If stalking Deputy

Manchi on his Reaper was the game Omi wanted to play tonight, that was the game they were playing.

He could at least try to enjoy himself.

And he totally did.

They swooped and darted from shadow to shadow. They made "whoops" and "chees" that dared the deputy to turn. But when he did, all he saw was the empty night and the quiet paths and steps of Glassblower's Gulch. One time, Omi even snapped her teeth at the Reaper's tail, then disappeared into a dumpster before it could turn around.

Abel's heart thundered in his chest at the risk of discovery, but a pure thrill flooded him too. It was easy to forget that he was being foolish and taking dangerous risks. When riding on the back of a dragon, everything was dangerous, but also anything felt possible. The danger of the game was the whole reason it was fun, and the fun made it much more dangerous.

Am I a daredevil? he asked himself. *Am I hooked on thrills like a gambling addict chasing a win at cards? And if I am, then what does that say about me? Are all my plots and plans really about doing what's right, or are they more about finding my next reckless thrill?*

These thoughts troubled him, and they also distracted him. He didn't notice Manchi landing at the bottom of the gulch, or that Omi had crept down to the ground to get closer. She lay perfectly still, belly flat on the cool sand, just outside the entrance to a sand mine.

The deputy tied up his Reaper and dismounted.

Wild cockatrices scattered at their arrival, clucking and screeching. Manchi looked in their direction. The little dragonets were excitable but also easy to ignore, which was what the deputy did now. He turned his attention to the midnight meeting that had brought him here.

"You weren't followed?" asked a voice from the shadows.

"Duh," Manchi replied, like it was the dumbest question ever asked of anyone. Except, of course, it wasn't, because he *had* been followed. Abel smirked.

This must be how undercover Dragon's Eye agents feel, Abel thought, which reminded him of his brother, which distracted him, so he didn't notice Omi creeping forward from the shadow. She was trying to catch a cockatrice that had scurried out of reach. He reined her back just before she burst into the open and gave away their hiding place in the deep shadows.

Manchi held a yellow perfume bottle, studying it in the moonlight. It was the one he'd taken from Kayda's parents, but it was no longer empty. Beside Manchi, his dark blue dragon snorted.

"It's untraceable?" Manchi asked the shadowy figure, who Abel guessed had given him the perfume bottle.

"It's all natural," the figure said. "Made from boiled cockatrice feathers and some other ingredients." Abel's spine tingled. He knew that voice. He squinted into the dark to make out the person to whom it belonged.

Her name was Ally, though he'd known her as *Instructor* Ally, the best seventh-grade teacher he'd ever had. She'd also turned out to be a dangerous Thunder Wings kinner. In addition to math, reading, and science, Instructor Ally had secretly taught Abel how to ride Karak.

When Abel betrayed the Thunder Wings, however, she'd been merciless and vengeful. Ally had even tried to destroy him and Karak in a four-kin battle for his brother's life.

He'd won, though, and she'd lost her teaching job. Turned out the school system didn't like employing kinners who trained their students in a life of crime and then tried to murder them. Ally had shaved her head since he'd last seen her. The lightning-bolt dragon symbol of the Thunder Wings was tattooed on the side of her scalp in metallic blue ink. It was the same symbol stitched in metallic thread on her long black leather trench coat.

I guess she doesn't have to hide being a Thunder Wing kinner anymore, thought Abel. But what was she doing in Glassblower's Gulch? And why was she giving the sheriff's deputy perfume?

"No one can trace it because it's just a pheromone," she said. At Manchi's confused look, she sneered. "Look it up on the internet. If you have internet here."

"We have internet," Manchi replied. "It just doesn't work."

Abel remembered what pheromones were: chemicals that dragons could smell that could alter their behavior. They'd lost control of ERDs at school because of a pheromone attack. Ally had been the one to subdue them and save the class. She knew all about pheromones. Abel knew nothing good could come of them.

Instructor Ally laughed. The Thunder Wings were the kin back in Drakopolis with the most technology and smarts—and they used the two in ruthless combination. They were spies and weapons dealers and dragon battlers, but also hackers and technicians. She could probably fix the internet in Glassblower's Gulch in twenty minutes if she wanted to.

Abel didn't think she was here to offer technical support.

"Don't worry," she reassured Manchi. "It will work. It's a special formulation. No dragon will be able to resist it."

"How do I use it?" Manchi asked.

"Just a few sprays on the sheriff," Ally explained. "Then, during the match, a few sprays in the air where the dragon can smell it. That's all. So easy even a child could do it."

"Hey," Manchi replied. "Didn't a *child* beat you in a battle last year?"

Ally took in a deep angry breath, and Abel tensed. It was one thing to spy on a corrupt sheriff's deputy and a vicious criminal in the middle of a secret midnight rendezvous. It was a whole other thing to find them suddenly talking about you.

"How *is* Abel adjusting to life here in the gulch?" she asked. "You got rid of his big brother?"

"As requested." Manchi gave a little bow. "The sheriff did just as we thought she would, and so did Silas. That do-gooder didn't stand a chance against a Candy Cane Reaper. Probably somewhere in its lower intestine by now."

This time it was Abel who nearly gave up their hiding place. He almost lunged from the shadows to rain down a flurry of fists on the cruel deputy, for all the good that would have done. And this time it was Omi who stopped *him*. Her tail curled around in front of him, and she flexed it ever so slightly, holding Abel back. *Did she know what he was about to do?*

There was a necessary bond between dragon and rider; they had to be able to anticipate and support each other without words, faster and clearer than language made possible. They understood the flex of one another's muscles, the prickles of skin and scales. Abel imagined this was a lot like being in love. It was how his parents communicated too. They could say more with a look than with whole paragraphs of words.

He and Omi had that now. They were connected. He unclenched his jaw and loosened his fists.

"Abel's failing in school, bullied constantly, and it looks like he's not sleeping," Manchi rattled off Abel's hardships like he was bragging. "The sheriff has made it clear he's an undesirable in town."

Ally smiled. "Lovely," she said. "Everyone will suspect he's responsible for the sheriff's murder, once they find the perfume bottle in his room. An act of revenge from a grieving and unstable boy."

Abel sucked in a breath. They were plotting to *murder* Sheriff Skint?! And frame him for it?!

"Once she's out of the way," Manchi said, "the rodeo and this little perfume will take care of the rest of the family. Can't have them interfering once I take over."

"We," corrected Ally. "Once *we* take over."

"Of course," said Manchi.

"Don't you forget it," said Ally. "The Red Talons have been partnered with your sheriff for too long. The moment Sheriff Skint has her 'accident,' they'll approach you to continue their arrangement. They'll offer you money and power. Don't forget that we offered first. It's the Thunder Wings' turn to run this town."

"You have my word as an officer of the law." Deputy Manchi loosed a belly-rumbling laugh, and Ally joined him, as if his badge was the funniest joke in the world. Silas would've been infuriated at this. He took his oath seriously. Or at least, he had.

Abel's head spun. This was too much information to process. Sheriff Skint was a Red Talon kinner, and her deputy was a Thunder

Wing. And though she'd sent Silas to the rodeo, Manchi had manipulated her to do it for his own corrupt plans.

The sheriff was being bribed by the Red Talons, and Manchi was being bribed by the Thunder Wings. They'd gotten rid of Silas because he wasn't the type to take bribes from anyone, and now they were out for Abel!

Abel and his family were pawns in some power game between the kins . . . again!

Without another word, Ally disappeared into the shadows. A moment later, she emerged riding a thin Moth dragon, a nocturnal long-wing. Moth dragons had no breath weapon, but they did have the ability to camouflage themselves, changing color to match their environments. Ally must have ridden the dragon all the way from the city. And with a snap of its wings, she was headed back. She wasn't even going to stick around to see if Manchi's plan worked. Somehow, that made Abel angrier. Did she care so little about him she wasn't even going to see if he got framed for murder and pulverized in the dragon rodeo?

Rude, he thought, watching her dragon's color change and change again as it rose through the gulch and vanished into the desert night.

He should've kept his eyes on the ground. When Abel looked back at the Cobalt Reaper, Deputy Manchi wasn't standing beside it anymore.

He was standing beside Abel. More like *over* Abel, and he had a poisonous cockatrice feather in his gloved hand.

"Isn't it past your bedtime, little boy?" Manchi said. Then he dropped the feather onto Abel's bare neck.

"Omi! Attack!" Abel called to his wyvern as the poison hit his skin, but Omi had flown off, chasing a firefly. He was alone.

He felt his skin crackle and sizzle where the feather hit it. He saw it turning hard and clear. He could see his own blood pulsing below the surface. It hurt so much that he couldn't even make a sound before his vision started to go white. He was about to faint!

"Omi," he whispered. Then darkness fell over him like he was slipping into a dragon's gullet.

17

ABEL WOKE UP ALARMED.

An alarm blared. Handcuffs dug into his thin wrists. He tried to raise them and felt the pinch tighten, heard metal clank against metal.

He opened his eyes beneath the glare of fluorescent lights and saw the source of the alarm: He was in a hospital bed, hooked up to a monitor. One of the sensors stuck to his chest had fallen off. A nurse shuffled in and fixed it without speaking, then shuffled out again. He heard a lock click in the door.

The air smelled rancid, like the locker room at school after a class in Basic Dragon Care. Dung and sweat and Wild Wingman body spray.

His eyes finally adjusted to the bright light. He saw his parents half asleep against each other on a too-small bench along the wall. On the other side of the locked glass door to his room, he saw the green uniform of a sheriff's deputy. The deputy's back was to the glass, but Abel recognized him by his size and his smooth, bald head.

Manchi.

Abel squirmed against his restraints, heart roaring in his chest.

Had the sheriff already been murdered? Had Abel already been framed? Where was Lina? And where was Omi?

"Calm down! You're safe." His father was at his side in an instant, hand resting gently over Abel's wrist to keep the cuffs from digging too deeply into his skin. His mother swung around to the other side, bleary-eyed from sleep and tears, but holding his hand in hers.

"You're in the hospital," she said. Then she glanced to the glass door and added quietly, "Though it's not much of a hospital, to be honest. But you're safe. The town doctor neutralized the poison."

Abel wrinkled his nose.

That explained the smell.

He was relieved his skin hadn't been "glassified" by cockatrice poison, but he'd learned from DrakoTek—which was based on extensive Dragonistics research by TimeHoard Gaming Company— that the cure for the poison was to play three cards together that players often didn't bother to keep in their decks: sweat, Water Wyrm dung, and Wild Wingman body spray.

Why would DrakoTek even make a Wild Wingman body spray card? Abel wondered.

"I'm so glad you're okay." Abel's dad let go of his wrist and hugged him awkwardly. A memory flooded back from when his dad was the one in the hospital bed, struggling through a rough case of Scaly Lung. Abel recalled stretching over to hug him in that crinkly plastic quarantine suit. His father had hated hospitals ever since, and now he had to visit Abel in one. The guilt gnawed at him.

"I'm sorry, Dad," Abel rasped. His dad wiped a tear off his cheek.

"Nothing to apologize for," he mumbled, though Abel caught a look from his mom, whose mouth had folded tight into a frown.

"I shouldn't have snuck out," Abel said.

"No," his mother said. "You should not have."

"But I swear, I didn't kill anybody!" he added hurriedly. Both his parents' faces folded like origami interrobangs.

"Who said anything about killing anybody?" his dad asked.

"I . . . Is the sheriff—um . . . ?" Abel glanced at Manchi's back against the door. "Is the sheriff okay?"

"Sheriff Skint?" Dad frowned. "Of course. Why wouldn't she be?"

"Why am I under arrest?" he asked.

"Arrest?" Their dad looked at the handcuffs and then the door. "Oh! You aren't under arrest!" He laughed a little. "The handcuffs were to keep you from spreading the poison on your skin while you were unconscious. If you'd touched it, you would've gotten a lot worse. When Deputy Manchi found you, he said you were writhing and scratching yourself."

"He says you were sleepwalking," Abel's mom added, then lowered her voice to a whisper. "What were you *really* up to?"

Abel swallowed hard. His throat was dry. He wondered why Manchi would save him and cover for him, after Abel had heard all about his plot with the Thunder Wings. He also didn't like the idea of telling his mom and dad everything while he was still handcuffed and the deputy was just on the other side of the door.

"I promise I'll tell you at home," Abel said. "Not here."

His dad sighed. "That's not gonna be so easy," he explained. "Sheriff Skint is keeping you here for a few days while we—" His father stopped himself. He couldn't go on.

"While we help Lina." Mom finished the sentence for him.

"What happened to Lina?" Abel tried to sit up in bed.

"Deputy Manchi caught her trying to steal the Cloudflayer freight dragon early this morning," his mother told him. "It flew off when he confronted her, carrying a week's worth of food, water, and supplies for the town. Unlike you, she *is* under arrest."

"She— *What? Why?*" Abel struggled against his restraints. If he wasn't under arrest, he really wanted to get out of his handcuffs and get as far away from Deputy Manchi as he could. "She wouldn't have done that," Abel said. "Isn't it suspicious that Deputy Manchi found me and arrested Lina on the same morning?"

"Shhh." His mother glanced nervously at the door. "Don't work yourself up."

And still, the voice inside Abel's head screamed, *Where is Omi??*

"The sheriff is questioning Lina now," his dad said. "She's going to want to question you too. They think . . ." Again, she lowered her voice. "They think there's illegal kin activity in this sleepy little town after all. And that Lina is part of it. They're saying she tried to steal the Cloudflayer for the Sky Knights."

"But the Sky Knights kicked her out!" Abel objected, maybe too loudly. "If anything, she'd be a Wind Breaker, and she's not even that!"

"Shhh," his mother urged again.

Abel took a deep breath. He'd been a Wind Breaker, not Lina. But also the Wind Breakers weren't even an official kin, with official rules for joining. Doing Wind Breaker things just *made* you a Wind Breaker. That made it hard to deny being a part of. Freeing a dragon *was* the kind of thing a Wind Breaker would do. It was the kind of thing Abel would do. But it hadn't been part of their plan, and he was sure that Lina hadn't done it. Manchi had framed her. This was all a part of his scheme to take over the town. Lina and Abel and Silas and their parents were all casualties of that scheme.

Abel needed to explain what was going on to his parents, but he had to be careful to keep his voice down too. No good could come of shouting while he was caught up in a conspiracy of kinners, full of thieves and double crosses. Especially not while he was hand-cuffed to a bed. "Lina is the only one who's *not* a kinner," he said quietly. "Manchi and the sheriff both are. She's a Red Talon, and he's a Thunder Wing."

This time, he understood the look that passed between his parents perfectly. It was a *we-have-to-get-him-out-of-here* look, mixed with *our-family-is-in-trouble* eyebrows, and underlined by *this-again?* frowns. Like all kids who get themselves in and out of trouble, Abel had become a master of interpreting his parents' looks.

As his father started hacking out worrisome coughs and wheezes, he felt his mother fidgeting at his wrist.

"Dad, are you okay?" Abel asked. His father stood. His face reddened, the coughs loud enough to shake the flimsy walls. Before turning to the door, his dad winked, then pounded on the glass for Deputy Manchi's attention.

"Water!" he croaked between coughs. Manchi's huge forehead furrowed, the creases deep as claw marks. But he left his post to get some water for Abel's sickly dad.

That was when Abel felt one pair of cuffs release. His mother quickly set to work on the other.

"Mom, since when do you know how to pick locks?" Abel marveled.

She smiled. "I was a young woman in Drakopolis, once upon a time," she said. "You learn some things."

"Got it!" Dad whispered as he picked open the locked hospital door. Abel's jaw dropped.

"Your mom taught me a few things." He blew her a kiss. Yuck.

"We trust you, and we're getting you out of here," his mom said. "Is there somewhere you can hide?"

"Kayda's place," Abel said quickly. If it was good enough for a Rose Thorn wyvern, it was good enough for him. He just hoped they wouldn't make him sleep on broken glass like she had. "But won't you get in trouble for sneaking me out?"

"We're already in trouble thanks to your sister," said their dad. "And after what happened to Silas—" His father's voice caught in his throat. It wasn't a fake cough this time. After a moment, he composed himself. "I'd rather one of my children be free," he stated firmly.

Abel nodded.

"Anyway, they already think *you're* a criminal and we're very bad parents," his mother added. "We'll just say you tricked us and escaped."

"Mom . . . I'm really sorry you're caught up in my troubles again." Abel sighed as he got out of bed and dressed under his hospital gown as quickly as he could.

"You're our child," she said. "Your troubles *are* our troubles. And we're going to solve them together. I have a letter to write to Drakopolis now. Just as soon as we stop them from feeding your sister to a dragon. Now get gone; that meathead deputy is coming."

Abel wanted to hug his parents, but there was no time. He couldn't possibly thank them for their faith in him—or their help with all the trouble he caused. All he could do was try to stay alive and make them proud. He was going to need Kayda's help.

He really hoped her family wouldn't slam the door on him the second he arrived. Although, if they wanted to stay safe, they'd be smart to do just that.

Luckily, they were a lot kinder than they were smart.

18

"ISN'T IT GOOD?" KAYDA ASKED Abel as he sat on a small stool in their storage closet, sipping the cold glass of soda she'd thrust into his hands. "We don't get Firebreather Soda out here because it's too expensive to fly in, so we make our own with fizzy water and long-wing spittle syrup, which some people think is gross, but it's, like, boiled and stuff and it tastes just like the real soda, so I don't mind. But my moms won't drink it, even though they grew up in the city and like all the chemical-tasting stuff. Grown-ups shouldn't drink soda, I think, because kids really should have some privileges that grown-ups don't, just to be fair. It's not fair being a kid most of the time. Oh, I'm sorry that I didn't talk to you in school. It's just that this town is even more unfair than most places, I guess, though I've never been most places, so I don't know for sure, but I think that—"

"Kayda, please, take a breath and give the boy some space." Kimber gently cut off her daughter's monologue, which was a great relief to Abel. It was like Kayda had saved up weeks of things to say, then spat them all out the instant they'd stowed him safely out of sight. "Abel's having a difficult day."

"Thanks for taking me in," he said. "I know it's a risk."

"What are they gonna go do, put us back in the dragon rodeo?" Kayda shrugged. "We'll show them!"

"We'll always help someone in need," Althea reassured him.

"But I'm certain they *will* come looking for you here. You won't be able to stay long."

"I know," said Abel. "I just needed a little time to think. And to be somewhere Omi can find me if she comes looking."

"Do you think she flew away?" Kayda asked.

"I dunno," said Abel. "I hope not. I kind of need her to carry a message to Drakopolis for me."

"To get help from your kin?" Kayda said. Her moms looked at each other nervously. No one liked to get caught up with the kins.

"I'm not really in a kin," said Abel. "I guess I'm loyal to the Wind Breaker ideals and stuff, but really, we're just some friends who help each other out."

"That's kind of what a kin is, right?" Kayda said. "And *we're* helping you out now, so does that mean we're in the kin too? Maybe we should get matching tattoos!"

"We're not in a kin, honey," Kimber said.

"We're not getting tattoos," Althea added.

Kayda sagged against the wall like a discarded trash bag. Abel wanted to give her some encouragement as thanks for protecting him. "I still need your help, though," he told her. "I think I know what Manchi is up to. There might be a way to stop him, save my sister, and free this town from Sheriff Skint and her rodeo."

"How?" Kayda asked.

The whole family perked up. Abel admired them, not only for their glassblowing skill, but for their bravery.

"Deputy Manchi made a huge mistake," Abel said. "He forgot the KISS principle."

"Ew," said Kayda. "Why would you want to kiss Deputy Manchi?"

"No," said Abel. "It's something Lina taught me. 'Keep it simple, scoundrel.' It means, if you're making sneaky schemes, it's best not to get too complicated with them. Manchi got too complicated with his, and we can use that against him."

"I think you better explain it to us," said Althea. "We aren't used to this."

"She's saying we're not criminals," Kayda clarified. "But we're doing our best."

Abel laughed. It felt good to laugh. He was amazed that he even remembered how. That was something pretty cool about being alive, he figured. Even when things were awful, if you still had breath in your lungs to breathe, you had breath enough to laugh.

He really hoped Silas was somewhere out in the wilderness—if not laughing, then at least still breathing.

"I have to drop some fireballs of truth on you here," he said. "Your sheriff works for the Red Talons kin."

Kayda's moms looked at each other with pursed lips, then back to Abel.

"Figures," they said.

Abel thought they'd be more surprised.

"Glassblower's Gulch is a rough town," Althea said. "It's not surprising it's ruled by rough people."

"Well, the Red Talons are in constant war with the other kins back in Drakopolis," Abel explained. "The Thunder Wings want to control this town and all the money from the mines and the rodeo. They've made a deal with Deputy Manchi to kill the sheriff so they can take over."

Kayda let out a bitter laugh. "Crooks offing crooks," she grunted. "Doesn't sound like a problem to me."

"I guess not," said Abel. "If you don't mind being ruled by crooks." Kayda nodded. "Anyway, Manchi wants to be sheriff, not a kin boss, so he can't just murder the current sheriff. Instead, he's going to use a dragon to do it, and he's going to frame me for it."

"How?" Kayda asked.

"With the dragon rodeo," said Abel. "He arrested Lina so he can put her in. Once she's there, he's going to use this perfume the Thunder Wings gave him to set the dragon on Sheriff Skint. And then he's going to make it look like *I* did it to help my sister. He'll be able to get rid of her, me, and my family and make it all look perfectly legal."

"That's why he wanted Silas gone," Kayda filled in the details. "Because your brother's honest."

Abel nodded.

"But it was the sheriff herself who put your brother in the rodeo," Kimber pointed out.

"Manchi knew she would," Abel said. "That's the thing about crooks. They're predictable. *She* couldn't have an honest officer on her force either."

Kimber shook her head, disgusted at the whole lot of sheriffs and kinners. "Our community deserves so much better than this," she said.

"How can we help?" Althea asked.

Abel took out his phone, which Manchi hadn't had the brains to confiscate. A smarter goon would've taken Abel's sole means of communication from him, but no one would ever accuse Manchi of being a smart goon.

"I recorded a message for my friends on here," he said. "Their pictures and addresses are on the lock screen. If Omi comes looking for me, I want you to give it to her and tell her to find them in Drakopolis."

"Tell her?" Kayda wondered. "Can she understand that?"

"She's young, but she's a reader," Abel said. "She can figure anything out if she's got the right tools. These addresses are all she needs."

Kayda took the phone from him. "What are you going to do?" she asked.

Abel took a deep breath. "I'm going to turn myself in to the sheriff as my sister's coconspirator," he said. "And hope I can trade my freedom for my parents'. After that, I just have to hope Omi gets my message through."

"That's a lot of hoping," said Kayda.

"Hope's not like ice cream," he said. "You can never have too much of it."

Kayda laughed again. "That means it's exactly like ice cream."

Abel set the soda down and stood. "Thanks for the hospitality. If my parents do manage to get away and look for me here, tell them I love them."

"I think they know that already, Abel," Kimber said.

"Still good to say it," he muttered. "Also, tell them I've got a plan. Whatever they see happen, tell them it's on purpose."

"*Will* it be on purpose?" Kayda asked.

Abel shrugged. He really hoped so.

He was going to lose at the dragon rodeo. And if Omi didn't get his message to his friends in the city, it might be the last thing he ever did.

PART THREE

"IS *THAT* WHAT I SMELL LIKE?"

19

"**YOU RAN AWAY FROM THE** hospital, just to turn yourself in?" The sheriff peered at Abel over her desk. Her office was a little shack at the top of the gulch, and her Rapid Assault Hog Dragon was sleeping just outside the window behind her. Its huge, spiked face filled his view. The window frame rattled with its every snore.

"I wanted to talk to you away from my parents," Abel said.

The sheriff raised her eyebrows. She waited for Abel to continue. A skilled interrogator knew that they didn't always have to ask questions. Most people would just fill the silence left for them, the way pockets just kind of filled with lint. Sheriff Skint thought herself a skilled interrogator. Abel was going to use that against her. She'd think he was confessing, while he was playing her like a hand of DrakoTek cards.

"My parents don't know anything," said Abel. "Lina and I, we were angry about what happened to Silas, so we plotted to get revenge. Lina was going to steal that Cloudflayer and burn up the rodeo grounds."

"And what was your part in this plot?" the sheriff asked.

"It was my idea," he said. "I was supposed to help, but I guess I was sleepwalking and those cockatrices got me. I'm just really lucky Deputy Manchi found me when he did." Abel laid on the act as thick as frostberry jam on a fresh-baked toaster cake.

His stomach grumbled. He hadn't eaten for way too long.

Never hatch a plot hungry, he scolded himself. Too late now.

"I wonder what Deputy Manchi was doing down there so late at night?" Abel asked as innocently as possible. He wanted the sheriff to wonder that too, but he couldn't just come out and tell her. She'd never believe him. Like the old saying went, *You can lead a dragon to treasure, but you can't make him hoard it.*

Sheriff Skint pursed her lips. Abel kept his face as blank and innocent as he could.

"Deputy Manchi is—"

"HORMPF!" A huge dragon snore cut her off. It shook the window frame, the plaques on the wall, and even the coffee right out of her cup—into a puddle on her desk.

She and Abel never broke eye contact.

"Deputy Manchi is not your concern," the sheriff finally said. Then she dabbed up the spilled coffee with a rag she kept near her desk. "You've just confessed to taking part in a conspiracy of theft and destruction. A valuable Cloudflayer was lost into the wild, with a week's worth of supplies. These are serious crimes, and they are in violation of your probation. I could have your whole family sent to Windlee Prison for this."

"But that's not how you do things here," Abel said. This was it. This was the moment. He was offering her a dare. He was the treasure, and she was the dragon.

Come on, he prayed. *Just reach out your greedy claw and snatch me up . . .*

"No," the sheriff smirked. "That is not how we do things here."

Yes! She was taking the bait! Abel nearly pumped his fist. He had to catch it in his other hand to stop himself from whooping.

"Lina and I will do your rodeo, if you let my parents go," he said.

"You're not really in a position to bargain," the sheriff replied. "I could put all four of you in the rodeo tonight if I chose to."

Abel nodded. "You could, yes, ma'am. But if you did that, we'd refuse to fight. We'll all get eaten up fast and you won't have any entertainment. Nothing to bet on. And the whole town would be disappointed in you."

Abel wasn't actually sure about that last part. This was a rough town and maybe they'd all cheer as four innocent people got eaten in one bite. But he was bluffing. It was like when you'd already played your best cards but had to act like you had a Reaper in your hand—or a Steelwing or something—so that your opponent held back *their* best cards. They had you beat, but if they didn't know that, you could bluff your way to winning.

Of course, if your opponent didn't fall for it, you lost. There was no chance Abel's parents would just let him and Lina get eaten without a fight, and no chance he and Lina would let them get eaten without a fight.

But the sheriff didn't know that.

She took a deep breath, and he worried she might say no.

"Yes," she said, to Abel's relief. "But I have one adjustment to your proposal." She picked up her coffee cup to take a drink, then remembered it had spilled and set it back down again. "You go in alone. I don't trust either of you, so you go first, and then, after you lose, Lina goes in."

"What if I don't lose?" Abel asked, which made the sheriff chuckle.

"You'll lose," she said. "Wanna see why?"

"Not really," Abel said, but he didn't have much choice.

As they walked, Abel took a sniff of the sheriff's shirt. She frowned at him.

"Just admiring your perfume," Abel said. "Is it new? Where'd you get it?"

The sheriff snorted. "Stop being weird," she told him. "Follow me."

Abel was under arrest now, just like Lina, so he had to follow Sheriff Skint where she took him. And where she took him now was a dragon holding cell deep in a cave on the edge of Glassblower's Gulch.

That's where he met his match.

A huge, angry, and freshly caught Bone Reaper from somewhere beyond the horizon.

"Abel, meet Skellor," the sheriff said. "Skellor, meet your midnight snack."

She smiled as the dragon roared in monstrous approval.

• • •

So that was how, just eleven and a half hours later, Abel came to be flat on his back in front of a charging Bone Reaper as a bloodthirsty crowd cheered for his imminent demise.

He hadn't been given armor, although he was supposed to have been.

Just before being sent on, Manchi told Abel he wouldn't need it, as an *experienced* dragon rider. "We don't have armor in your size anyway," he lied.

The sheriff didn't object. Abel wasn't allowed to see his sister before the match either, "to avoid any kind of conspiracy between you two." Abel assumed she wasn't given armor either. The sheriff didn't care what became of them, and Manchi wanted them dead.

Abel figured the deputy would plant the evidence in his apartment after the dragon killed him, his sister, and the sheriff. There wouldn't be anyone left to contradict him. Who was going to question the law when everyone who could've was in the belly of a dragon?

Abel heard the click and crunch of a new bony spike about to fire. He rolled as it sliced the air and crashed into the glass, cracking spiderwebs across the surface. Then the huge Reaper charged!

Abel waved his hands frantically, calling for relief. Three blasts of the sheriff's whistle followed, and on cue, the Dragon Distraction Divas burst from their dugout by the side of the bleachers, a riot of color and chaos.

This was the moment he'd find out if his pleas had been heard or if his world was about to crash down on him like a fifteen-ton dragon.

Although the Divas were dressed up in outlandish costumes—giant mirrored helmets with bedazzled dragon horns, huge silk wings, and garish makeup like dragon scales and jets of fire—Abel knew them immediately. His heart soared.

"You did it, Omi," he whispered to himself. He scanned the crowd for any sign of his wyvern, but of course she wasn't there. Or at least, not where he could see her. This would be too tempting a place to play hide-and-seek for the little dragon. But he knew she'd made it to Drakopolis and back, because the three Divas doing pirouettes, head spins, and the Floss were *not* the regular Divas. They were Abel's friends: Roa and Arvin and Topher!

Omi had delivered his message and flown them here to help!

Topher—dressed like an exaggerated human-sized version of a Cloudflayer—tripped over his tail while trying to do a handstand.

Arvin, the most skilled Diva of the group, had to catch him and help him up before the Bone Reaper attacked them.

Of course, Skellor was just as stunned by their sudden appearance as Abel was delighted. It was the Bone Reaper's first rodeo too, and it had likely never seen humans dressed up like this before.

The distraction gave Abel time to get to his feet and prepare for his next move.

Abel thought back to the message he'd recorded on his phone for them.

Hey, friends, it's your old pal Abel, out here in Glassblower's Gulch. If you're getting this, it means you've met my friend Omi. Don't be alarmed. She won't try to kill you on purpose, but I'm gonna need you to ride her to the gulch and get to a midnight dragon rodeo in secret. Instructions are attached to this message. The kins are here, and they're using this town to fight their war, Thunder Wings versus Red Talons. Yeah, Arvin, your mom's goons are getting paid off by the sheriff, and her deputy is trying to take over for the Thunder Wings. Innocent people are caught in the middle. If we don't do something to stop them, it won't matter who wins. I need your help—one more caper. It's not gonna be safe, but if we do it right, we might help some dragons out too . . .

Abel was really proud of Omi. The young wyvern had done what he'd trained her to do, and no one had died in the process.

Yet, anyway.

As the Divas left the field, Arvin made eye contact with Abel and winked. Roa, dressed kind of like a Rose Thorn wyvern, gave him a thumbs-up. Topher scrambled after, trying not to fall again. Abel saw Deputy Manchi in the crowd, taking out his little yellow perfume bottle and glancing around before he spritzed the air in Skellor's direction.

"Pheromones away! Brace yourselves," Abel said, even though no one else could hear him. It just felt good to have a team again. He hoped, in a few minutes, they'd all be able to hug in the safety of the desert outside Glassblower's Gulch.

It was that or they'd be dragon feed.

Sheriff Skint blew her dragon whistle to restart the action.

In the dugout, Arvin was frantically fiddling with a device hidden in Topher's helmet that sprayed another scent. If Roa had done their job, the smell would cancel out the pheromones and match the smell to Abel. He'd told them to use the T-shirts he'd left behind to make it, the same way Manchi's perfume used cockatrice feathers. He just hoped his smell said "friend" to Skellor and not "food."

There was nothing else Abel could do now but play his part and hope.

He leapt into the air and squeezed his eyes shut as its huge claw swung at him.

His feet never hit the ground.

The dragon's claw wrapped around him, enveloping him in its warmth.

If Skellor had wanted to, it could've crushed him into a paste and licked him off its fingers like peanut butter, but instead, the darkness concealed him with surprising gentleness. Abel took a calming breath and tried to slow his racing heart. He peeked out at the small circle of light at the top of the dragon's palm. He wondered if this was the last view his big brother had seen. He wondered if it was the last he'd see too.

The crowd shrieked as the dragon charged at Sheriff Skint. Then, the moment before impact, it leapt into the air. Abel was airborne in a wild dragon's claws and Manchi's murderous plan had been thwarted!

Next, Omi erupted from behind the stands with a mighty roar. On her tail, she had a big spray bottle made from what looked like an old fire extinguisher. She was spraying a new and powerful cloud of scent behind her. Skellor, picking up the smell, gave chase. Skellor nearly bit her tail off before she dodged away.

"Good girl!" Abel yelled toward Omi. "You having fun?"

"CHEE, CHEE, CHEE!" the wyvern chirped in gleeful reply. Only for a dragon could all this violent chaos be a grand good time, Abel thought with a laugh.

No one in the stands was laughing.

People panicked and scattered, diving for cover. Abel saw that the little wyvern had spent the time since they last saw each other in a few different ways. Not only had she flown a secret mission to deliver a recorded message to Drakopolis and flown his friends to the gulch under cover of darkness; she had been growing too.

Omi was at least five tons by now, and big enough to carry a half dozen people on her back if she had to.

Which was a good thing, because she *did* have to.

She dove to the ground and spat a blob of acid at the bleachers, clearing them of the last, lingering spectators. Then Omi lowered her wings to let Arvin, Roa, and Topher climb onto her back. She looked over at Lina, standing still amid the chaos around her, absolutely stunned. Abel's parents held each other in total terror in the front row, where Deputy Manchi had been guarding them.

Now he was gone and they were free to escape.

The Bone Reaper growled, sniffing the air.

"Run!" Roa shouted across the way at all of them. Lina and Abel's parents did just that. They ran to Omi and climbed onto her back. The not-so-little-anymore baby wyvern launched into the sky and screeched at the Bone Reaper, who screeched a reply.

It loosened its grip on Abel. Letting him climb its ankle, up its leg, and scramble in midair onto its back.

On Omi's back, Lina had settled into the best piloting spot at the base of the wyvern's neck, while Arvin and Topher and Roa showed Abel's parents how to hold on to the different spikes to keep from falling off.

"Nicely done!" Lina yelled across at her brother.

"It wasn't exactly simple!" Abel yelled back. His plan had involved secret messages, midnight flights, Diva costumes, and an experimental perfume scent to tame a wild dragon that Abel now had to figure out how to ride. His plan had left the KISS principle far behind.

Still, he was so happy to see his friends, he could've kissed all of them.

"It's about to get more complicated!" Roa yelled over at him. Two new dragons had taken to the air from opposite sides of the arena. Sheriff Skint was perched on the back of her Rapid Assault Hog Dragon, and Deputy Manchi on his Cobalt Reaper.

"Get them!" the sheriff yelled, still completely unaware that her own deputy had been trying to kill her.

Omi screeched again. She darted off into the dark, spraying more perfume in her wake. Skellor followed her, weaving happily through the thick perfume cloud, playing in it.

"Oh, flaming starlight." Abel gagged and coughed as it flew him straight into the fog of perfume. "Is *that* what I smell like?"

Skellor didn't seem to mind. The Bone Reaper was loving it.

Sheriff Skint's RAHD and Manchi's Cobalt Reaper followed them, twirling around each other, looking for a clear shot. They were *not* having any fun at all.

What had started as a rescue operation had now become a high-speed evacuation.

20

WHAT KIND OF BREATH WEAPON *does a Hog dragon have?* Abel wondered, though he didn't have to wonder for long.

From behind him, he heard a low, rolling snort that grew suddenly louder—thunderously loud!

"ROAWUPP!" He turned his head just as a giant blob of mucus the size of a dining table erupted from the Hog dragon's snout.

"LAND IMMEDIATELY!" the sheriff's voice blasted over a loudspeaker.

The Bone Reaper dove out of the lethal loogie's path, corkscrewing toward the desert floor. Monitors fired jets of flame from their burrow holes, and the dragon weaved in and out between them. The flames scorched Abel's shirt, reminding him that he wasn't wearing any armor or even his beloved riding jacket. A T-shirt was poor defense in a dragon duel.

"Omi! Dive!" Abel yelled, though there was no way the little dragon up ahead could hear him. The blob of mucus slapped into her tail with a wet *splurch.*

"Ahh!" Topher yelled.

"EEEEE!" Omi screeched.

"Ew!" Roa cried.

All of them were suddenly silenced as the mucus curled around the wyvern's body and enveloped her in a gooey, pale green blob. The blob crashed from the sky and bounced along the ground.

Monitor lizard flames sizzled off it and bits of glass broke away from the desert floor, but the mucus itself provided cushioning to the dragon and her riders.

Skellor chased after the bouncing ball of dragon slime until it came to rest and oozed open. Roa, Arvin, Topher, and Abel's family gasped for breath. The humans flopped off Omi's back onto the hard ground. Omi tried to stand and flap up again, but the goop weighed down her wings. She couldn't take off. She gagged and spat up Hog dragon snot, and she tried to wipe it away from her eyes with a clawed wing. Abel's heart broke to see the playful young wyvern in such agony.

The Bone Reaper landed beside her, and Abel waved for the people to climb onto its back. Skellor's claws were big enough to carry Omi, if Abel could figure out how to tell the feral dragon that's what he wanted . . . and if it would obey.

It didn't matter. Because just then, the sheriff arrived on her RAHD and Deputy Manchi on his Reaper. Abel was surrounded. The deputy and the sheriff were on opposite sides, angled so they wouldn't hit each other when they fired their breath weapons. He'd been triangulated. Of all the shapes you could encounter in battle, triangles were just the worst.

"Nice try, kid," the sheriff told him. "But you're alone out here and I'm the law. And I've had just about enough of you and your family."

"We surrender!" Abel raised his hands over his head.

"Too late for that," the sheriff replied. She called over to Deputy Manchi. "Fire at will. Leave nothing but ash."

A ball of flame flared in the deep blue of the Cobalt Reaper's fearsome maw.

"Sheriff! Don't trust him!" Abel yelled, in one last desperate attempt at saving his friends. "Deputy Manchi is trying to kill you! He knows you're a Red Talon. He wants to take over Glassblower's Gulch for the Thunder Wings."

The sheriff's eyes darted between Abel and Manchi. She hesitated. It wasn't much, but doubt was creeping in. "Nonsense," she eventually spat out.

"So you aren't on the Red Talons' payroll?" Abel asked.

"Oh, she is," Arvin called up. "And if she incinerates me or my friends, she'll regret it."

He peeled off his helmet to show his face to the sheriff, though he was still covered in Dragon Distraction Diva makeup. She clearly had no idea who he was.

"I'm Arvin Balk," he clarified. "The only child of Red Talon boss Jazinda Balk. *Your* boss."

The sheriff winced. She was stuck now in a very bad position, which was just where Abel wanted her. She couldn't air-fry Arvin without getting in trouble with the Red Talons. Now she had to hear Abel out.

"Deputy Manchi gave you that new perfume you have on, right?" Abel asked. The sheriff didn't deny it, though she didn't answer either. "It's made from cockatrice pheromones, so you smell like food. Whoever the Bone Reaper smells it on, it wants to eat! The Thunder Wings were going to have it eat you and then blame me for it—by planting the perfume in my apartment. I'd get eaten; my family would go to jail; and Manchi and the Thunder Wings would take over all the mining, snuggling, and gambling in Glassblower's Gulch."

"Did you just say 'snuggling'?" Deputy Manchi shouted.

"I meant 'smuggling,'" Abel said. "I misspoke."

"You *said* 'snuggling,'" said Deputy Manchi.

"You know what I meant," Abel snapped. He turned his attention back to the sheriff. "He poisoned me with cockatrice feathers after I heard his plan. The only reason he let me live was to frame me. He knew you thought I was a crook, so you wouldn't believe any accusations I made."

"But you *are* a crook," the sheriff said. "And I don't believe your accusations. Deputy Manchi is loyal. Always has been."

"And you did say 'snuggling,'" Deputy Manchi repeated.

"Let it go!" Abel threw his arms up.

"So you admit it!" Manchi pointed an accusing finger at him.

"You're just trying to distract Sheriff Skint from your treachery!" Abel yelled back.

"No," said Deputy Manchi, an oil-slick grin sliding across his face. "I'm not trying to *distract* her." He turned his dragon's mouth toward Sheriff Skint. "I'm trying to *delay* her until my backup arrives."

Just then, swirling down like tornado, came a flight of a dozen dragons—Reapers and Widow Makers and Yellow Stingers and even a long-wing Infernal. They fanned out to surround everyone, while the Infernal circled overhead.

Their riders were Thunder Wings, one and all, and Ally led the charge.

Abel's former teacher rode the back of her old Yellow Stinger now. No more sneaking around on a Moth dragon. Yellow Stingers were fighting dragons, and this one was clearly experienced. He'd seen it battle in Drakopolis. Both Ally and the dragon looked very pleased with themselves.

"Abel, Roa, Topher," she said. "My former students! How lovely to see you out here beyond the reach of help." She nodded at Abel's parents. "Nice to see you both as well."

"You were *not* a good teacher," Abel's father snapped at her, though that wasn't exactly true. She was the best teacher Abel had ever had, if you could ignore the whole merciless-kinner thing.

It was admittedly hard to ignore.

"*It's true?*" Sheriff Skint gasped at her deputy. Aside from the peril she suddenly found herself in, it looked like her feelings had been hurt.

"The boy wasn't lying," Deputy Manchi said. "Though I realize now I should've just let the cockatrice poison turn his skin to glass. He's a troublesome little dork, isn't he?"

"He's not a dork!" Arvin defended Abel, which made Abel's heart do a double tap against his ribs. Arvin, with his amazing makeup talent, his effortless cool, and his position as the heir to the most powerful criminal kin in Drakopolis, was the one boy whose opinion mattered to Abel. He nodded thankfully at his friend. Arvin nodded back.

"How sweet," Deputy Manchi said. "Unfortunately for you, I'll get extra credit from my new boss for killing you. So . . . Ally, may I fry this sad little flock of wannabe Wind Breakers?"

Ally took a deep breath. Maybe she still had some affection for her former students, enough to feed some small morsel of mercy that lingered in her heart.

"Go for it," she told Manchi. "Start with the sheriff, though, please."

Nope. No mercy morsels there.

"With pleasure," Deputy Manchi replied. "Sorry, boss. Nothing personal."

"Oh yes, it is, Deputy," said Sheriff Skint. "Very personal."

Deputy Manchi shrugged. He wasn't the sentimental sort. Flame rose in the Cobalt Reaper's mouth, but suddenly a blood curdling screech cut the night sky.

The Infernal circling overhead had been attacked by two lightning-quick Stoneskins, snapping at its wings and tearing at its belly.

Two dozen *more* dragons dove from the clouds, led by a huge Diamond Colossus, one of the rarest long-wings in the world.

It was ridden by none other than Jazinda Balk.

"Mom!" Arvin cried out in joy.

Her favorite henchmen, Grackle and Sax, flanked her on matching Ruby Widow Makers. They aimed their mouths right at Manchi.

"I wouldn't let your dragon so much as sigh if I were you," she warned the deputy.

"And I wouldn't move a muscle if I were you," Ally warned her. The Yellow Stinger had its eyes locked right on Arvin and his friends, breath weapon at the ready. "Or your son's ashes will fit in a shoebox."

"If you hurt so much as an eyelash on my son . . ." Jazinda Balk said, smooth and sharp, like her words could slice steel, "you will suffer as no one has ever suffered in the history of Drakopolis."

"If you haven't noticed," Ally sneered, "we aren't *in* Drakopolis."

"Mom, how did you find me here?" Arvin asked while keeping very, very still. He didn't want to upset the huge black-and-yellow dragon currently eager to fire just feet from his fragile flesh.

"I have a tracker hidden in your earring," his mother said. "And another in your phone, and a third in your nose ring. Why do you think I let you get all those piercings?"

"A shared respect for fashion?" Arvin suggested meekly. Jazinda

Balk *was* very fashionable. Her current combat outfit was a black-and-red full-body jumpsuit studded with diamonds to match her dragon's scales.

"I had to keep tabs on you," she told him. "And when I got a message of concern from one mother to another, I had to come to your aid." She winked at Abel's mom.

"Mom?" Abel gasped.

His mother nodded. "When your father got nowhere with his letters to the authorities, I wrote one to the only mother I knew beyond their authority."

"And I did what any caring mother and responsible crime boss would have done," Jazinda said. "We parents have to keep track of our hatchlings, no matter how we feel about the flock they choose to fly with."

"Um, right," said Abel. "Thanks?"

He wasn't quite sure whose side she was supposed to be on here. The Red Talons had tried to kill Abel countless times. The sheriff was one of them, and it was almost accidental that they were on the same side now. The only reason Abel and his family weren't already cooked to a crisp was because of Arvin. Neither of their mothers exactly approved of their friendship.

There was a reason the kins were called "kin." "Kin" was another word for "family"—and family, whether by birth or choice or criminal affiliation, could be *complicated*.

"So we're in a classic Hydra's Hitch," Ally said. "Who knows what that is?"

Her voice had dropped into teacher tone, which Abel figured some adults just couldn't help, no matter the circumstances. If there were kids around, they were going to quiz them.

"I do," said Roa, looking over at their former teacher and even raising a hand. There were some *kids* who just couldn't resist being in perfect-student mode, no matter the circumstances. They were going to ace any quiz. Roa was one of them. "It's from the myth of the many-headed dragon whose three heads disagreed over a small goat they all wanted to eat. They couldn't attack each other because they shared a body, but they couldn't agree on a solution either, so they argued for thousands of years. They argued so long, they turned to stone. That's the myth that explains the volcano with three peaks on the horizon."

"Very good," Ally praised Roa, which made them smile in spite of themself. "What's the lesson there, do you think?"

"If you've got power, try not to be stupid with it?" Topher suggested. He hadn't ever been the best student in the world, but sometimes he saw right through to the important lesson. Ally even laughed.

"You do realize in this scenario we are the small goat?" Roa said. "Anyway, it's a myth. That's not really how volcanoes are formed, and there are no three-headed dragons."

"Myth or not, no one is making a small goat out of my child!" Jazinda Balk yelled. "Arvin, step away from your friends and join your mother, please."

"I'm not leaving them," Arvin said, much to Abel's relief. He climbed right up onto the back of the Bone Reaper and wrapped his arms around Abel's waist, squeezing so hard it nearly took Abel's breath away. "If you fry Abel and his family, you'll have to fry me!"

"Thanks," Abel said over his shoulder.

"We're scales on the same serpent, my friend," Arvin whispered in his ear. "I'm not gonna let them lay a talon on you."

Roa and Topher climbed up too, then Lina and Abel's parents.

Whatever happened next, it wouldn't be on Abel alone.

On the ground, Omi spat the last of the Hog dragon goo out. She snarled at the dozens of bigger dragons around her.

They all roared back in one bone-rattling voice. Poor little Omi curled up into a ball under her wings, just like Percy did when she'd scared him. Omi hadn't realized what a small dragon she still was.

"Where'd you get a baby Rose Thorn wyvern anyway?" Roa asked.

"A friend gave her to me," Abel said.

"You're making new friends here?" Roa frowned. Were they jealous? Of Abel? "I mean . . . I'm glad. It just hasn't been that long, you know?"

"Maybe we can catch up another time?" Topher suggested, gesturing at the Thunder Wings and the Red Talons all around them.

"Let's just fry them all, huh?" Deputy Manchi suggested. "We can win."

"We're outnumbered," said Ally. "We would not all survive."

"Why don't we settle this the Drakopolis way?" Jazinda's goon Sax suggested. "With a battle. One-on-one. Thunder Wings versus Red Talons for control of Glassblower's Gulch."

"Sheriff versus deputy," Jazinda added. "Seems to me this is a small-town disagreement, so the small towners should settle it."

"How do I know you'll honor the results?" Ally demanded.

"How do I know *you* will?" Jazinda replied. "Where's your boss anyway?"

"I'm the kin boss now," Ally said, sitting taller on her dragon. "I had a dispute with our previous leadership, and he ended up on the losing side."

"I respect that," said Jazinda. "Stop aiming your dragon's maw at my son and his . . ." She cleared her throat and made a sound like a gecko being stepped on. ". . . *friends*, and we'll let these two officers of the law battle."

"To the death?" Ally suggested.

"Of course," Jazinda agreed.

"Hey!" the sheriff objected. "What if *we* don't agree?"

"I've no problem with it," said Manchi—and then to Sheriff Skint, "Sorry, boss."

"Fine," she agreed quickly, like she was clicking on the terms and conditions to a shopping website. "To the death."

"Um? Excuse me?" Abel's dad called from the back of the Bone Reaper. "So . . . what happens to us? If you don't mind my asking."

The kinners all looked at one another for suggestions. Overhead, the stars shimmered. It was a beautiful night. Abel was amazed how lovely the sky could be while horrible events happened in people's lives below it. It was a good reminder that the world did not revolve around him. If it did, the sky would be full of thunder and lightning, like the storm raging inside him right now. He could feel vengeance and justice slipping away. He'd gone from the brave hero of a story he was creating himself to a quiet victim on the back of a dragon while the powerful decided his fate.

"Winner gets them," said the sheriff.

"Agreed," said Manchi.

"Not my son," said Jazinda.

"Fair enough," said Ally.

"I'm not leaving my friends!" objected Arvin.

"Sweetie, I'm going to protect you," the boss of the Red Talons said gently. "Even if that means Grackle and Sax have to knock you out and drag you away from your little boyfriend."

"I'm not his—!" Abel started to say.

"He's not my—!" Arvin said at the same time, though neither of them finished the sentence. Each waited for the other to say the rest. Everyone else just kind of stared. They both fell quiet again.

"Okay, adolescent drama aside, can we get on with this?" Ally asked. "I'd like to get back to Drakopolis as soon as flaming possible. I'm a city girl. All this nature makes my skin crawl."

"Red Talons, stand down!" Jazinda ordered her kin.

"Thunder Wings, you too," Ally ordered. "But if Abel and his flock of miscreants try to flee, light 'em up."

Dozens of dragon eyes rested on Abel's Bone Reaper and on the smaller wyvern beside it.

"What are we supposed to do now?" Topher whispered. "Just watch them battle for our lives?"

"I could try to steal a dragon while they're distracted?" Lina suggested.

"I could fake a medical emergency?" Abel's dad chimed in.

"How would that help?" his mom asked. "They don't really care if we live or die."

"I'm just brainstorming," Dad replied.

"You're a lovely man but a terrible criminal," Mom told him.

"Well, I don't see anyone else coming up with any nifty schemes," Dad said.

"'Nifty,' Dad? Really?" Lina grunted.

"Sorry," he said. "'Sneaky'? 'Groovy'? 'Sus'? I don't know young people's lingo for 'scheming.'"

"Just say 'scheming,'" Lina told him.

"Sometimes, doing nothing and waiting for an opportunity is the best course of action," their mom said. "What do you think, Abel?"

Abel was proud that his mom wanted his opinion. He felt a little grown-up right then, but the feeling also made him a little sad. The flip side of growing up was making grown-up choices, and he didn't know the right one here.

Abel watched the Hog dragon and the Cobalt Reaper circle one another, riders' eyes locked, preparing to fight. It occurred to him that he didn't have a lot of good role models for how grown-ups should act. That's why he always wondered what Dr. Drago would do. But Dr. Drago had never been in a situation like this. There was nowhere else to look for guidance. He had to trust his friends. He had to trust his family. He had to trust the voice inside himself that told him what was right.

"I think whoever wins," he said, "is gonna have to fight us next."

Lina patted his back, and his mother squeezed his shoulder. He gripped Skellor's horns tighter and felt Arvin grip his waist. Roa and Topher were holding hands. Everyone was locked in their own thoughts as the sheriff's and the deputy's dragons roared.

The two dragons launched themselves into the air and straight for one another's throats, and all Abel could do was pray. Pray for what, he didn't yet know.

21

THIRTY TONS OF DRAGON SLAMMED into each other just overhead. The air rippled with heat.

"I trained you and supported you!" Sheriff Skint yelled from the back of her snorting Hog dragon. Its wings beat the air and its claws grappled with the Cobalt Reaper's.

"I found a kin who could make *me* rich, just like you did!" Manchi replied. "You can't blame me for learning what you taught me!"

"Learn this!" Sheriff Skint yelled, and tugged her dragon's reins. Ten blobs of snot, each the size of a computer screen, shot out of its snout and slammed into the Reaper—enveloping its claws, covering its eyes, and nearly knocking Deputy Manchi from his saddle.

"Yes!" Lina cheered.

The Reaper shot back with a streak of blue-hot fire that singed the Hog dragon's scales and sent it squealing away.

"Yes!" Lina cheered again. Apparently, she was rooting for both of them to suffer, and neither of them to win.

Abel glared at her. He didn't much care what happened to the riders, but he hated to see dragons suffer because of humans. It was unfair that in fights between people, dragons had to get hurt and to do the hurting. He felt Arvin wince when the Hog dragon recovered and rammed at full speed into the Reaper's side, nearly knocking it out of the sky. Roa groaned. None of them wanted to see a single dragon injured, not even these two.

A jet of flame flared out of the Cobalt Reaper, spraying wildly and making everyone on the ground duck for cover. Little Omi scurried underneath Skellor's wings. The Bone Reaper let her stay there.

The two battling dragons circled in the sky. The kinners kept their eyes on them, each rooting for their side. It was an odd image for Abel, two big groups of kinners sitting calmly on their armored dragons under the stars, cheering for uniformed officers of the law who were fighting on behalf of the criminals below.

Only four kinners weren't watching the battle. On one side of Abel's dragon, Jazinda Balk stared at her son while, beside her, Grackle looked lightning bolts at Abel. On the other side of Skellor, Ally and one of her Thunder Wings goons stared right across them at the two Red Talons. All four of their dragons had their breath weapons ready, all fixed on Abel and his family.

There would be no escaping, whatever happened.

"I'm sorry I brought you out here," Abel told his friends, tears welling in his eyes. "And I'm sorry, Mom and Dad, that I couldn't save Silas. Lina . . . I'm sorry I forgot to keep it simple. I'm not a very good scoundrel."

He looked down from the Bone Reaper's back to where Omi's head was poking out to watch the battle.

"And I'm sorry to you too, Omelette," he said. "I shouldn't have trained you. I should've just let you escape while I still could. I let you down."

"Chee, chee," the wyvern said quietly, which Abel realized he didn't actually know the meaning of. He'd thought the sound was a cheer. Was it maybe also forgiveness? Was it a question or an idea? For all the time he spent with dragons, he realized he didn't really understand them at all.

Boom!

Sheriff Skint had thrown a stun grenade at her deputy, but the Reaper batted it away with a wing, knocking it to the glass ground. The explosion sent monitor lizards scattering from their burrows, bumping into each other in panic and confusion. The Hog fired another blob of snot. The Reaper vaporized the snot with fire. Neither dragon could get an advantage. Their riders would push them past exhaustion as they tried.

"The problem is us," Abel said philosophically. "It's not the law or the criminals. It's greed. It's jealousy. It's people. It doesn't matter if it's Drakopolis, Glassblower's Gulch, or the total wilderness of the Glass Flats; wherever people bring their feuds and fears and frustrations, dragons will be forced to fight. We can't save the dragons until we save the people from their worst selves."

"Deep," said Topher.

"We can't save people from themselves," said Arvin. "We can't even save *our*selves from other people!"

"I just don't know what to do," Abel whined, letting himself collapse against his friend, hot tears pouring down his cheeks. "I failed everyone. *Again*. For good this time."

"No, Abel, you didn't fail anyone," his mother said.

"If anything, we failed you," his father said. "You're a good kid with a good heart, too good for this brutal place."

"We're only here because I got in trouble in Drakopolis!" Abel cried.

Ally, on her dragon's back, smirked at his agony. His sadness turned to anger. He wanted to shoot a giant spike right through her treacherous face. If he was going to go down, he wanted to go down fighting. If he couldn't stop people from being their worst selves, maybe he should just embrace his worst self too.

"What are you thinking about?" Roa whispered. They'd noticed his grip adjusting on the dragon's horns. They knew him too well. They could tell he was up to something.

"Don't do anything foolish," Arvin pleaded.

"Abel . . ." his mother said slowly, which was a parental catchall warning not to do whatever it was he wanted to do, from swiping a cookie from the jar to waging a losing war.

"You should all get down from Skellor," he whispered, staring at Ally as hard as he could. She stared back.

Ally shook her head at him, and the leather of her gloves creaked as she tightened the grip on her Yellow Stinger's reins. He heard Arvin suck in his breath. The boy turned his head to see Jazinda and Grackle locking their safety harnesses, preparing for combat.

The dragons battling in the sky screeched and tangled, but Abel didn't look up this time. His fight was here, on the ground. For now.

He braced himself.

"You have to get down," he told the others again as calmly as he could.

"Abel—" Lina started, but he shook his head.

"When you get a chance, climb on Omi," he said. "She'll do her best to get you out of here if you make her think it's a game."

"Don't," his father pleaded.

"If I'm going to pick a losing fight, I'm doing it alone," Abel said, trying his best to keep from crying. He couldn't save himself, but at least he might save the people he cared about.

"But you're not alone," Roa said.

He turned around to smile at his best friend. "That's really nice, Roa. But I can't let you all do this."

"Not us, pimple brain!" Roa said. "Them!"

They pointed up, and Abel followed the path of their finger toward the stars just beyond the dragons battling.

At first, Abel saw nothing but the night sky. There were some stars out of place. They were moving. A whole field of stars shifting together, and when he squinted, he saw the faintest outline around them. It looked like a dragon's wings, a living constellation.

The outline turned and circled toward him, like the sky was . . . not falling but *flying* to him. His breath quickened; his heart raced, and he saw a sunrise among the stars, a perfect orange circle blazing in a sea of night.

A wave of warmth washed over Abel as the blazing sun grew brighter.

It wasn't a sun, but a dragon's breath, and the stars weren't stars, but the camouflage on a Sunrise Reaper's wings. He'd seen this sunrise before. He knew this Reaper. He raised both arms to the falling sky and cheered "Karak!" as loud as he could.

His beloved Sunrise Reaper, the first dragon he ever rode, had come back for him.

Behind Karak, he saw a massive flock of dragons erupt from the horizon, blotting out the stars that had hidden Karak so well. There were a hundred or more, and they swirled in from the sky like . . . well, like . . .

There was no simile for this. No figure of speech could capture a flock of wild dragons descending on a battle in wide-winged fury.

Omi peeked out from below the shelter of the Bone Reaper's

wing, wide-eyed at the cloud of dragons. There were so many, they blotted out the night.

It was only when the flock swooped in low, driving Sheriff Skint and Deputy Manchi to the ground on their own terrified dragons, that Abel saw the dragon just beside Karak. A Candy Cane Reaper flew with a rider on its back, the only human among hundreds of wild wings.

"Is that—" Lina gasped.

"Our big brother." Abel smiled as Silas, alive and thriving, buzzed past them with a cheer.

"Ep ep!" he yelled, before circling high again over Karak's head.

Karak's eyes met Abel's, and the dragon screeched, then let loose a flood of fire, forcing the Thunder Wings and Red Talons and every one of their dragons to flatten themselves against the ground in fright.

Among the flames, Abel sat up tall.

FAMILIES COME IN ALL KINDS, Abel thought. *There are those you're born into, the siblings you may have and fight with, the parents you've got or don't; the bonds you form with friends along the way, friends who become closer to you than you ever thought strangers could be. There are families by birth and families by choice, families with one parent or two, with grandparents or none, one mom or two dads or two moms, stepparents or foster parents.*

Some people made families in uniform, like Silas with his fellow agents, or like Jazinda Balk with her criminal kin. Different people meant different things when they said "we." It was just a question of how big the heart's imagination could be.

Abel's heart, he realized on seeing Karak again, was big enough for dragons.

While Silas and his Candy Cane Reaper still circled overhead, pinning the Thunder Wings and Red Talons down, Abel leapt from Skellor's back and ran to Karak the moment the huge Reaper landed.

He stood in front of the Sunrise Reaper's snout, gazing up.

"I thought I'd never see you again!" he cried.

Karak lowered his huge black head to Abel. The dragon's face alone was taller than two Abels, and his wingspan could've covered Abel's entire apartment. He could've swallowed Abel without even chewing. And yet the moment their eyes locked, the dragon flopped sideways to the ground, rolled over, and let Abel rub the underside of his jaw. The Reaper cooed like a house pet.

"Um," said Arvin, taking his turn to be speechless.

"Oh yeah, this is Karak," said Abel. "He was the first dragon I ever flew into battle." Abel gestured to Arvin and to Omi and to his family. "Karak, you know Topher and Roa already. And Lina, 'cause she was the one who stole you originally . . ."

Karak's eyes narrowed at that. Lina had gone up against Karak for the Sky Knights in their first battle. A dragon's trust, once lost, was hard to win back.

"She's cool now, trust me," Abel reassured Karak. Though it was more to reassure his sister that she wasn't about to get scorched to cinders.

"This is Arvin, my . . . er, friend," Abel stumbled. "Don't mind the tattoo. He's not really a Red Talon. Or the makeup. He's not really a dragon."

Karak snorted.

"And this is Omi!" Abel pointed under the Bone Reaper to the curious but frightened wyvern hiding out below Skellor's belly. "We've been training together."

Karak sat up straight, tall as a three-story building, and cocked his head. There was a low snarl.

"No, no, not like that," Abel said, understanding his old dragon's alarm immediately. "She's not gonna battle. I trained her to carry messages. She was always gonna go free."

Karak relaxed again. Abel did not doubt their friendship, but he knew Karak wouldn't approve of any dragon being forced to battle by humans. But he also was here to support Abel, which meant he approved of dragons *choosing* to fight for humans.

He'd come with an armada to help, after all, and he'd brought Silas.

It was then that the Candy Cane Reaper swooped in for a landing. Silas slid off the dragon's back as casually as climbing off a city bus. He met Abel's eyes across the glass.

It occurred to Abel that the last time he'd seen his brother, Silas was bloody, his shirt was torn, and he was clutched in the claws of this same Candy Cane Reaper.

How had he tamed it? And where had he gotten new clothes? Or bandages? Or even, like, food? No way Silas had been eating raw monitor lizard or glass cat.

There were so many questions Abel wanted to ask. But before he could, Silas broke into a run and nearly tackled him. He wrapped his arms around Abel with bone-crushing affection.

"I thought you were a goner—" Abel started, feeling a sudden surge of tears he'd have normally been too embarrassed to let Silas see.

"And let you get all the glory?" Silas laughed, though his voice was gravelly with tears too. "Never."

His big brother felt warm and familiar, and it occurred to Abel that they hadn't hugged like this in years. The smell of burnt hair and BO reminded him why.

As he was about to pull away to make what he thought was a clever comment about Silas still *being* alive but *smelling* dead, Lina and both his parents suddenly wrapped *themselves* around the two brothers.

"Family hoard!" Dad shouted, just like he had when they were all still little. Abel and his siblings would then fall into a pile on the floor, hugging so hard that Percy could come along and lie on top of them like a dragon in its lair.

"Hey, what about Percy?" Silas asked, looking between his whole family.

"Kayda's looking after him," Abel said. "Until we get back . . ."

"Right." Silas nodded. "Back . . ." He rubbed the uneven patch of whiskers on his chin. They weren't really growing into the beard he might've been hoping for. Still, Lina and Abel were way too relieved he was alive to make fun of him for it. "We've got some things to take care of first," he told them, gesturing at the Thunder Wings and Red Talons.

The kinners on all sides were terrified. It looked like Deputy Manchi was crying. He was trying to hide under his Cobalt Reaper, while his Cobalt Reaper tried to hide under him. Obviously, this was difficult for a fifteen-ton medium-wing dragon to do.

"Ouch! Stop it!" Manchi snarled at the dragon, whose snout kept knocking him over and rolling him around. "Stop it, you brute!"

Karak ran his large eyes over the crowd of kinners and their dragons, the two uniformed officers with theirs, and then looked Omi and the Bone Reaper up and down. He snorted and screeched in a few quick bursts, which made everyone jump, even Abel. A chorus of shrieks and snarls erupted from Karak's flock. Some dragons snapped at each other; others shuffled their feet or flapped their wings in place. The deputy's Cobalt Reaper roared, and the sheriff's Hog dragon let out a series of grunts that sounded almost like pleas.

"What's happening?" Topher wondered.

"I think they're having a . . . debate?" Abel said, and looked at Roa. They knew more about dragons than anybody Abel had ever met.

"There are theories of dragon language," Roa said. "Their jawbones and horns carry vibrations to their brains in subtler ways than human ears. Some researchers think that when we hear roars and screeches, dragons are hearing thousands of different sounds. It's not a language as humans could understand it, but they suggest it is a language nonetheless."

"That's *just* a theory," Ally chimed in, ever the teacher. "Others believe the sounds are purely instinctual, with none of the characteristics that make a language, like grammar and vocabulary. The roars and grunts carry no greater meaning than what they sound like to us. Instinct, not intellect."

"This sounds like a City Council meeting to me," Abel's father added, not knowing much about draco-linguistic theory but knowing a lot about local government.

"What do you think this council of dragons is debating?" Topher asked.

"They're debating whether or not to let these kinners live, aren't they?" Abel asked.

His brother nodded.

The tables had turned on Ally very suddenly, but she didn't show alarm. She glared at Abel and clenched her jaw, resolute. She was too proud to beg, and she wasn't going to cower either.

"Please!" Deputy Manchi cowered and begged. He crawled away from his dragon and scurried on all fours across the hard ground to plead at Abel's feet.

"Don't ask me," Abel said. He hitched his chin toward Karak. "Ask him."

Manchi turned his head to the huge Sunrise Reaper, whose black scales and folded wings sparkled with starlight. He hesitated, then crawled over to Karak's giant foreclaw and rested his head on it, blubbering.

"Some champion you've got there," Jazinda Balk called toward Ally.

Sheriff Skint just shook her head sadly at her traitorous deputy's pathetic performance.

"Please, noble dragon," the deputy pleaded at Karak. "Spare me and my beloved Manchini!"

"He named his dragon Manchini?" Arvin whispered in Abel's ear. "Like a little Manchi?"

Abel burst out laughing, even though it wasn't that funny. But once he started, he couldn't stop. It was like when someone made a face in school during a test or passed gas at a funeral. Totally inappropriate to laugh, and totally impossible to stop. Abel's whole body shook.

Karak looked up from the deputy and cocked his head at Abel, puzzled by the outburst.

Arvin put a hand on his shoulder. "Dude, it wasn't that funny."

"I know!" Abel waved his hands in front of his face. His stomach hurt from it, but he couldn't stop laughing. Sometimes, when the feelings were too big, too complicated, and spinning him like a 7-g turn on a racing dragon's back, all he could do was laugh.

Deputy Manchi's pleading brought out a new round of cacophonous grunts and roars and shrieks from the flock of dragons. Finally, Karak bent his neck back, gazing straight into the night, and shot up three perfect rings of fire. They rose like bubbles in a swimming pool, and then he shot a jet of flame through the center of all three.

The flock fell silent. The humans fell silent. Even the wind fell silent.

"Judgment time," Silas whispered. He'd spent enough time in

law enforcement that he knew the vibe of a sentence being passed. The Thunder Wings and Red Talons seemed to know it too. Even Lina. It was a gift experienced criminals had—sensing a shift, knowing before it happened when something was about to go down.

Abel noticed a few of the kinners slowly reaching for weapons, as if a human with an electric switchblade stood a chance against a hundred dragons.

Through the thick silence, Omi chirped and padded over to Karak. She looked small below the big Reaper, though she was now bigger than Abel's bedroom. She chirped again up at him, and Karak snorted two little jets of flame from his nostrils.

Whatever that answer meant to whatever Omi had asked, it made the young wyvern extremely happy. She practically hopped from foot to foot, chittering the whole time, and walked over to Abel. She lowered her wing for him to get on.

Abel looked up at Karak. If he was going to ride a dragon out of here, he wanted to be on the back of his old friend. But Karak bobbed his head once, like a nod. This was a bit like the T-shirts Abel had given his friends. Omi was young. She needed to know she had not been forgotten. Karak and Abel would have time together later.

He climbed on Omi's back.

"It's okay, Mom!" Silas called over to their parents, who were still watching from atop Skellor. "We're all gonna go for a ride. They're taking us somewhere . . . new." He cleared his throat. Silas didn't sound quite like himself, but in a good way. He sounded *humble*.

"What about them?" Abel gestured toward the Red Talons, Thunder Wings, and the sheriff. Lastly, he looked at Deputy Manchi at Karak's feet.

The big black dragon raised one claw and used it to knock the deputy onto his butt, out of the way. Then he let out one great roar.

Karak launched himself into the sky, and every wild dragon followed with their own bone-rattling ruckus.

In seconds, the entire flock was airborne. The Bone Reaper hesitated just a moment, then joined them. Only Abel and Omi remained on the ground.

Arvin shouted down as they left, "Sorry, Mom! I think you'll be okay, though!"

Jazinda Balk watched her son fly into the night with Abel's family. Then she dropped her gaze to Abel on his wyvern. Her Diamond Colossus could swallow Omi whole. Abel feared she just might do it too, until she exhaled and her shoulders slumped. Suddenly, Jazinda didn't look like a ferocious kin boss anymore. She looked sad.

"Watch out for my son," she told Abel. "If he gets hurt, in mind or body, no flock of feral dragons will keep me from my vengeance. I'd burn the world to bone and ash for the ones I love. Savvy?"

"I would too," Abel vowed. He held her gaze a moment longer, then squeezed his legs and ran Omi past her, launching the wyvern with a screech over her head. Then he circled over Deputy Manchi, Sheriff Skint, and the two rival kins. They were on their own now. The puzzled kinners and their dragons craned their necks up to watch him as he turned and joined the huge flock heading for the horizon.

Some people might've felt small, surrounded by so many huge creatures, but Abel felt safe up there with them. He felt like part of something big and fast and powerful. Omi darted around, diving and swooping, seeing how close she could get to the bigger dragons without slowing down. She was having a blast!

Some of them growled when she got too near, others snapped at her, and more than a few fired their breath weapons, which got way too close to Abel for comfort. Dragons, he remembered, played rough.

"Hey! Don't forget you've got a passenger here, Omelette!" he warned her, using her full name to make sure she knew she was in trouble. Of course, having now heard dragon language being used in a way he'd never imagined it before, he wasn't sure she even thought of the name humans called her as her own. *What*, he wondered, *do dragons call themselves to each other? And can I learn to call them by their real names too?*

Abel's heart raced as they flew through the night, led by Karak, with Silas on his back. They flew across the Glass Flats, farther into the wilderness than Abel had ever dreamed of flying. He saw strange landscapes of sand and stone, mountains and caves, and whole forests bursting from colorful glass. Jets of flame flared between the trees, and lakes of lava bubbled in the ground.

Wherever they were headed, it was no human landscape.

This was a land for dragons.

AS THE SUN ROSE ON the flock crossing the desert, Abel saw gleaming mountains looming before them. A long string of colorful glass mountains stretched in front of them, and as they flew closer, he saw the mountains were dotted with caves.

The flock broke apart like a flood crashing into a gutter, the dragons scattering into different caves. Silhouettes moved behind the thick walls. It was like watching a shadow puppet show, dragon shapes growing and shrinking and curling around one another, until most of them had vanished deeper into the mountains, where the glass was too thick to see through.

Karak settled on a flat plain in front of a huge cave entrance with a smooth ramp leading up to it. Just beneath the surface, the ramp was filled entirely with jewels arranged in a swirling pattern that looked just like the three rings of fire Karak had blown with a straight line up the middle. Dragons had their symbols, Abel thought, just like the kins.

The surface above the jewels was perfectly smooth and solid. It looked like they'd been piled there before the glass was melted over them. It would take a craftsperson of immense strength and skill to do that.

No, not a craftsperson. *Crafts-dragon?*

There were enough precious stones under that glass to buy half of Drakopolis. Abel noticed that the walls around the entrance itself were also filled with jewels, like the whole mountain had been decorated, then encased in glass.

"Karak?" Abel gasped. "Is this your home?"

The Reaper exhaled slowly, the way he did when the answer to a human question was too obvious for a roar.

"Cool place," Abel added, remembering the pride all dragons have. "It sure beats the abandoned can factory where I met you."

This time, Karak snorted sparks, which was his way of laughing. They scorched Silas's jacket as he walked over to Abel and Omi. Silas was normally a stickler about his clothes, but he brushed the sparks off his shoulders and kept walking without slowing down.

"We should probably go inside," he said. "There's a lot you need to see."

Karak had already started to make his way up the ramp. He glanced over his shoulder and bobbed his head for the humans to follow.

"Do you even know how cool this is?" Roa practically skipped up the ramp. "No one's ever been inside a wild dragon's lair, let alone a whole dragon *city*. And did you see the symbol? I swear I could get a university-level degree out of this."

"I can't believe they're thinking about school right now," Topher said. "Oh, wait, I absolutely can believe that."

"We learn at the Academy that dragons don't have, like, cities," Arvin said. "They don't form flocks unless they're trained to."

"You believe everything you were taught in '*school*'?" Topher asked him, putting the word "school" in extra-sarcastic quotes. Arvin was a Dragon Rider Academy kid, while Roa and Topher went to an overcrowded municipal school in a neighborhood that had more kinner gambling parlors than grocery stores. It had been Abel's school too, until exile.

"We were all taught the same thing," Abel pointed out. "And we used to believe it too."

"Speak for yourself," said Topher. "I never believe anything I'm taught."

"Touch a lot of hot stoves, then, huh?" Arvin grunted, a burn Topher didn't quite understand. He was a clever inventor, but his humor was more of the laughing-when-someone-falls-on-their-face variety than the clever-wordplay variety.

Walking up the ramp toward the cave, he nearly fell on his face himself.

"Tell your little friends to step carefully," Silas offered. "The ramps are slick for those of us without claws."

"Wait." Abel stopped walking. "'*Us*'?"

Silas smirked at him.

"Come inside," Silas said. "And prepare to have your minds blown." He paused and mussed Abel's hair. "Those of you that have minds." Despite all that had happened, he was still Silas, and he was not going to save the day without offering an insult to his little brother.

"Silas! Manners!" their dad scolded, because *he* was still their dad and he was not going to let Silas get away with anything, ever. Even if the whole family was about to walk into a dragons' lair.

• • •

"Okay, so this is definitely a dragon city," said Arvin, squinting at the bright firelight reflecting off the heaps of jewels and gold and glass and metal piled into precious miniature mountains inside the giant mountain cave. There were openings up and down the walls, where dragons perched to watch over their vast and varied treasures. Paths wove and wound among the massive treasure mounds, where

Abel saw, to his absolute shock, humans walking calmly.

"Flaming fingernails!" Roa cried out. "Are these dragons *sharing* their hoards? And are people walking freely among them?"

Silas nodded.

"This goes against everything we know about dragon behavior!" Roa marveled. "Everything we're taught. They're not supposed to cooperate with each other. They're not supposed to *share*!"

"Yeah," said Silas. "I was surprised too. When that Candy Cane over there scooped me up, I thought for sure I was a goner. Then, when it carried me here, I thought I'd be a prisoner in some kind of collection. I did *not* expect to find a—"

"Civilization," Abel finished his brother's sentence.

"A *rich* civilization." Topher pointed at the treasure heaps: gold and silver, jewelry beyond counting, fancy furniture, and stolen electronics. Any luxury items humans prized, the dragons had hoarded them by the ton. That also explained where Silas had gotten his outfit. Abel counted at least four building-sized heaps of designer clothes. This was a shopper's paradise, except that nothing was for sale.

"How do they keep it all from falling down?" Abel's mom wondered.

"Engineering," Topher said with awe. "Dragons are brilliant engineers . . . ?"

"My mom could steal the whole city and not come close to being as rich as this," Arvin said.

"But she's sure trying," Topher whispered. Roa elbowed him in the side.

Abel trotted away from his friends to catch up with Silas and Lina, who were walking down a steep slope into another cavern. He felt a smile rising, seeing the two of them getting along. It'd been years since they were close, one a dragon thief, the other a cop. And all it took to heal their relationship was nearly dying at the hands of two murderous kins, a corrupt sheriff, and a flight of wild dragons.

Family therapy would've been easier, Abel thought as he caught up to them.

"Silas, how many humans live here?" he asked. "How do they know what the dragons want? How do they, like, get clothes and food and stuff? How does this all work?"

"Whoa, Abel, slow down," Silas told him. "Everything's gonna get answered, but I'm not the one to do it."

"Who is? Is there, like, a leader?" Abel imagined someone like Dr. Drago, friend to all dragons, sitting on a golden throne, commanding humans and dragons with kindness and grace. Whoever it was, was a real-life superhero. What kind of person could rule a civilization of dragons, after all?

It was embarrassing to admit, but Abel even imagined himself sitting on a great dragon throne.

They turned around the corner of an especially high tower of riches—jewelry and electronics mixed together. Beyond it was a wide corridor with human guards lined up on either side of it. At the end was a huge door to what Abel imagined was the throne chamber, where the ruler of the dragons awaited them.

Karak stood beside the door, settled onto his haunches.

The guards wore mismatched clothes in every color of the rainbow and had decorated themselves in shiny medals and jewels. They all held huge electric stun spears. The spears wouldn't have done much against a dragon attack, but they'd stop any humans who tried to storm the chamber up ahead.

Behind the human guards, there were big pillars with platforms on top. Dragons perched on those, also bedecked in jewels. They were all different sorts of dragons too. Abel gasped in recognition of a few of them.

"These are the dragons I freed from the lab in Drakopolis," he marveled.

"They're the mutants the Sky Knights made," Silas confirmed. Abel looked up at them in awe. There was the dragon with no eyes, whose face was entirely spikes. There was the dragon who shot poisonous rainbows, and the dragon that breathed lightning, and another that made acid fog. Lina looked down at her feet, ashamed. She'd been the thief who'd delivered most of these dragons to the Sky Knights, where they'd had their DNA hacked.

Abel had freed them and set them loose in the city, where they'd almost gone on a rampage of death and destruction. That is, until Brazza, his racing dragon, had found a way to calm them and guide them to freedom.

Abel stopped in his tracks. His heart skipped a beat, found it again, and then danced to it in his chest.

He looked from the dragons and the guards to Karak and his brother. "Does that mean—"

With one huge foot, Karak pushed the great doors open, and Abel saw the ruler of the dragon city sitting atop her own hoard. Behind Abel, Omi chittered nervously, but a grin split Abel's face from ear to ear.

"Brazza!" he shouted. For a moment, he forgot his friends, his family, his young wyvern, and the guards. He ran straight past them all to hug the snout of the moodiest, strangest, fastest dragon he'd ever known.

And Brazza lowered her huge pink-and-blue head to let him.

ABEL COLLIDED WITH BRAZZA, WRAPPING his arms around her snout as wide as he could. She pressed back against him a little, her scales warm and hard. He closed his eyes and felt her face against his cheek. He felt like he was flying with both feet on the ground.

After a long time that somehow felt not nearly long enough, he pulled away and wiped the tear streaks from his face. First Karak and now Brazza. This was too much joy after so much sadness.

"I never thought I'd see you again," he told her. "When you left Drakopolis with that flock, I thought that was goodbye." Brazza closed her eyes and bowed her head to him, confirming she thought the same.

The hoard shifted under Abel's feet, and he nearly fell over. That was when he noticed what Brazza's massive treasure hoard was made of. She hadn't collected gold or jewels or electronics or designer clothes. Her hoard—which filled the huge chamber and in some places piled a few stories high—was made entirely of books. They weren't even piled haphazardly. She'd arranged them by color and by size. Abel burst out laughing.

"You did love to read with me," he said, scanning the titles at his feet. Famous novels, histories, biographies. Abel didn't know there were this many printed books in the world. He downloaded all his books onto his phone. But you couldn't exactly build a dragon's hoard on a single hard drive, could you? Dragons hoard objects, not data.

"Brrrrp?" a sound came from over Abel's shoulder. He opened his eyes and turned to see Omi making her awkward two-legged way up the book heap. Though only half the size of Brazza, she was fast becoming a fearsome dragon herself. "Brrrrp?" she said again.

"Yeah, um, Brazza, this is Omelette . . . er . . . Omi," he introduced her. "And, Omi, this is Brazza. She's, or like, she *was*, um . . ."

Why am I so embarrassed? He felt weird introducing the newest dragon he was riding to the two who had come before. Dragons could get jealous, and he didn't want any of them to think he was choosing favorites. Of course, he missed how powerful he felt on Karak's back, and how fast he could fly on Brazza's. And he and Omi were just getting used to each other, but she sure was fun.

Karak made his way into the chamber and sat opposite Brazza, waiting for the rest of the humans to catch up. The Bone Reaper from the rodeo had already gone back to its own cave. This was where it had come from, after all. Abel had helped it home. He sort of wanted to tell Brazza that, but it felt a little like bragging.

Can you brag to a dragon? he wondered. *You can definitely brag about a dragon. They love compliments.*

Finally, he told Omi, "Brazza is the fastest dragon of all time. She's one of a kind too. We used to race together."

"We did more than race, I think."

A voice like silk crackling in a bonfire shook the pile of books around him. The hair on the back of Abel's neck stood on end. The breath stopped in his lungs.

Brazza's big golden eyes stared down at him.

"Did you just—"

She nodded.

Roa gasped, and Lina's jaw flopped open. Arvin coughed, and Abel's parents grabbed each other's hands. Abel was stunned silent.

"I've learned to speak your language," Brazza said, though her voice sounded more like a chorus of voices all at once. "Although my vocabulary is voluminous, I am not particularly adept at your vernacular. For example, what does it mean to 'vibe'?"

Abel swallowed. "I . . . um . . . I . . ."

Dragons don't talk, his brain screamed at him.

You are talking to a dragon, reality screamed back at him.

"Are you okay, Abel?" the dragon asked. "Do you need a soda?"

"Did she just offer him a soda?" asked Lina. His dad nodded, dumbfounded.

Abel sat down right there on the pile of books. "This is a lot to take in."

Brazza made a series of roars and grunts that were actually comforting. They were the sorts of sounds you might expect from a dragon, though most of the time Abel had known Brazza, she'd made no sound at all.

Omi screeched at her in response and scampered away.

"I sent her to bring you something to drink," said Brazza. Abel looked up at her, then over to Karak, who snarled.

"Karak says you look tired and I should let you sleep. Do you need to sleep?"

Abel shook his head. "I don't think I could sleep if I wanted to."

"You have questions," Brazza confirmed.

"I have questions," Abel repeated.

"When I saw your brother arrive here," Brazza began, answering a question he had not yet asked, "and learned what had become of you and your family, Karak and I arranged for your rescue as quickly as we could."

"But how— I mean— How can you—?" Abel's next questions jostled over each other and tangled in his brain so that they came out in useless jumbles of words.

"It's amazing what can happen when you find your voice, isn't it?" Brazza told him. She took a deep breath and exhaled, ruffling the pages of the books all around her. "I'm very grateful you helped me find mine. Do you remember?"

"Of course," said Abel. When he'd first gotten Brazza, she'd been an angry, isolated dragon in a cage at the Burning Market.

"I am not from Drakopolis," she said. "When I was young—as young as Omi—I was taken from the wilds and sold in the city. I was put to work battling and racing for so long, I forgot where I came from. Forgot what I knew . . . until you reminded me. I came from here, Abel. I knew this place, and your trust in me reminded me of it, of a place where humans and dragons lived together in harmony, not domination. So I returned.

"But the place I found was in disarray. Dragons waged war on any humans they found," Brazza said. "They captured long-distance riders hauling freight across the flats. They took out entire tourist flights. And yes, they took people from the rodeos at Glassblower's Gulch." Brazza snorted. "Those they didn't eat right away, they brought here as prisoners, just more treasure to hoard. The humans did *not* live well."

Karak looked down at his paws, embarrassed. He'd been here longer. Abel couldn't imagine his own dragon hoarding humans, but Karak hadn't done anything to stop it either.

"Don't blame Karak," Brazza said. "He was newly free. He had never lived anywhere but Drakopolis, where humans reign over dragons. When he came here, he saw the free dragons reigning over humans and he thought that was how it should be. Power dominates. This he understood."

"But you didn't?"

"You treated me as a partner, not a beast to dominate," Brazza explained. "I knew humans were capable of this. And I learned why this place had fallen so far. You are right that I am one of a kind, but I'm not the first. There was a Sire before me, who could speak to dragons and to humans. But when I was born, he began to die. The hatching of a new Sire is always the death knell of the previous one. The Sires are a sort of bond for the community, and to have more than one would invite conflict and factionalism. As I grew strong, he grew weak . . . but when I was taken away, he was already gone. There was no Sire anymore, and the community fell into conflict. Such is always the way when we stop being able to communicate. On returning, I started us speaking again."

"That's all it took?" Arvin asked, then added a quick "Your Highness."

Abel mouthed "Your Highness?" at Arvin, who whispered back, "I've never spoken *with* a dragon before! Much less a dragon queen!"

"Please, call me Brazza," Brazza told him. "I remember you. I like your makeup. A noble dragon queen yourself."

Arvin smiled. It wasn't every day a Dragon Diva outfit got complimented by an actual dragon. In fact, it may never have happened before in the history of the world.

"How's ours?" Topher asked, pointing at himself and Roa.

Brazza looked them up and down, then snorted once. "Dragons do not lie," she said.

She turned back to Arvin. "But to answer your question, I reminded us of our best selves. The work of living up to it continues."

With that, she lifted her head toward the roof of the cave and roared. It came out as several sounds at once, like a chord or a chorus, a dozen voices in one.

In reply, Karak raised his own head and roared. So did the guard dragons outside the chamber. Soon, every dragon in the entire mountain lair was roaring in harmony. But the moment Brazza stopped, they did too.

"Our language is more complicated than yours," Brazza said. "It moves faster. What takes hours to explain in your words takes seconds in ours."

Abel thought about his fit of uncontrollable laughter before, when he was feeling too much all at once—relief and fear and sadness and joy—and it just came out as a gut-busting cackle. Maybe a dragon's roar was the same way. It didn't mean *nothing*; it meant too much, sort of how you had to get a joke to laugh at it. It couldn't be explained.

Maybe only a giant dragon brain could understand all the things a dragon's roar meant at the same time. Maybe the bigger you got, the better you got at understanding the ways your heart could roar. Maybe that was the real work of growing, and it had nothing to do with size. Brazza wasn't the biggest dragon here, but she understood the most, which made her powerful.

"So are you, like, the ruler here?" Abel asked.

Karak roared at Brazza, and she roared back. Soon the Reaper and all the guard dragons were rumbling and roaring, and this time even Abel could understand their meaning. This was dragon laughter, which sounded a lot like a wrecking ball hitting a violin factory.

"We do not have a ruler as you understand it," Brazza said. "I am merely the *facilitator*, the only dragon who can speak to humans and dragons. No dragon would submit to a *ruler*."

"But people rule over dragons in our city," Abel pointed out.

"Yes, they do," Brazza agreed sadly. "It wasn't always like that. In ancient times, before my Sire's Sire's Sire was sired, humans and dragons built the city together. It was much like this place."

Abel thought about the ancient Lace Wing skeleton that was found surrounded by humans. So that wasn't a dragon hoarding humans as prisoners, but a dragon who lived among them! That wasn't evidence of dragon brutality, but of dragon-human cooperation!

He felt like someone had just turned on the lights in his mind, but he hadn't even known they were off. History as he'd learned it *wasn't* history how it had happened. What else, he wondered, hadn't he been told?

"I see the questions on your face," Brazza noted. "But not everything you know is a lie. Humans and dragons were not all living in harmony. There were dragons who believed they should not help the humans, and there were humans who believed they should not trust the dragons. They fought, and the humans, sneaky as they are, won."

"How could humans beat dragons?" Abel asked.

"Your kind is not as fragile as we dragons like to believe," Brazza said. "First, the people killed our Sire, and then they used the confusion to divide the dragons from one another. They made them fight for food, allying with some of them, used the conflict to bring the rest of my kind to heel. They could not speak with us, but they mastered speaking *to* us—ordering us, controlling us, manipulating us. They built Drakopolis on the backs of the dragons they captured and told stories about how it was the natural order, how dragons, on their own, would only fight. They controlled the breeds so that no dragon Sire would be born. They did not want anyone even *imagining* a different possibility. The possibility of unity. The possibility my voice might offer. They silenced me to silence us."

"So they keep us at each other's throats," Silas added. "The Dragon's Eye versus the kins, the kins versus each other, and everyone ruling over the dragons."

"We are not without conflict here," said Brazza. "But here we are free. We are a society united by one goal: the liberation of all dragons. We plan and enact to achieve that goal, but we do not *command* anyone. If a dragon wishes to raid Glassblower's Gulch or submit to their rodeo, they are free to do so. If a dragon wishes to attack Drakopolis, they are free to do that too, however futile it might be. If a dragon wishes to stay in the wilds and never interact with the civilization of humans again, they may do that, as long as they treat the humans who live among us with the same respect we treat one another."

"So the humans are free here too?" Lina asked.

"Yeah," Silas answered for Brazza. "There's a human committee that organizes clothes and food, and anyone can petition the dragons for anything they need—or with any ideas they have about how to help the cause. The only thing they *can't* do is try to tame a dragon."

"So they're free to leave?" Topher asked.

"We are," Silas said. "If we can find a dragon willing to give us a ride."

"Many have gone back to Drakopolis over the years," Brazza told them. "They're sworn to secrecy about this place, but you know some of them already."

"I do?" Abel asked.

Karak shot a jet of flame up to the roof of the cave. There, Abel saw a huge symbol of a laughing dragon made of tiny rainbow jewels.

"The Wind Breaker kin?" Abel asked.

"The first operatives ever to return from here to Drakopolis created the kin," Brazza said. "All who are committed to the liberation of humans *and* dragons may pledge themselves to it, as you have before, Abel. As I think you will again."

"So the Wind Breaker kin was founded by dragons?" Abel asked, awestruck. He had pledged himself to the Wind Breaker kin when he thought they were just a group of humans who didn't follow unjust rules. He hadn't known they were a kin of humans and dragons with a much bigger purpose.

"'Kin' means 'family,'" said Brazza. "And we have made a family of a most unconventional kind here. Our goal is to grow it. To protect it. The kins as you know them—the Sky Knights and Red Talons, the Thunder Wings, and even the Dragon's Eye police force that Silas served—they all say 'we' when they really mean 'I.' *We want power; we want money; we want freedom; we want order . . .*" Brazza narrowed her eyes. "But when the Wind Breakers say 'we,' we mean everyone. Our goal with each operation is to expand who we call 'we,' not to narrow it."

Abel couldn't help but smile. He'd had the same idea himself.

"So?" Brazza looked over the ragtag group in front of her. "Will you join us? Help us in the liberation of all dragon-kind?"

"Of course!" Abel and Arvin and Roa and Topher all said at the same time.

"Now, hold up a moment," Abel's mother interrupted, picking her way up the huge mountain of books. "You are not joining a revolutionary organization founded by dragons without talking to your parents first, young man. You're too young!"

"I don't think my mom would say yes," Arvin pointed out. "Without dragons, she loses her wealth and power."

"And my parents are worried enough about my safety," Roa added. "They want me to go to veterinary school."

"My mom doesn't care what I do." Topher shrugged. "I'm in."

"Abel, we won't make this decision for you," Abel's dad said, making his way up the pile himself. "But you haven't even finished middle school. I want you to *think* if this is really how you want to spend your childhood?"

"Kids your age should be trading DrakoTek cards and whining about chores and having their first crushes," his mom told him. "Not trying to dismantle the natural order of the world."

"There is nothing *natural* about the order of your world," Brazza snarled.

Abel stepped forward and rested his hand on her huge snout. "My mom didn't mean to offend you," he said. "She's just worried about her kids."

"You know, Mom," Silas said, "I started at the Dragon Rider Academy when I was younger than Abel."

"And I started stealing dragons for the kin when I was his age," Lina added. "Abel's better than both of us."

To Abel's surprise, Silas didn't disagree. Both his siblings looked at him with pride. He couldn't help blushing.

"Just because the path he's on is new doesn't make it wrong," Silas added.

Their mom sighed and took their dad's hand in hers. "We're not great parents, are we?"

Abel gasped and looked at his siblings, who'd frowned. What

were they supposed to say to that? He stepped away from Brazza to hug his mom. "You are, Mom, I swear. You raised us to do what's right, even when it might cost us something."

"Not your freedom," their dad said. "Not your life."

"Yeah, even that," said Abel. "What's the point of believing in something if I only act on it when it's easy to? You two taught me that."

"We did, didn't we?" Their dad smiled through his tears.

"We did," their mom agreed, then looked up at Brazza. "So if my kids agree to help your cause, will you promise that they take no unnecessary risks?"

"Of course," said Brazza. "Only necessary ones."

"And make sure they get enough to eat? Get enough sleep?" she added.

"Mo-om!" Abel groaned. "She's an ancient dragon of immense power, speed, and wisdom. She's not gonna give me a bedtime!"

"I will," Brazza told his mother kindly, ignoring Abel's objections. "And after a rest, we're going to start with the liberation of Glassblower's Gulch."

Abel smiled. That was just what he was hoping to hear.

Brazza rose up on her back legs and spread her wings wide. Karak did the same, followed by both rows of guard dragons.

Together, they roared so loud the mountain shook.

Abel didn't need Brazza to translate.

It meant war.

PART FOUR

"OUR BROKEN HEARTS
BREAK BONES."

THE PROBLEM WITH WAGING WAR on Glassblower's Gulch was that it was *already* at war.

After a restless night's sleep in one of the caves—which was amazingly comfortable and well furnished, with luxury home goods hoarded from Drakopolis—Abel awoke to the cacophony of a dragon council.

He wouldn't have normally called it a "cacophony," because that wasn't a word he used, but the first thing Roa said when they woke up and popped their head out from under the luxurious silk sheets on the king-sized bed each of them had to themselves was "What is that cacophony?"

"That means 'loud noises,'" Lina explained, popping out of her own king-sized bed.

"I know what it means," said Abel, though he hadn't known. He slipped his feet into fancy velvet slippers and made his way to the cave door, still wearing bright orange pajamas.

The king-sized beds were arranged in a circle around the edge of the huge round chamber. The room had been carved into the glass for a dragon's use, then repurposed for human comfort. Each bed had a night table and dresser of its own, a solar-powered lamp, and a mixture of silk sheets and fur covers for the cold cavern nights.

There was a thick woven rug in bright geometric patterns in the center of the floor. A skylight above cast the morning's glow through the multicolored glass of the mountain. It would've been a very serene, very huge bedroom, if it weren't for the roaring dragons just outside.

In a dragon council, every dragon who wished to speak would have their voice heard. It was a loud process. Every dragon in the mountain city had gathered for the discussion. Some stood on treasure piles, others flapped in the air above, while more sat on their haunches in the paths between piles, humans perched on their backs and heads and necks for better views.

In the center of it all stood Brazza and beside her, little Omi, who had grown less little overnight. She looked proud and confident before the great council of dragons.

"What's going on?" Arvin asked, rubbing the sleep from his eyes. He wore his pajama shirt open, showing the Red Talons symbol tattooed from his collarbone up to his neck.

What kind of a parent lets their thirteen-year-old get a kin symbol tattoo? Abel wondered before he answered his own question: *The leader of the kin.*

How could the two of them really be friends? He was glad they were, but he didn't fully understand it. Arvin caught him looking at the symbol and buttoned up his shirt, embarrassed.

We don't choose our parents, Abel thought, *but that doesn't mean we don't care about them.* Even Arvin's dangerous mom was still his mom.

"This is a war council," Silas panted as he jogged up a narrow path cut into the side of the cave, breathing heavily in a designer tracksuit. Apparently, he'd gotten up early to go for a run. Abel would never understand people who chose to run for fun, especially if it meant waking up early. "Your little wyvern scouted

Glassblower's Gulch last night after we went to sleep. She reported back that the sheriff and Deputy Manchi are at war, with the Red Talons on one side of the gulch and the Thunder Wings on the other. They've got about twenty-five fighting dragons apiece now. It's not one-on-one battles anymore. It's flame and fog and acid and everything else. People are hiding in their homes, but it's brutal."

"When dragons battle in the sky, their flame rains down on you and I," Arvin recited the lyrics to a sad old song.

"What's that mean?" Topher wondered.

"It means," Abel explained, "that a war between dragons hurts the innocent people below them. In this case, the citizens of Glassblower's Gulch."

"So the dragons here are deciding whether or not to intervene," Silas explained. "From what Brazza translated, there are some who want to let the two kins fight it out, then attack whoever wins. Some dragons don't want to get involved at all, while others want to go right now and liberate the dragons while the humans are distracted."

Abel looked over the loud council and saw Brazza listening as other dragons got up to speak.

A gray short-wing Knuckler screeched and roared something that sounded like a tin can stuck in a garbage disposal. Then a medium-wing Dazzler dragon, with frilly wings and scales every color of the rainbow, reared onto its back legs and roared out something that sounded like that same garbage disposal breaking.

The two dragons dove for each other and clashed, claw to claw, horn to horn. The Dazzler was bigger but less of a fighter. The Knuckler, true to its name, bent its front claws into fists and delivered lightning-fast punches to the Dazzler's chest.

Abel saw Karak building a ring of fire in his throat, but nearly as

soon as the skirmish between dragons started, it stopped. They settled down next to one another like they hadn't been fighting at all.
The flame died in Karak's throat. Abel couldn't tell who won.

He looked at Silas, who shrugged. "I haven't been here that long,
though I know that Knuckler isn't the biggest fan of humans. I was
warned to stay out of her way."

"She probably wants to let Glassblower's Gulch burn," Roa said.
They loved dragons, but they had no illusions about dragon senti-
mentality. Dragons bonded with their riders and maybe a trainer or
two, but not many would care about humans in general, not humans
they'd never even met.

Brazza suddenly launched from her spot and flapped up to Abel
and his friends. The entire meeting of the dragon flock fell silent to
watch her.

"Would you be willing to speak?" Brazza asked him. "You are
considered a great friend to free dragons everywhere. Your words
might convince him."

"Convince who?" Abel asked.

"Whom," Roa whispered under their breath. This time Topher
elbowed them in the side. "What?" Roa said. "If he's gonna talk to
all these dragons, he should really know when a word is the subject
or object of a sentence."

"Please, no grammar lessons in a cave full of arguing dragons?"
Abel pleaded.

"Your friend Roa is correct," Brazza told him. "Convince *whom*?
'You' are the subject of the sentence, and 'whom' is the object you
will be convincing. In this case, I am referring specifically to
Karak."

"Karak!" Abel startled. "You mean Karak—"

"Doesn't want to help the humans of Glassblower's Gulch," Brazza confirmed. "He is leading a faction of dragons who believe we should not risk a single free dragon's safety to fight for a town that would subject our kind to these brutal rodeos. Nor does he wish to liberate the dragons who are fighting for the kins, until those dragons show a willingness to liberate themselves."

"But that's unfair!" Abel looked across the cave to Karak standing in the midst of a group of Reapers and short-wings. The Knuckler stood right at his side. Karak met Abel's eyes across the cave, and it looked like the huge black dragon shrugged.

"Karak, as you know, does not care much for humans," Brazza said.

"Neither did you," Abel told her.

She snorted, then extended a foot for him to climb on. "I came to realize that our freedom is tied to theirs. We might be powerful enough to free ourselves from humans, but we will never be free as long as humans feel they must subjugate us to have power over one another. Unity is the only sensible choice."

"It's funny how we agree on so much," Abel said, climbing onto her foot. "I realized the same thing just yesterday."

"Why is that funny?" Brazza asked. "I do not understand the humor."

"Well, not funny *ha-ha*," Abel tried to explain. Language was one of those things people used all the time without ever thinking about how it worked, like cell phones or bathrooms. "But, like, funny *hmmm-hmmm*."

"Human language is strange," Brazza agreed. "Perhaps because human people are strange."

Abel smiled. The dragon curled her big paw around him to glide him safely to the cave floor. She added in a whisper, "Not all dragons share my affection for humans. Some might wish to do you harm."

"Not Karak," Abel said, though his certainty wavered. How well did he really know his old dragon? They'd trained and fought together, though not for very long before Abel set him free. He thought he had earned Karak's loyalty, but he couldn't be sure.

"He only speaks of you with love," Brazza reassured Abel. "But a dragon's love is a dangerous thing. You do not want to disappoint a dragon who loves you. Our broken hearts break bones."

Abel's stomach dropped as Brazza set him down in the middle of the dragons' council. Omi quickly rushed to his side and glared at the crowd of dragons around them. There were a few humans scattered throughout the crowd, and they looked at Abel with some curiosity. He thought he recognized an old bus driver from Drakopolis among them, and his heart leapt with joy when he recognized an old friend from his neighborhood.

"Shivonne!" he cheered. She had been the host and manager at the all-night laundromat/casino across the street from his apartment building. She sat on the back of the very Cloudflayer that had been released from Glassblower's Gulch. Deputy Manchi never could have predicted it'd find its way here.

Shivonne was a Red Talon but had really been a Wind Breaker double agent. Abel didn't know she'd left Drakopolis. Maybe she'd been found out. Abel wished he could hear the story of how she escaped the city, but he was surrounded by dragons waiting to hear him speak. He had to figure out what to say.

His brain was doing that thing again, getting distracted because he was anxious. He hated public speaking and didn't think he was very good at it. He'd faked stomach problems more than once to get out of giving book reports, and that was when he only had to speak to his teacher and the other middle schoolers. They weren't the sort of audience that could literally eat you if they didn't like what you had to say.

There is always someone rooting for you in a crowd, Roa had once told him before a school presentation. *Just look for the friendly faces. Even if it's only one person, talk to them, and you'll be okay.*

And if that doesn't work, Topher had added, *picture your audience in cartoon underpants. No one looks scary in cartoon underpants.*

Abel didn't think he could picture hundreds of dragons in cartoon underpants, so he looked up and across the cavern to his friends and family outside their sleeping cave. He looked to Shivonne and then to Omi. He looked around the cavern for the faces of any of the other dragons he'd freed from Drakopolis and found he was not without allies here. He could do this. He *had* to do this. For the people of Glassblower's Gulch. For himself. For what was right.

He had to convince the dragons not just to go to war, but to stop a war that wasn't theirs.

26

"UM," HE SAID, WHICH WASN'T the best start to a speech. "So, some of you, like, know me already?"

He paused to look at Brazza so she could translate, but she just stared back at him, waiting for him to say something worth translating. He figured dragons didn't have a word for "um." When the smallest of your kind weighed at least four thousand pounds and most of you could spit death from the sky, maybe you didn't need words for doubt and insecurity.

Abel, on the other hand, was a whole heap of doubt and insecurity stuffed inside a sack of skin and bones. He felt like a human question mark, when what he needed to be was an exclamation point.

Stop thinking about punctuation! he yelled inside his head. *Speak!*

"So, yeah, I'm Abel?" He heard a squeak from Omi beside him, which he was pretty sure was dragon embarrassment. If he lost Omi's loyalty, he was in real trouble. "I'm Abel!" he said louder and with more confidence, standing up straight like his mother always had to remind him to do. Shivonne gave him an encouraging fist pump from the back of the Cloudflayer.

"I came to Glassblower's Gulch from Drakopolis," he said. "I was *sent* to Glassblower's Gulch because I chose the freedom of dragons over my own safety and the safety of my friends and family." He nodded up toward his friends and family, and the dragons followed his gaze, then looked back at him. "I've never asked for anything in return," he said, locking his eyes on Karak, "and I'm not asking now. Each of you is free to make your choices. You don't owe me anything. But I want to tell you why I think we should go to Glassblower's Gulch right away and stop the war."

Abel cleared his throat again. He wished he had a glass of water. Didn't public speakers usually get water?

"There are good people there," he continued. The dragons growled and snarled. Some snorted flames. One blasted the ceiling with a rainbow that sizzled where it hit. "There are!" Abel shouted. "And bad people too, sure! And people who are trying their best but do bad things and people who aren't trying very hard at all but do good things almost by accident. The point is, they're just people, and they need help. Y'all are dragons, and you're super powerful and stuff." He wished he was more articulate. "You have the power to help, just like when I was in Drakopolis, I had the power to help some of you. Not all of you were nice to me, remember? Some of you tried really hard to kill me, in fact." He looked at the Bone Reaper from the rodeo. He found the eyes of a bright red Ruby Widow Maker who had shot jagged gems at him in his first battle. The dragon looked down at its front paws, bashful.

"Even the dragons I call my friends tried to murder me at first," he said. Both Karak and Brazza looked away from him, which was as close to an apology as a human would ever get from a dragon. "But it's what you'd been taught your whole lives. It doesn't make you less worthy of your liberty. And the same is true for us. Humans mess up. We hurt each other and ourselves, but it's because we're told we *have to* in order to survive. These are hard lessons we're taught." He met Shivonne's eyes again, remembered something she'd told him a long time ago. "We can't let hard lessons make less of us."

He looked up at Brazza and then at Karak. "If we have the power to help those who need help, and we choose not to because we've decided they don't *deserve it* . . . well . . ." He stopped. Abel wasn't sure what point he was making. "Well, then what's the point of being powerful at all? Power is for helping or else it's just another word for 'bullying.'"

He stopped talking and looked up at Brazza. She stared at him for a long moment, then lifted her head and roared out her translation, which was about two seconds of roaring. He really thought he'd made a more complicated argument than a two-second roar.

Afterward, the cave was silent.

"Are you sure you got it all?" Abel asked her. "I said a lot of stuff."

"It wasn't that complicated," Brazza replied.

"Oh . . . Okay." Abel blew out his cheeks and put his hands in his pockets to keep from fidgeting. "So what now?"

"They're thinking," Brazza said.

"When they're done thinking, what happens? Is there, like, a vote?"

Brazza grunted, and even her grunt harmonized with itself. As if Abel needed a reminder he was chatting with someone who was decidedly *not* human. "Not exactly," said Brazza. "We don't vote. We act."

And in a great flurry of grunts and snarls, the dragons did just that. The air of the cave suddenly filled with wings. Dragons flapped this way and that. Some had people on their backs; others waited for the humans to climb down before they took off. Soon, just about every dragon had changed places.

Almost all of them stood or perched or flew to one side of the huge cave. Only a handful had flown over to where Abel stood.

"Um?" he said again.

"These dragons have chosen to go with you to liberate Glassblower's Gulch and put a stop to the fighting between the two kins," Brazza explained. "The others will not be going. They do not think this a good action, but they will not stop you either."

Omi was still at Abel's side, as ever. The Candy Cane dragon that had taken Silas was there too, and it had flown Abel's friends down to him. The Ruby Widow Maker had joined his side as well, and Shivonne on the Cloudflayer. His parents sat on Skellor the Bone Reaper, as if riding a clear-scaled Reaper that looked like a living dragon skeleton zombie was the most normal thing in the world. They didn't even look nervous. They *were*, however, still in their pajamas.

Abel looked at the hundreds of pairs of dragon eyes staring at him from across the cave, dragons of all shapes and sizes. Some he recognized, and some he didn't. Some he'd freed from Drakopolis, and some he'd never seen before in his life.

His heart sank when he saw Karak in front of that large group. The Sunrise Reaper was tall and proud as ever, but he wasn't standing on Abel's side. He had not been convinced.

Karak *roared*, and it sounded like stone cracking.

Brazza translated, though she didn't need to. Abel understood.

"He says he will always know you are the best among humans. And he will always call you a friend. But he will never again fight in a human battle."

"That ungrateful sewer snake!" Topher grumbled, but Abel shushed him.

In truth, Abel also felt betrayed and disappointed, but he understood too. "Karak almost died fighting in our battles," he said. "I set him free so he wouldn't have to anymore, not so I could call him back whenever I wanted him to fight. I get it."

"Still," Topher said. "He should want to come help you!"

"Neither of us has ever been a harnessed dragon forced into battle," Abel said. "I don't think we get to tell him what he should want. I don't think we can possibly know."

Arvin put a hand on Abel's shoulder.

Brazza nodded. "You are a wise young man," she told Abel. "As I have always known."

Abel wiped a tear from his eye. "Have not," he laughed. "You tried to smear me on the side of a skyscraper the first time I ever rode you."

"Well, I didn't know you well then," she said. "I do now, Abel the Liberator."

Abel grinned. He'd never had a cool nickname before. It was even cooler that a dragon had given it to him. He looked at Arvin and wondered if he'd share the name of his tattoo artist. Abel would definitely get "The Liberator" tattooed on his chest or something.

One look at his parents, however, reminded him that was never gonna happen, no matter how many dragons he freed. Also only a dork would get his *own* nickname tattooed on his chest.

"At least I'll have you on my side," Abel told Brazza.

The long silence that followed was worse than Karak's roar.

"Wait?" Abel's voice broke. "I don't?"

"I am not a fighter," Brazza said. "I cannot go to battle. My community will not allow me to risk myself. I must stay here."

"They won't *allow* you?" Abel shook his head. "Then you aren't really free at all."

"I serve something larger than myself," Brazza said. "And submit myself to serve my community so that all may be free."

"But that's not freedom!" Abel objected. "I didn't set you free so that your own kind could keep you prisoner!"

The pink-and-blue dragon lowered her head to him, nearly knocking him over. When she spoke, her voice rumbled in his bones. She spoke slowly to make sure he understood every word.

"You do not dictate the meaning of my freedom, Abel!" Brazza growled. "I choose my path, and this is my choice. A community is not a prison, and serving my community is not a prison sentence. You savvy?"

Abel nearly choked on his own tongue as he nodded and told her, "Yeah. Savvy. Sorry. I didn't mean to . . . I just . . ." He smiled to break the tension. "You just said 'savvy'! You *do* know human slang!"

Brazza snorted what had to be a laugh, but the force of it made Abel stumble.

"It is easy for one as old as I am to forget how young you are," she said. "We place a lot on your narrow shoulders. I hope not too much."

He felt every dragon in the cave looking at him, and every human too. He took a deep breath and spread his arms open as far as he could. "Wings wide, Brazza," he said. "We got this."

The dragon sat back on her haunches and looked down at him with something like pride, he thought. It was the same way his parents were looking at him now too.

"I will be here rooting for your victory," Brazza continued. "If you are in danger, send a signal. Karak will be there in a flash to rescue you."

"But not to help the town," Abel confirmed. He met Karak's huge orange eyes across the cave. The dragon bowed his head in acknowledgment. He would always protect Abel. He would not, however, follow Abel's commands.

"Correct," Brazza confirmed without a hint of emotion.

"I understand," Abel said. "Thanks for . . ." He let the sentence trail off. He didn't quite know what to say. Could someone disappoint you but stay your friend? If so, which one of them was doing the disappointing here? Brazza probably thought Abel was rushing into a dangerous situation without thinking it through, like he always did. He definitely thought Brazza was being more loyal to some ideal than to real people and dragons who needed help. They weren't likely to ever agree on the right thing to do here, but they were both trying their best to do the right thing. Knowing that about each other was enough, he realized. They couldn't give total agreement, but they could give each other grace. He knew how to finish his sentence. "Thanks for being my friend."

"Likewise, Abel," Brazza said, her voice harmonizing with itself like a song.

Abel turned his back to her, to face the ragtag group of humans and dragons who were going with him to Glassblower's Gulch. Omi lowered herself to her belly and stretched out a wing so Abel could climb on. He sat straight, with his legs on either side of her neck, holding on to one of the spines running down the center. He felt like a general astride his trusted battle partner.

"So, who's, um, like, ready?" he asked, sounding a lot less the part of general than he looked.

"Ep ep!" Silas shouted the Dragon Rider war cry.

"Savvy!" Arvin and Roa and Topher shouted the kinners' war cry.

ROAR! erupted the dragons on his side of the cave, all of them thrusting themselves from the ground in unison, toward the opening at the top and the bright blue sky above.

"Wings wide, Liberator!" Brazza cheered him on, and the other dragons joined her in a chorus of roars, a raucous reminder that, in spite of their disagreements, they were all on the same side.

Abel and his little air force would either come back heroes or never make it back at all.

27

ABEL DIDN'T WANT TO WAIT another minute before charging into Glassblower's Gulch. He thought of Kayda and her parents and Percy stranded down there as Thunder Wings and Red Talons battled for control above the town.

Roa, as usual, slowed him down. They insisted he think through a plan *before* flying into the fire.

"We have to assess our assets and liabilities," Roa said.

They'd landed their dragons and assembled outside of town, far enough away that they wouldn't be seen but close enough to see the pillars of smoke rising from the gulch. When the wind changed direction, Abel could even hear the distant roar of fighting dragons.

The Ruby Widow Maker growled in the direction of the battle. The Bone Reaper narrowed its eyes toward the town, sniffing the air, while the Candy Cane Reaper licked its lips, thirsty for a fight. Omi—now the same size as the others—was distracted by a cloud in the shape of a drumstick drifting by. Abel had to tap her gently on the leg to get her to pay attention again.

"Assets means the breath weapons, equipment, and other skills we have," Silas said. "The armor we got from the hoard is an asset, and our helmets and utility bags and supplies, but also Omi's playfulness, the Widow Maker's ferocity, the Bone Reaper's . . . um . . ."

"Bones," Roa said.

Silas nodded. "You know, Roa, for someone who never trained at the Academy, you've got a good head for command."

"You know, Silas," Roa answered back, "for someone who spent his youth as a lackey for the secret police, you've got a good head for rebellion."

They'd meant it as a compliment, but Silas frowned. He didn't *like* being a rebel, but he liked injustice even less. Abel was proud of his big brother. It was hard to go against everything you thought you believed to do what you knew was right.

At least, Abel hoped it was right. He'd hate to have made a mistake by convincing everyone he cared about to follow him.

"Okay, well, Mom and Dad have no fighting experience," he said. "I think they might be lia—what's the word?"

"Liabilities," Silas and Roa said at the same time, then looked at each other. Having two know-it-alls on a team had its advantages *and* disadvantages.

"Sorry, Mom and Dad," Abel said. "But it might be trouble in battle if we have to worry about protecting you. Maybe you should wait here, outside of town."

"Like a bivouac," Silas said.

"That means a temporary camp, in normal-person-speak," Roa clarified.

"Thank you, Roa," said Abel's mom. "I know what a bivouac is. What I don't know is why my children suddenly think their parents are incapable of contributing."

"Because you're inexperienced," said Silas.

"And worriers," said Lina.

"And kinda . . . old?" Abel added.

Abel's mom stepped forward, looking every bit as defiant as Lina did when they argued. "Well, I have a thing or two to say about—"

But their dad touched her shoulder.

"They're right, you know," he said. "Not about the old part, obviously. But we'd be worried about them the whole time. And my health isn't what it was. Also, neither of us has ever flown a dragon before."

"We flew dragons all the time in Drakopolis," their mom said.

"I don't think riding the number 9 bus counts, Mom," Lina said. "It's an herbivore, for one. And you were just passengers."

Their mother looked around at all of them like she wanted to argue, but then she relented. "If that's the consensus of the group, I'll respect it," she said. "We'll make camp." Then she pointed a very stern motherly finger at Silas and Lina. "You watch out for your little brother, or you will see just how ferocious your old mom can be."

"Ep ep!" said Silas.

"Savvy," said Lina.

"I don't need them to babysit me," Abel grumbled, but he liked the idea that his mom was still trying to watch out for him. Even dragon-riding liberators could use their parents' support from afar.

"Of course you don't, honey," his mother said, but she made *yes-he-does* eyes at his older siblings.

"Don't worry, I'll look out for him." Arvin clapped a hand on Abel's shoulder. "All of us will."

"I made them the best armor I could, ma'am," Topher pointed out. He'd taken a lot of the luxury goods from the hoard in the dragon city and designed some ingenious battle dragon armor. There were thick leather pads from high-end jackets, silk straps holding armor made of the passenger doors from luxury dragon-riding compartments, and more gem-studded spikes, blades, and battering rams than Abel could've ever imagined coming from piles of fancy junk. Topher could be obnoxious in his way, but he was a genius when it came to design. In a more just world, he'd have scholarships to the fanciest colleges. In Drakopolis, he was a failing student at a mediocre middle school, always just on the edge of expulsion.

"So we've got six armored dragons with breath weapons," Abel said. "And the kinners don't know we're coming. We've got the element of surprise. What else?"

"Ourselves," said Arvin. He was dressed in wild swirling patterns of color. Arvin wore a leather riding jacket that was dizzying to look at and blue-lensed sunglasses that shone like the noon sky. And for once, Abel and the others were dressed just the same.

It had been Arvin's idea. Attacking in daylight, over the colorful glass, they'd be hard to spot and even harder to focus on.

"We have two objectives," Abel said, trying to sound as much like a military leader as he could. Silas nodded his approval, so Abel continued, even though he felt a little silly talking like he was in *KINWARS 2: The Rec-KIN-ning*. "We want to evacuate as many human civilians as we can back to our—"

"Bivouac," Roa said.

"Bivy-whack," Abel butchered the word, but kept going. This was war, not a vocab test. "Where Mom and Dad can look after them." He nodded toward his parents with a *see-how-useful-you-are* look.

His mom stuck her tongue out at him, but she also smiled. She was up for the job. She'd already begun unloading supplies from the Widow Maker's bags and setting up a first aid clinic. Dad was even getting to work on a play space for little kids.

"Our other goal," Abel said, "is to stop the kins from fighting each other and give their dragons the choice to leave. The ones who do, Lina can lead back to the dragon city, where Brazza will welcome them and tell them what's what."

"And the ones that don't choose freedom?" Roa asked.

"We'll have to fight them," said Abel. "And we'll have to win."

"Not everyone is capable of liberation," Lina quoted the Sky Knights motto. "But everyone deserves the opportunity."

The Sky Knights only meant it about humans, but it worked for dragons too. Anyway, Lina wasn't a Sky Knight anymore. They were all Wind Breakers now.

Some more than others. Abel wrinkled his nose.

"Oh, flaming feet! What is that smell?!" Topher groaned just as Omi finished gulping down a monitor lizard she'd chased from its hole with a snort of acid breath.

"Wyverns have famously bad gas," Silas pointed out. "It's the trade-off for their breath weapons."

"It's like a backward breath weapon!" Topher gagged and tried to bury his face in his jacket. "Her name's Omelette? More like rotten eggs!"

Omi cocked her head at him, then looked at Abel, wondering if she'd done something wrong.

"It's okay, Omi," Abel said. "You're good. Topher's just being dramatic. Anyway, here's what we're gonna do . . ."

Abel laid out their battle plan, drawing lines in the dirt and working out signals to each other, since they didn't have cell phones or radios. He'd ride Omi, while Shivonne would be on the Cloudflayer to evacuate the civilians.

"You have a way of making people feel welcome," he told her.

"It's what I do best," she agreed.

Silas and Lina, on the Candy Cane Reaper and Frost dragon, respectively, would stand by to attack when Abel gave the signal. Arvin would ride the Widow Maker to the Red Talons and try to persuade his mother to stand down. Roa and Topher would go to the Thunder Wings on the Bone Reaper, either to talk them down or to distract Ally long enough to get the civilians out.

"What happens if my mom won't back down?" Arvin asked. "Or if your old teacher isn't distracted long enough?"

"She's not old," Abel's dad interjected. "She can't be more than thirty-five."

"I meant '*former*,'" said Arvin.

"But also, Dad, thirty-five *is* old," added Lina.

"What does that make us?" asked their mom.

Lina, Silas, and Abel all looked at one another, avoiding parental eye contact. The others looked at their feet or the sky or the dirt under their fingernails. Even the dragons looked uncomfortable, and they were all, like, ancient.

"Ugh, kids today! No respect for their elders!" Their mom shook her head. "Whatever. Tell your elderly parents the rest of your plan."

"Okay, thanks, Mom." Abel smiled at her. "And you really look great for your—"

"Don't you dare say '*my age*,'" she cut him off.

"So for my plan, I'm going with the KISS principle," he said, which made Arvin's cheeks flush. "It means 'keep it simple, scoundrel,'" Abel clarified. "And the simplest thing to do with a fleet of armored dragons is to battle."

"Oh, right, of course," Arvin recovered. "KISS. Keep it super simple. I like that."

"Scoundrel," Abel said. "Keep it simple, scoundrel."

"We're not scoundrels," Arvin told him. Apparently, he was sensitive about it. Maybe being a crime boss's son could be a real touchy subject when you didn't want to be a criminal at all.

"Okay, keep it super simple," Abel amended the acronym.

What Abel *didn't* say was that there wasn't anything simple about flying dragons into battle. Not for the dragons forced to fight, and not for the people clinging to their backs. It'd be a sad day for all of them if bloodshed ever became simple.

But simple or not, scoundrels or not, it was time.

"Wings wide, Wind Breakers!" Abel called encouragingly. He scampered up Omi's side to the saddle at the base of her neck. "Today needs heroes!"

Omi bent her legs and launched into the sky. It would've been such a cool moment if she hadn't also passed more gas as she did it.

Abel sighed. *Why do dragons always ruin my best lines?*

"**THAT'S GOOD, OMI,**" **ABEL WHISPERED** to his wyvern as she weaved her way through the wreckage of Glassblower's Gulch. "Just keep low."

The Red Talons and Thunder Wings had taken up positions on either side of the canyon, trading fog and frost and fire from one side to the other, slamming their dragons into one another in the open air between the high canyon walls.

The people below had closed their shutters like it was midnight, and retreated as far into their cave-like homes as they could. Still, for some, it was clearly not enough.

Abel saw heavy metal shutters melted from their frames, the apartments inside scorched black. Another apartment had been flooded with a wyvern's poison gas. The furniture and decorations were intact, but the potted plants were dead and a sickly green mist lingered in the air. Abel really hoped whoever lived there had gotten out in time. He didn't see any bodies, and he really didn't want to.

Omi flew slow and silent. Even she sensed this wasn't a game. They had to keep out of sight. Abel flew for Kayda's house. He wasn't sure it was fair to rescue someone first just because they were friends, but in a war, fair and unfair got as blurry as a counterfeit DrakoTek card.

Abel leaned to the right and nudged Omi's reins, settling her on the ground behind a huge abandoned freight car. It was half-filled with sand from the mines, the kind used to make the concrete they sold in Drakopolis. That was what this war was really about, wasn't it? Which kin got to make money from the mines in this town?

The money flowed out from Drakopolis and back to Drakopolis again, and the various factions all fought over it. But no matter what, it never went to the people who lived *here*, the ones who did the actual work of mining. Those were the people hiding in their homes right now.

Abel wondered how many buildings back in the city were built out of material that was taken from this town. He wondered how people could sleep at night if they knew the concrete and steel that held their homes together was held together by the suffering of innocent people and battle-scarred dragons.

He wondered if they would care once they knew.

He hoped so.

"Okay, Omi. You remember the way?" he whispered. The wyvern craned her neck around to look at him. The gold spikes on her face had hardened and sharpened. In her armor, she looked like a full-grown fighting wyvern. She nodded her head, then straightened out and flapped through the shadows at the bottom of the gulch.

She weaved around wreckage and ruins, glided over upturned dumpsters and burned piles of garbage, then pressed herself to the ground just as the shadow of a patrolling dragon passed over them.

Abel held his breath, looking up into the glare of the sun. He could see the silhouette of the sheriff's Rapid Assault Hog Dragon sweep over the canyon. Two black Stoneskin short-wings flanked her tail, watching out for Thunder Wing patrols.

In the distance, he heard a screech that made the spines along

Omi's neck twitch. The patrol wheeled off to chase it down. A moment later, Abel heard the roar of dragons fighting, but he couldn't see the battle. Abel hoped it was Red Talons versus Thunder Wings, and not one of his friends who'd been intercepted.

He looked behind him and raised a fist, the signal for Shivonne to come forward on the huge Cloudflayer. There was no hiding a dragon that big. They just had to hope that Arvin's camouflage worked well enough and the kins were distracted by fighting each other.

Even with Shivonne trying to steer, the Cloudflayer simply plowed through the middle of the gulch, smashing the debris in its path, knocking down clotheslines and power lines as it came.

"This is not gonna go as smoothly as I hoped," Abel said. But he urged Omi forward. The Cloudflayer followed in its own destructive way.

It only took a few minutes to reach Kayda's parents' shop.

"It's a ghost town," Abel said sadly.

"I don't think so," Shivonne told him as she sidled her much bigger dragon up beside his. He looked up at her, against the overhead sunshine. "Ghosts don't like to hang around their own graves."

Abel shuddered, but he knew what she meant. This place might be a graveyard.

"Stay sharp, Stable Abel," she encouraged him. "Wings wide, savvy?"

"Savvy," he said.

Shivonne steered the long-wing into the shadow of a freight elevator tower that led into one of the mines. It curled up inside its wings. If you didn't look too closely, it might just look like a giant boulder rolled out of place.

Omi, however, wasn't going to hide like that. She was too excited to be back at the place she was born. Forgetting her size, she rushed the door and smashed into it with her snout. Nothing else would fit through. Less than a month ago, Abel had snuck her out of there in a small box. Now not even her nose made it through the door.

She shoved a little, cracking the doorframe, then sat back, puzzled.

"Growing up's hard for everyone," Abel told her as he slid off her neck. "Just remember all the cool stuff you can do now. I'll be a few minutes. You stand guard and warn me if any unfriendly dragons come our way." Omi growled, and Abel corrected himself. "I mean, um, dragons ridden by unfriendly people. Sorry."

Omi snorted and turned to take up her guard duty, head swiveling side to side and up and down, scanning the gulch in every direction. Just before Abel stepped inside the shop, the shadows of six more dragons raced over the top of the gulch, screeching to join whatever battle was underway on the other side. He really wished he could get a text message from his team telling him they were all right.

Just complete your mission, he heard Silas's voice in his head. *Do your job and trust us to do ours. We'll get through this! Ep ep!*

Of course, if it were the real Silas talking, he would have called Abel a snot-brain or something too.

Move fast and don't get caught, he heard Lina say, which was much better advice and much more in character.

Cover your mouth when you sneeze, his mom added, which was good advice, just not helpful right now.

"Shh, everyone!" he said to himself, earning one quizzical head cock from Omi. "Sorry. Just talking to . . . er . . . myself."

He stopped stalling and stepped into the dark of Kayda's family glassworks.

The place was a mess. Shelves toppled, shattered glass everywhere. There were scorch marks on the walls, but those might've been there before. He couldn't remember. The place was quiet.

"Hello?" he said. "Anyone here?" He got no response. He walked deeper into the dark shop, fancy combat boots crunching on broken glass.

Crunch. Crunch.

He was grateful for the dragon's hoard of expensive clothes. The soles of his regular sneakers would've been torn to shreds in here.

"It's me . . . Abel!" he called. "Kayda? Percy?"

Crunch. Crunch.

"I'm here to get you all to safety," he said. He wasn't sure why, but he felt like he was being watched. The hair on the back of his neck tingled. A trickle of hot sweat raced down his spine. He worried that his friend was gone already and it was Deputy Manchi lying in ambush for him.

Crunch. Crunch.

He stopped walking and listened.

Crunch.

He froze. That last crunch wasn't his.

Someone was in the room behind him, between him and the door. He clenched his fists. Abel wondered if he'd be any good in a fight without a dragon to back him up. For all his kin battling, he'd never actually been in a person-to-person brawl. He didn't really even know how to throw a punch.

He saw a heavy green glass sculpture of a Moss dragon resting across the toppled shelf next to him. One of its wings had snapped off to a jagged edge.

Crunch. Crunch.

The sound got closer. In one quick move, he bent and grabbed the broken sculpture, whirling around and throwing it like a missile at his attacker.

Whoosh!

A crystal-clear candlestick sailed straight for him at the same time, zipping over his head and smashing against the wall.

Crash!

"Ahh!" he shouted. The green sculpture smashed into the wall beside Kayda, breaking into a billion jagged pieces.

"You!" Abel shouted.

"You!" Kayda yelled.

"Why'd you sneak up on me like that?" Abel demanded.

"Hey, you were the one sneaking into *my* place dressed like you're going to war at a nightclub," she said. "And also I thought you were dead!"

"I might've been if you had better aim." Abel nudged the sharp pieces of broken candlestick with his toe.

Kayda looked over her shoulder to where the dragon sculpture had made a dent in the wall. "Thank thunder both of us have bad aim," she said. "So, anyway, you're alive? And that huge wyvern outside—that's Omelette?"

"Omi," Abel corrected.

"Okay," Kayda said. "Is your brother still alive too?"

"Yeah," said Abel.

"Thank him for me," she said. "For saving us at the rodeo."

"I will."

Abel expected her to launch into one of her long monologues, peppering him with questions about where he'd been and how Silas had survived, and dumping information on him about everything that had happened in the last few days to bring such massive destruction to the town . . . but she didn't say anything else.

"You're awfully quiet."

"Yeah, war has a way of replacing words," she said flatly.

"Right," Abel told her. He spoke like he understood, but he didn't really. He'd never known war. The kins in Drakopolis fought all the time, and he'd fought with them, but life in the city stayed pretty normal. Businesses were open, and kids went to school. Maybe some people got hurt or went to jail, and maybe a dragon blew a hole in a wall once in a while, but if you weren't involved and kept your head down, it was easy enough to pretend nothing was going on.

Here, though, it didn't matter who you were or where you kept your head. In just the last few days, it looked like the fight between the sheriff and her deputy hadn't spared anyone. The town was a wreck, and yet the fighting raged on.

"Are your parents okay?" Abel asked.

Kayda nodded. "They're upstairs with Percy. He's fine. They're all fine. I was out looking for food."

"You're hungry?" Abel reached into the pocket of his cargo pants and pulled out a Chocovore-brand Chocolate Charcoal Protein Bar. He tossed it to her—and missed just as badly as he had with the statue.

Kayda rolled her eyes, but she picked it up and brushed the glass off the wrapper with her gloved hand. "Thanks."

"I've got a transport dragon waiting outside too," he told her. "A Cloudflayer."

"The one your sister stole?"

"She was framed," he said.

"Yet it ended up with you anyway?" Kayda quirked an eyebrow. "Coincidence?"

"Dragons do what dragons do," he said, which didn't really explain anything, but sounded like wisdom. "Anyway, it can carry a lot of people. Do you know where any others are?"

"Everyone's hiding in the mines," Kayda said. "There's too much fighting the higher up you get. Funny how high up used to be the nice apartments, but now they're the front lines. Dragons and kinners shooting at each other all day and night."

"Can you gather everyone and get them onto the Cloudflayer?" Abel asked.

"Yeah," said Kayda. "Where are we going?"

"A place you're not going to believe," Abel said. "A city where dragons and people live together."

"That's Drakopolis," said Kayda.

"No," said Abel. "I mean as equals. A city founded by dragons."

A tiny smile popped up on Kayda's dirty face. She nodded. "Cool. You coming?"

"Eventually," said Abel. "Omi and I have something to do first."

"Something dangerous?" Kayda asked.

"Very," said Abel.

Kayda nodded. "You're gonna fight Sheriff Skint and Deputy Manchi and both the kins, aren't you?"

"Not if I can help it," Abel said. "I'm gonna try to get them to declare a cease-fire."

Kayda shook her head. "Those two only understand violence," she said.

Abel sighed. "Well, Omi and I can do that too, if we have to."

Kayda nodded sadly and then rushed across the glass to give Abel a hug. "Thanks for coming back for us," she whispered in his ear. She pulled a small glass carnation from her pocket, glittering orange and in perfect condition, then pressed it into his hand.

"I'm not sure I can take a piece of glass into battle on a dragon's back," he said. "Seems kind of unsafe?"

"It won't break," she said. "It's my lucky charm. And you're going to give it back to me when we see each other again."

Abel looked down at the smooth glass petals and delicate stem. Kayda wrapped her fingers around his to close his palm over it.

"Fly safe," she told him. Then she left to find her parents and the other citizens of Glassblower's Gulch, shoving the protein bar into her mouth as she ran.

Abel stepped back outside. He waved at Shivonne. It was the signal that the rescue mission was underway and passengers would be arriving soon. Then he climbed up onto Omi's back.

He was just in time. At that moment, two black Heartrender Reapers slammed into the ground in front of Omi.

"Thunder Wings," Abel whispered. They wore the colors on their leather riding jackets—gray, pale blue, white, and purple— and they had the lightning dragon emblem on their helmets.

Abel really wished he'd already gotten his helmet on. They gave him no time before they attacked.

THE HEARTRENDERS CHARGED AND THEIR riders fired stun guns straight at Abel. He swung his body around Omi's neck and hung underneath, dodging the rippling waves of energy that could knock a full-grown adult out cold. Who knew what damage a direct hit would do to a kid Abel's size? Nothing he wanted to find out. The pulses rippled the air over the wyvern's head as they passed, making Omi snort like she'd gotten water in her nose.

The stun guns couldn't hurt her, and Abel could dodge them, but he stood no chance against the breath weapons from two dragons.

An image flashed in Abel's mind. He pictured Roa sitting across from him on the playground, dealing out DrakoTek cards. Abel's own flock of armored wyvern cards was lined up in front of him as the first Heartrender slapped on top.

In the card's illustration, its eyes were rolled back in its head, gleaming white from lid to lid. Its great maw was open, revealing row after row of needle-sharp fangs.

He had to play a minimum +3 defensive time reaction, but he didn't have the right cards. Abel's entire flock got wiped out by one blast of white-hot Heartrender fire.

That was the game. This was real life.

The first Heartrender's black eyes rolled back in its head, gleaming white from lid to lid. Its great maw opened, revealing row after row of needle-sharp fangs. White flame blossomed in the Heartrender's mouth.

"Lie down on my count!" Abel yelled at Omi. "One, two . . . THREE!"

He let go of her neck as she flattened herself to the ground. On the three count, just like in the DrakoTek card game, a streak of flame erupted with the speed of a switchblade and sliced the air where Omi had been. It cut through the empty air and hit the front of Kayda's family's shop. He saw where these dragons got their names: There was a charred black gouge deep in the wall where the fire had hit, like a sword slice. It would be enough to rend a human heart clean in two.

Abel was still rolling away from where Omi's huge neck had come down when the second Heartrender's black eyes rolled white.

"On three!" Abel yelled again, and sure enough, on the count of three, another blade of fire spat from the dragon's mouth. This time, Omi shoved herself off the ground and into the air. The flame passed under her and cut into a huge piece of steel mining equipment. The machine sizzled and then collapsed, sheared in half.

Omi screeched as Abel looked up at her. The two Heartrenders moved their heads toward the noise, but Abel noticed their eyes were still white. They tilted their earholes in Omi's direction, not their eyes.

"They can't see when they shoot," he marveled. "Their flame must come out so bright it blinds them, so they roll their eyes back to protect their sight."

Even as he watched, though, their eyes rolled back around to gleaming black. The dragons looked at the entrance to one of the mines. There, Kayda was sheltered with a crowd of people, preparing to make a dash for Shivonne and her long-wing carrier dragon. She held Percy in her arms. Omi chittered, seeing her little playmate again.

One of the Heartrenders lowered its head to the level of the opening, straight at Kayda and everyone behind her. The people were trapped and defenseless.

The other Heartrender looked at Shivonne. It lined its head up to aim at the Cloudflayer, whose back was to it. The long-wing didn't have enough room at the bottom of the gulch to turn its massive body around.

The two Reapers rolled their eyes back white in their sockets once again. Even knowing they had three seconds before the flames would come, there was no way to dodge in time.

But three seconds where they couldn't see might just be enough time for Omi.

"Remember the monitor lizards?" Abel shouted. "Let's play!"

Omi understood. She dove and smacked her massive feet into the first Heartrender's head, like she was snatching a lizard from its burrow.

"One, two . . ." Abel counted.

The people in the mine shaft screamed.

Instead of lifting the Reaper up, which she couldn't have done anyway, Omi turned its face so it was looking right at its companion.

"Three." Abel grimaced just as the first dragon fired its flame straight into the second one. Shocked, it raised its head and roared, letting loose its own blade of fire harmlessly into the sky. Its rider dove for safety as the other one shouted a warning, but they couldn't shout loud enough over the roaring.

Omi dove again and scooped the fallen Thunder Wing rider off the ground. She landed in front of Abel, pinning the kinner below her huge foot, and lifted a single taloned claw. She used it to flick the terrified kinner's helmet clean off.

"Ahhh!" he screamed. Abel recognized him immediately. His name was Jusif. He was a teen who'd had a lot of fun bullying Abel when Abel was first learning to ride dragons. Jusif wasn't having any fun now. "Please, Abel, call her off!" he cried out.

Without its rider, the injured Heartrender was now coiled around itself, shielding its wounded side with its wing and whimpering. The other one lowered its rattled head and aimed at Omi.

"Tell your friend to fly away!" Abel barked.

The rider on the other Heartrender hesitated, but apparently, Jusif's desperate look and Omi's hungry snarl convinced them. They turned their dragon, and it bent its legs, then jumped into the sky. The Cloudflayer finally got a clear view of it. It kept its eyes locked and its breath weapon ready until both dragon and rider were gone from sight.

"Send yours away too," said Abel.

"I can't just—" Jusif whined.

"NOW!" Abel yelled. Jusif whistled three quick bursts. His dragon snorted angrily, stomped its foot, then launched itself into the air. It flew a little crooked but made its weary way up the gulch and over the top, leaving Jusif behind.

Abel shook his head and spat in the dirt. "That didn't take much convincing," he said. "Guess your dragon didn't like you that much."

"My dragon follows instructions," Jusif replied. "Unlike the ones you fly. You don't know how to control a dragon properly."

"Seems like I'm doing an okay job now," Abel said as Omi's talon hovered just over Jusif's face.

"You're gonna regret this," the kinner told him. "When Ally gets ahold of you, she's going to have you burned to charcoal."

"She's welcome to try it," Abel said. "But I'm not in her seventh-grade class anymore. She doesn't scare me."

"She should," Jusif replied. "She didn't take over the Thunder Wings kin by *not* being scary. Now, let me go and maybe I can talk her into sparing your life."

Abel laughed. It took guts to make threats when you were lying underneath a wyvern's foot, but Jusif never lacked for guts. He lacked good sense, sure. Basic human kindness too. But guts, he had. If he wanted to keep those guts inside his body, he'd do what Abel said.

"Omi's going to let you up," he explained, squatting next to Jusif and taking the stun gun off his belt. He popped the battery out and threw it in the opposite direction. It skittered across the ground to rest just next to the huge Cloudflayer. "You're going to walk right over to that wall and sit on your hands."

Abel didn't know why he had to sit on his hands, but he'd seen it in one of those cop shows on TV, the ones that always made the Dragon Safety Officers look way smarter than they were in real life. He figured if it was good enough for TV, it was good enough for Jusif.

"And you're not going to move, or the Cloudflayer will—" Abel tried to think of a good threat that would keep Jusif following his instructions.

"Flay me?" Jusif suggested impatiently.

"Right, yeah," said Abel. "Flay the skin off you like a boiled tomato." He added that last bit with a flourish, proud of his simile. "So if you don't want to be turned into sauce, you won't move until all the civilians are gone, savvy?" He was really getting the hang of the whole metaphor-versus-simile thing.

Jusif nodded.

Abel whistled and waved at Kayda to start the evacuation. She and her moms left the mine and started helping people onto the Cloudflayer's back while Shivonne kept the big dragon calm.

Abel climbed onto Omi. He listened to the distant sounds of dragons fighting in the air and decided it was time to check it out. If his friends were already in the fight, he wanted to help them. And if it was just the kins fighting each other, he'd keep them distracted until the Cloudflayer got all the innocent people free.

"Ready to have some more fun?" he asked his dragon.

Omi leapt into the air to play, still treating it all like a game.

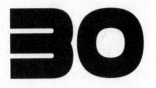

THERE WERE AT LEAST TWENTY dragons in the sky over the gulch. Their bodies crashed into one another, claws sparking off armor, wings beating against the riders in their harnesses. The riders themselves fired missiles and stun guns through it all. The air was an absolute chaos of fog and fire, ice and mist, jagged shrapnel and bolts of man-made lightning. Wind and wings and wild roars.

At least Abel remembered his helmet this time. He popped it on, using the high-tech display in the visor to scan the scene above. Far from the battle, he saw Arvin's Ruby Widow Maker flapping in place on the opposite side of Glassblower's Gulch. It was next to his mother's Diamond Colossus, scales sparkling as it watched the fight. Abel zoomed in to see Arvin frantically arguing with her, pointing and shaking his head. His mother had her lips pursed, like her son's anti-war tirade was irritating her. The Diamond Colossus had its brilliant silver eyes fixed on the fighting itself, the dragon's jaw grinding back and forth. Most long-wings breathed fire, but this breed exhaled a poison similar to cockatrice feathers'. It turned any living flesh it hit hard as diamond, which might've been cool, except it also turned internal organs hard as diamonds. A diamond heart looked good in a jewelry commercial, but it was not very useful for actually keeping a person alive.

The Colossus wanted to use its weapon. It looked pretty clear Arvin wasn't going to convince his mother to back down.

Abel scanned the horizon in the other direction and saw the Bone Reaper lying down. For a moment, he was afraid the ferocious Reaper had been killed. His stomach dropped to the floor and did a split like a gymnast. But then he pulled it back together when he saw the dragon breathe.

The Bone Reaper was held down by huge magnetic anti-flying cuffs, and neither Topher nor Roa was on its back. Abel scanned, trying to catch sight of them, but they were nowhere to be seen.

What he did find was the wounded Heartrender dragon and its rider, seated beside Ally on the back of her Yellow Stinger. They were talking—and then the rider pointed straight at Abel. Ally was wearing her riding glasses, which had all the same features of Abel's helmet. She zoomed right in on him, snapped her fingers, and pointed. Then she mimed ripping a throat out. It was a pretty offensive gesture on the edge of a battle, especially from your former seventh-grade teacher.

Then she pointed up. Abel followed her finger.

Deputy Manchi was on his Cobalt Reaper, Manchini, fighting against the Red Talon kinners Sax and Grackle on their Widow Makers. Abel's friends were tied up on the Cobalt Reaper's back. They'd been taken prisoner and thrown right into the heart of the battle.

As Abel watched, Manchi rolled his Reaper into a backflip to dodge a blast of bright red jewels from Sax's Widow Maker. Then he nearly caught an electric crossbow bolt Grackle fired, only escaping it when the Cobalt Reaper swatted the bolt from the air. Abel couldn't hear the sound from this far away, but the dragon screeched with pain.

Two more Red Talons were heading in to help. Sheriff Skint too had just broken away from a Green Flame Flinger short-wing to take on Manchi and Manchini. No way he'd survive being so outnumbered, but he didn't look like he was about to back down.

Manchi would go down fighting, and Topher and Roa would go down with him, tied up like meat in a butcher shop.

Abel had to stop the Red Talons.

Through his viewfinder, he saw Ally still looking at him. Her eyebrows were raised like she'd just asked a math problem in class, one Abel should've been able to answer if he'd been paying attention.

Abel was *rarely* paying attention in math class, but he didn't miss much in a dragon fight. She was forcing him to take her side.

He nudged Omi to fly toward Jazinda and Arvin Balk. The lithe young dragon weaved her way through the aerial melee, dodging flame and fog and jagged gems, as dragons fought all around her. She came in fast and snapped her wings open for a quick, stomach-turning landing.

"You have to call off the attack!" he pleaded as soon as he was close enough, pointing to where Topher and Roa were held captive on the Cobalt Reaper.

"You've got some nerve," Jazinda Balk scolded him, "to turn my own son against his kin and then demand I risk losing a war to save two kids I don't know."

"Well, you *do* know them," Abel said. "They helped me beat your dragons more than once."

"Not helping," Arvin muttered. "But, Mom, please? If it wasn't for his mother reaching out to you, the Thunder Wings would've gotten me for sure. You owe them."

"I owe the parents, not the son and his little friends," she replied.

"They're my friends too," Arvin argued back. "You're always telling me I need to be assertive if I'm going to lead. So I'm being assertive now. You'd do anything for your kin, right? Well, these kids are my kin, and I demand you call yours back at once!"

Jazinda pursed her lips, then looked from Abel to the sky and sighed. "Oh, the things I do for my child."

She whispered some orders into a bracelet. Without the slightest hesitation, every Red Talon in the air broke off their attack and retreated, leaving the Thunder Wings stunned and confused. Flames fizzled in dragon mouths, ice melted on frosted maws, and poison faded harmlessly from dragon snouts.

Only Sheriff Skint didn't retreat as ordered. She was still aimed right for Manchi.

"Call her off!" Abel said.

"She's on the payroll but doesn't exactly work for me." Jazinda shrugged. "And that deputy technically works for *her*. I consider this a matter between coworkers. I won't interfere."

"Mom!" Arvin objected.

"Don't press your luck," she said.

"I'll do this myself!" Abel snapped. He and Omi took off again to intercept Sheriff Skint. The wyvern raced as fast as her young wings would fly, corkscrewing into the air.

"I'm coming too!" Arvin shouted. Abel turned to see Arvin and his Ruby Widow Maker just behind them, matching Omi turn for turn. The boy had chosen friendship over safety.

"Don't get killed fighting a fight that isn't yours!" his mother yelled after him.

"Any fight alongside my friends *is* my fight!" Arvin yelled back, though the wind had probably snatched his words away before they'd reach his mother's ears. Still, Abel had heard them and couldn't help but smile. Arvin's Widow Maker looked hungry for a fight.

That was the thing about dragons; as much as Abel believed they had a right to peace and self-determination, most of them still loved a bloody battle. Maybe that's why they got along so well with people. They could gleefully bring out the worst in each other.

Abel dared a glance toward Glassblower's Gulch and saw, happily, that the Cloudflayer was making its way toward safety with huge, confident wingbeats. It carried what must have been the whole town on its back, over a hundred people. That was a lot, even for a Cloudflayer, but dragons didn't like limitations. Abel was certain that the long-wing would do everything in its power to get those people to safety.

Sure, war could bring out the worst in people and in dragons, but it could also bring out the best. In fact, Abel was counting on it.

"Now, Omi!" he yelled. "The signal!" His partner let out her cheerful cry.

"Chee! Chee! Chee!" She lifted her neck and flapped her wings. They swooped straight up into the sky, higher and higher, until the altitude made Abel's feet tingle and his belly tighten. Without a phone, the only way he could signal Silas and Lina to move in was by getting high enough for them to see him. He had to shut his eyes, though, because as much as he loved dragon riding, his fear of heights still lived in him. From time to time, it liked to remind him it was there.

As they reached the edge of the clouds, the air was so thin and cold, Abel feared he'd pass out. Omi's wings snapped open. She was vertical and perfectly still, like a statue in the sky.

The plan was to hover a moment so her wide-winged silhouette would be clear against the sun. Then she'd fly back down to the fight.

Except this was the highest Omi had ever been in her life. Abel realized too late that she couldn't possibly resist the chance to play.

"Oh no, oh no, oh no," he whispered. Abel wrapped his arms around her neck and pressed his cheek against her scales, shutting his eyes and holding on for dear life.

With a happy screech, Omi snapped her wings. Then she back-flipped with them flat against her body, nose pointed straight down, testing how fast she could dive.

Abel's stomach wrapped itself around his brain, or at least that's what it felt like. He was no doctor, but he was pretty sure all his internal organs were now tangled.

WHOOSH!

Omi had turned herself into a missile, speeding for the hard ground. Abel wasn't wearing a suit to protect him against g-forces. He felt the speed pressing his body back, pulling the blood away from his brain. His vision started to narrow. He couldn't even worry about the ground rushing up to him because he was pretty sure he'd be unconscious before Omi crashed into it.

She was young, so she might not know how to pull up in time. But she was also a dragon, so if she crashed, she'd be fine. Abel, however, would be the texture of a smoothie—one of the chunky ones with carrots and beets.

"Pull up!" he groaned through gritted teeth, desperate to keep himself awake. "Please . . ."

But Omi was too lost in the thrill of the dive to hear him, wind whistling through her horns.

"This . . ." He gasped. How could he get through to her? "This isn't . . ." Abel strained to get the words out. His lungs could barely get any air. "This . . . isn't . . . FUN!"

Suddenly, Omi opened her wings and swung her tail, slowing with a sickening sideways swing.

Abel flopped down against her neck again, catching his breath. "Thank you," he muttered. "Thank you . . ."

They were still pretty high up. Down below, Arvin's dragon was about to slam into Sheriff Skint's at the same moment that Manchi's Cobalt Reaper was going to hit them both with its fire.

Abel had to break them apart, but how? He was too far away! Also, he was still dizzy from the high-g dive. *So* dizzy that he was seeing double, in fact. Arvin and the other dragons swirled and blurred below him.

It was then that he let go of whatever he did have left in his stomach. Abel watched as his own unintentional breath weapon plummeted toward the fight.

He couldn't have gotten a better shot if he'd aimed.

His vomit splattered right onto Deputy Manchi's head. It hit with such surprising speed—and probably smell—that Manchi yanked the dragon's reins and sent his fireball high. The bright blue flare startled the sheriff and made her veer off.

Abel had stopped the fight in the most disgusting way possible. War was not pretty, but victory didn't have to look cool to be a victory.

Victory was also short-lived.

The dragons prepared to go at one another again. The Thunder Wings had also regrouped, preparing another attack on the Red Talons, who would be glad for the excuse to get back in the fight.

Abel's 3D yawn had only paused the hostilities, not ended them. His friends were all still in danger.

"Dive, Omi!" Abel said. "But maybe . . . like, a little slower this time?"

Omi dove, only a tiny bit slower. At the same time, Silas and Lina sped in low over the flats on an intercept course.

By taking Topher and Roa hostage, the Thunder Wings had made it clear they weren't willing to back down or give up control of the town. And the Red Talons weren't about to let themselves be attacked just because their boss's kid asked them to.

The fighting was about to start again, and Roa and Topher weren't going to survive it if Abel didn't get them free right away.

"Remember my friends?" Abel asked Omi. She dipped in the air a little, which Abel hoped was her way of saying yes. "We're going to have some fun with them, okay? Our goal is to get them onto your back. Savvy?"

Another midair bob, meaning yes.

"Great," said Abel. "The game starts on my count of one, two . . ."

Omi didn't wait for three.

She shot into the air like a popped balloon, twirling and swirling as Abel held on tight.

OMI CORKSCREWED TOWARD THE COBALT
Reaper. Abel kept his head low against her neck, both for protection and to keep himself from getting airsick again. The closer their bodies were, the less jolting her wild ride would be.

Manchi saw him coming, but at the same moment, he saw Sheriff Skint circling back on him, her Hog dragon preparing its blast of mucus.

He was already dripping with the contents of Abel's reverse breakfast. Perhaps the thought of dragon snot on top of it was too much for him.

He reined in his dragon and began a retreat toward Ally and her Yellow Stinger, who were racing up to defend him. If Manchi got behind her, his hostages would be in even more danger than they were now.

Still, Abel had to dodge the missiles the Thunder Wings were firing at him before he could do anything about it.

Boom, boom, boom.

Omi weaved between explosions, twirling and diving to avoid their blast radii, and using her claws and wings to knock other projectiles out of her way. Dragons fired their breath weapons from all directions. Though Abel felt the mix of hot and cold, smelled the sulfurous stench of poison, and even the crackling zip of jagged gems snapping past his helmet, Omi's wild flying protected him.

Why are they focusing all their power on me? he wondered a moment before he saw the answer.

Ally knew he would try to rescue his friends, and she knew rescuing them would keep him distracted. While he and Omi were dodging a barrage of attacks, her dragon had swiped both Roa and Topher off the Cobalt Reaper's back. They were now in the Yellow Stinger's claws.

Omi saw her goal being carried away and dove, sliding underneath the Cobalt Reaper and giving chase. A huge blob of Hog dragon mucus smacked into Deputy Manchi from above just as they passed.

ROAR! Sheriff Skint's dragon thundered in fury.

"BLARGH!" Deputy Manchi cried out. He tumbled off his Reaper's back and dangled from his harness, covered in slime. His dripping Reaper, fed up with the indignity of so many different fluids coating its scales in so short a time, bolted away. It seemed completely unconcerned that its rider was hanging upside down from its side. The Cobalt Reaper raced for the horizon, and Deputy Manchi's gurgling cries vanished into the gulch.

Sheriff Skint didn't chase her old deputy. She now had her sights set on Abel. The Hog dragon spat another blob.

Omi dodged, and a Thunder Wing missile blasted the mucus apart in the sky. As Omi chased the Yellow Stinger, Ally launched bombs from its tail, forcing them to duck and weave.

The wyvern sliced through the smoke. Omi came in low, trying to get underneath the black-and-yellow dragon so that Abel could reach up and free his friends from its claws. Abel didn't want to hurt Ally's dragon if he could help it, but he had a little stun gun that could shock the Stinger's feet and make them open.

Of course, the newly opened claws might then just slash him to shreds, but at least his friends would be free . . . if Omi caught them.

There were so many different things happening at the same time. Abel couldn't worry about all that could go wrong. Normally, a stressful situation would set his mind to catastrophizing and his thoughts to wild distraction, but he was totally sharp.

Maybe that's why Omi liked these high-stakes games so much. They were dangerous, but they made your mind and body feel totally focused on the moment. There was no worrying about homework or that weird zit or whether or not your crush felt the same way or what happens after a dragon bites you in half. There was no worrying about anything at all. You were living in your OODA loop: observe, orient, decide, act. Over and over again, until you'd won or were eaten. It really helped you focus.

Oops.

Or not.

Abel realized a moment too late he had, indeed, been distracted thinking about how not distracted he was.

Come on, brain! he scolded himself. *Work with me here!*

He hadn't noticed Ally's dragon perform a midair loop-de-loop. Omi chased her, but she'd let go of Abel's friends at the same time, tossing them down to the Thunder Wing on the Heartrender. The dragon caught them both in one foot and was now flying in the opposite direction.

Omi had to break off chasing the Yellow Stinger partway through the loop. She dropped toward the Heartrender, which meant Ally was suddenly behind them. Which was not a good place to have a dragon ridden by your murderous former seventh-grade teacher.

WHOOSH!

The first blast of flame went just over Abel's head. He heard the paint crackle on his helmet. Omi jackknifed down, then spun up, folding her wings as she zipped between two Pincer short-wings.

She came up below the Heartrender, weaving from side to side to stop Ally from getting a clear shot. Abel was just below his friends, almost close enough to reach up and grab them from the Heartrender's claws.

"Um, little help?" Roa shouted down to him.

A geyser of flame streaked by, shot by a Thunder Wing below. Another from Ally's dragon cut the air between them.

"A LOT OF HELP!" Topher screamed.

Abel had his stunner out but couldn't reach the Heartrender's foot. Omi was doing her best to dodge attacks from every direction *and* get close enough for Abel to rescue his friends.

He'd have to stand on Omi's back, but his safety harness strap kept him tethered too low.

"Steady, girl . . ." he told Omi. Abel bent down and undid his clip, then stood, unsecured, hundreds of feet in the air. Abel tried to balance like a sky surfer. Sky surfing was not a sport he had *ever* wanted to try.

The ground below them looked way too far and also way too close. The air was filled with smoke and flame, dragons swirling and tangling everywhere he looked.

He tried to look only at his friends.

"You can do this!" Roa assured him, locking their eyes on him, keeping him focused. Abel noticed Topher and Roa were holding hands. He really wished he had a hand to hold right then. Or a handle.

Omi lurched; Abel jumped and zapped the Heartrender's claw.

It yelped and opened its hand, dropping Roa and Topher onto Omi's back.

The problem was, they also fell into Abel, knocking him clear of Omi. A snotty blast from Sheriff Skint caught Omi's tail at the same instant, spiraling her away.

Abel fell. The air snatched his friends' screams as they lunged to catch him but missed his fingers by an arm's length or more.

He plummeted.

The world through Abel's helmet moved in slow motion.

Omi tried to turn, to catch him, but a stream of the Yellow Stinger's fire cut off her path.

Time became like ripples in a puddle on the sidewalk; on the outer ripple, he saw his parents around the dinner table. Lina and Silas were there too, all of them laughing. On another, he saw Roa in school with him, trading DrakoTek cards before class. He saw the moment he met Karak, his first dragon, looming in the dark of an abandoned can factory. And he saw Arvin in full Jewel dragon costume, performing as Ruby Scales in the military academy dorm. He saw Brazza; he saw Kayda; he saw the rodeo and the city of dragons, and everything and everyone he'd ever known, rippling out from the center of his vision.

So this is what it's like to die, he thought. *Weird. It's like falling.*

No, you sewer-soaked stooge! his brain yelled back at him. *You're actually falling!*

His brain's rudeness snapped him back to the moment. Abel fought to orient his body and get control of his limbs. He decided that instead of dying, he was going to aim.

He flipped himself over in the air like he'd seen videos of

Long-Wing Leapers do, except they made it look so easy. When *he* turned in the air, he just kept turning, until he was spinning out of control. Sky, then ground, then sky, then ground.

Okay, now maybe you are *going to die*, his brain told him. *Nice knowing you. Thanks for wearing a helmet.*

"No!" he yelled. Abel thrust his hands out. He'd caught a glimpse of scales looming up and just hoped that meant a dragon.

His arms nearly jerked out of their sockets as he caught the edge of a passing Short-Winged Pincer's tail. The dragon and its Red Talons rider turned to look at him in shock as he dangled there. Then the Pincer snapped at him, peeved to have an uninvited guest.

Abel let go, falling straight but controlled this time, to land on the back of a Thunder Wings Frost dragon who had been passing below. He landed behind *that* rider, who turned to him and immediately pulled a switchblade.

Abel saw his own surprise reflected in the kinner's helmet, just below the Thunder Wings symbol.

"Oh, sorry, wrong stop." He smiled and then leapt sideways into the sky, timing his jump so his feet hit the side of a Sawtooth Reaper's wing on its downbeat. Abel bent with the motion, and as the wing went up, he jumped, stretching his arms over his head and letting both his wrists get snatched by the Ruby Widow Maker he'd seen racing his way.

It was a perfect catch.

Arvin leaned over the side of the dragon and smiled down at Abel. "I didn't know you could do parkour!" he shouted.

"Neither did I!" Abel shouted up. "But I *have* watched a lot of videos of it. I think the dragons did most of the work for me, though. I, um—AHH!"

He was falling again. Arvin's Widow Maker had been hit with a blast of flame and startled into dropping him. The Heartrender was still after Abel, even as Sheriff Skint was now after Topher and Roa on Omi's back.

Oof.

Abel belly flopped onto a white-and-pink dragon. He looked up to see Silas in its harness, piloting the Candy Cane Reaper through the chaos in the air. The Red Talons had rejoined the fight, dragon battling dragon, kin versus kin. Grenades exploded against shock waves from stun guns; fire breath boiled ice breath to steam. Screeches and screams came from every direction.

"You sure know how to keep people busy!" Silas shouted over the din. "I almost didn't catch you."

"Thanks," Abel grunted, which was as much as he could get out. He was sweaty and winded and dizzy—and not the least bit in control of the situation around him. "Omi," he added, barely above a whisper, hoping his brother would know what he meant. He just wanted to be back on his dragon, to feel like he was doing more than falling around the battle.

"On it," said Silas. They flew fast through the fight, firing cotton-candy-colored flames to clear their path. Arvin's dragon was battling the Heartrender breath for breath, ruby shrapnel from its mouth against white-hot fire. Arvin was mostly playing defense, because he didn't want to hurt a dragon, even an enemy one. Jazinda, however, had fought off all the dragons around her and flew an intercept path toward her son. He saw her coming and fell away, drawing the Heartrender to chase him deeper into the fracas of the fighting kins. The Thunder Wings rider didn't know it, but Arvin was actually protecting him from his own mother.

How long he could do that was anyone's guess.

Violence just created more violence. Hurt dragons and hurt people kept hurting one another. With this many figures fighting in the sky, that was a lot of new wounds opening and old grudges growing. It wouldn't end, not by force of flame and claw. Fire couldn't put out a fire.

"Drop me onto Omi!" Abel shouted.

"Ep ep!" Silas confirmed. "I'll take care of Sheriff Skint." He leaned forward in his saddle and sped his dragon up. After closing the gap with stomach-punishing speed, they fell in behind the sheriff and her slime-spitting RAHD.

ROAR! The Candy Cane Reaper loosed an earsplitting sound. The Hog dragon and its rider both looked over their respective shoulders, at which point Abel stood. He ran down the length of the pink-and-white Reaper's tail, legs wobbling with fear but never faltering.

When he reached the end, Silas's dragon cracked its tail like a whip. Abel jumped with the motion, leaping over Sheriff Skint and her dragon and right onto Omi's back, where Topher and Roa caught him.

"I didn't know you did parkour!" Roa shouted.

"Neither did I," he repeated. "I just watched a lot of videos of it. I think the dragons did most of the work for me, though. Because I—"

"Watch out!" Topher tackled them both against Omi's scales as a streak of ice sliced the air. A Short-Wing Frost Wyrm chased them.

Omi bent her head to look right at it and snarled, showing the beginning of a blast of acid breath. The Frost Wyrm ignored its rider's commands and veered away. Meanwhile, Silas and his old boss circled, tangling and breaking, blasting and dodging.

"You were an officer of the law!" Silas shouted in rage and heartache, so loud Abel could hear it all the way from Omi's back.

"And I still will be after you're dead!" Sheriff Skint replied. "Who do you think will write the official report of all this to the Dragon's Eye? Me!"

"But you're a crook!" Silas objected.

"Not if I say I'm not!" Skint's dragon bobbed its stout head and spat a trick shot from underneath. The mucus blob hit Silas's dragon right in the face, choking it. The Candy Cane Reaper thrashed and panicked, falling from the sky.

Silas had to jump free as they crashed into the ground, rolling to safety and then rushing to pull the mucus from his dragon's clogged throat in double armfuls. He crawled all the way into its mouth to help it breathe again.

Sheriff Skint then came for Omi.

They had to put an end to this fight. Neither side could win, but both sides were inflicting intense damage.

Abel and Omi had one last trick up their sleeve.

The kins all thought they were fighting a serious dragon war, with all their weapons and kin symbols and oaths for vengeance. The sheriff thought she was winning. The kinners thought they would get control. None of them knew that Abel and Omi were going to make them all look ridiculous.

If there was one thing kinners and cops alike hated, it was being made to look ridiculous.

ABEL GAVE OMI THE SIGNAL to start her favorite game.

"Let's do the numbers!"

The Hog dragon was hot on their tail, which was just where Omi wanted it to be. Abel reached into the utility pack they'd loaded with spray paint cans back in the dragon city. He picked out a bright orange color with metallic glitter, something that would really catch the sun and sparkle.

Roa and Topher clipped themselves into the safety cleats on Omi's saddle.

"Here we go!" Abel said. "Moss dragon, eleven o'clock!"

"Not the clock thing!" Topher groaned. "Can't you just point to where it is?"

"He still doesn't know how to read a clock," Roa said with a sigh. "We're working on it."

"I do know!" Topher objected. "It just takes me a second. Anyway, there. I see it." He shook his spray can. "Let's do this thing."

With the Hog dragon still chasing them, Omi flew just below the bright green Moss dragon that was circling and trading shots with a Sapphire Widow Maker. Blue jewels sizzled against green burning swamp gas in midair.

The dragons were so preoccupied with each other, they didn't pay any attention to the young wyvern that raced under them, or the three kids who stood up on its back and sprayed a big number 1 onto the Moss dragon's belly.

Without even slowing, they hit the underside of the Sapphire Widow Maker with the number 3.

"What about two?" asked Topher.

"Odds and evens," said Abel. "Lina and Silas are doing evens."

Somewhere on the other side of the flying fracas, Lina and Silas had begun tagging the bottoms of every dragon they came across with even numbers: Red Talons and Thunder Wings alike. The rival kinners were confused, but they were also so busy trying to kill each other, they didn't do much to go after the kids who were tagging their dragons with harmless paint. Abel and his friends even got under Sheriff Skint to write 11 on the Hog dragon's belly armor.

Only Arvin hadn't begun tagging anything. His job was to put the number 36 on his mother's Diamond Colossus, but he was still trying to keep her from blasting the Heartrender to smithereens. Even as the Heartrender was trying to slice *him* in half with its jets of flame.

"I think Arvin's in trouble," Topher noted just after they tagged the belly of a Steelwing with the lucky number 13 (and nearly had their heads all bitten off in the process).

Abel saw Arvin diving toward the ground on his Widow Maker. The Heartrender's eyes rolled back to fire at him. Arvin's mother was just behind them, but being on such a huge dragon meant she was slower. There were too many other smaller dragons fighting in between for a clear shot. As Arvin sped up, she fell farther and farther behind.

"We should help him, right?" Topher suggested.

"I think he's got it under control," Abel said. Arvin's Widow

Maker skimmed the ground—and then Arvin did something very surprising for a rider to do in a dragon battle.

He jumped off.

Arvin hit the hard glass ground in a roll and pulled out his own spray can as he did. His Widow Maker pulled up without him. The Heartrender was going so fast it flew right over him in pursuit. Arvin's mom didn't even see him; she just followed the dragons, flying over her son a moment later. When she rose again into the open air, her dragon had the number 36 on its sparkling diamond-scaled belly.

Arvin looked in Abel's direction. Abel zoomed in on him through the helmet and laughed. Arvin was giving the Wind Breakers salute—the tip of his thumb in his mouth and his cheeks blowing out. It looked ridiculous, which was the point. Dragons didn't care if they looked cool; they *were* cool no matter what they did. Ridiculousness took real confidence.

"They're all tagged," Abel said. "Let's do this!" He tapped Omi on the neck three times, then shouted, "Number seven!"

Omi immediately turned and flew through the battle, seeking out the Greytoe Pincer they'd tagged 7.

When she found it, she flew up underneath and bopped it with her snout.

"One!" Abel shouted. Omi flew fast, seeking the first dragon they'd tagged, the Moss dragon. It was still fighting the Sapphire Widow Maker when it got snout bopped.

It stopped fighting for a moment, to stare after Omi in confusion.

"Is this really going to work?" Topher wondered.

"Dragons like to win," Roa explained. "It's in their nature. Once they think another dragon is beating them, they'll want to win at whatever competition is taking place. So we're giving them a new game to play."

Topher smiled. "You really are brilliant," he said.

"I see a problem; I figure out how to solve it," they replied. "Just like you with your designs." This time Topher blushed.

Abel rolled his eyes. If those two got any mushier with each other, he was going to throw up again. He didn't need his best friends canoodling behind him while he was trying to end a war. He focused on flying.

"Odds!" Abel barked. Omi started looking for *any* odd-numbered dragons and bopping them on their bellies one after the other. She weaved through their weapons, dodged their claws, and smacked three, five, seven, and nine, *chee*ing with delight each time. Abel didn't know if she was really having fun or just acting like it because she knew the plan, but when she went to hit the Steelwing with 13 painted in hot pink across its belly, a Purple Frostspitter dropped down from the clouds and beat her to it.

The Red Talons rider on its back was yelling and tugging the reins, but as Abel knew, when a dragon decided it wanted to play a different game, you had best let it. Otherwise, it might scrape you off like gum from the sole of a shoe.

Omi roared; the Frostspitter roared back, and Abel couldn't help but think of competitors trash-talking each other. He felt like he was getting the gist of dragon language after all. They raced side by side, hunting for the dragon numbered 15, a very confused Green Cloudscraper, ridden by a very confused Thunder Wing.

By number 17—a Red Dracario ridden by a Red Talon who was covered in prison tattoos—four other dragons had joined the fun.

They raced and weaved and spun and twirled, goading each other with snarls and chirps.

Grackle rode a Ruby Widow Maker just like Arvin's, but with the number 19 blazing in green paint on its belly.

He and his dragon had figured out the game.

"Don't you dare!" Grackle yelled, first at Abel racing in, then at his own dragon, who, once bopped, decided to join chasing down number 21. "AHHH!" He tugged the reins to no avail.

"Change it up!" Abel shouted. "Evens!"

A Goatmouth with an angry Thunder Wing on its back turned first, found the Heartrender with number 2 on it, and beat Omi to the bop. She made a sound like cheering, then found number 4 and regained her lead. Abel noticed Arvin's mother's dragon on the ground making huge claw marks in the glass desert, even as Jazinda Balk scolded it and tried to get it to fly. Her dragon was keeping score!

Before long, all the fighting had stopped and every dragon was playing Omi's game. The riders on both sides were helpless to stop them. There were nearly fifty dragons zipping this way and that, trying to bop each other's bellies, like a game of tag where anyone could be "It" whenever Abel shouted out a different number. Just to see if they could do it, he tried a math problem.

"Nine plus three minus one!" he yelled. Omi hesitated.

Grackle's Widow Maker tried to bop an orange wyvern with 12 on its belly, but the wyvern knew that wasn't right and shot poison at him.

Surprising everyone, the Goatmouth was the first to turn and find 11 on the belly of Sheriff Skint's Hog dragon, then bump it.

"How are dragons better at math than I am?" Topher groaned.

"No offense," Roa said, "but dragon dung is better at math than you are."

"How is that not offensive?" Topher replied.

"You know I think you're great at other things," Roa said.

Abel didn't tell them that he'd used the calculator display in his helmet to make sure he had the right answer, even though it was, like, first-grade math. He spotted Ally reining her Yellow Stinger on the ground. She looked up at the scene, stunned. She'd probably never imagined dragons could do math. A lot of the kinners looked stunned.

This will show them, Abel thought. *This will show them that their dragons are more than just violent beasts. They're thinkers with minds as capable as our own.*

"Two times five plus one!" he yelled. Every other dragon went to bop the Hog dragon again. Sheriff Skint was jostled right out of her saddle, left dangling from her harness.

"Twenty minus twelve plus three!" Abel yelled.

The Hog dragon got hit again. It snorted loudly as Sheriff Skint yelled.

"Nine plus two!"

Again, the Hog dragon. Again, Sheriff Skint screamed.

"I think she's had enough," said Roa.

Abel agreed. He wanted to show he was a good sport. And show that dragons were capable problem solvers. "No number!" he yelled.

Omi snapped her head around to stare at him, eyes wide.

"What?" Abel laughed. "Don't play with fire if you don't like it hot!"

She snarled and dove just as every other dragon tried to bop her from below. Omi was the only dragon without a number. She was "It."

Omi raced and twirled, dove and dodged, crying out gleefully as she flew. Abel and his friends whooped with the rush of speed until they all got jolted from below.

Ally's Yellow Stinger bopped Omi, joining the game.

"Fire! Shoot her!" Ally was screaming in the saddle, but her dragon had no interest in attacking. It wanted to keep playing.

Despite the protestations of the Red Talons, the Thunder Wings, and Sheriff Skint, the game went on. Arvin's Widow Maker joined the fun, with Arvin back on board again, and every time Arvin and Abel made eye contact through the fray, they both laughed. Abel learned he could use his helmet display to locate the dragon numbers, then suggest directions to Omi through the reins. Arvin kept up and even beat him to a dragon or two, so he'd probably figured it out too. They were competing with each other, and it was . . . fun!

"Keep up, mama's boy!" he yelled at Arvin when they got close.

"Eat scales, Unstable Abel!" Arvin yelled back, and their dragons roared trash talk at each other too.

They were all laughing in their own ways.

A few kinners gave up trying to fight and helped their dragons play. The game was a chance to remind them all that they were hooligans, not an army. No one joined a kin to go to war all the time. It was supposed to be fun! What good was hooliganism without a laugh or two?

The sun was setting by the time the dragons had tired themselves out and landed helter-skelter around the Glass Flats to rest. Thunder Wings and Red Talons mixed together without any fighting.

At least among the dragons.

The moment they landed, their exhausted riders leapt off and drew weapons, ready to start a bare-knuckle brawl with each other between the mounds of slumbering dragons.

Omi was the youngest among them, and yet they'd all kept up with her. Abel knew from the one time he'd babysat the upstairs neighbor's toddler that little kids played the hardest. He guessed that was true for dragons too. They'd all worn themselves out. The humans, however, still held their grudges when the fun was done.

"Don't fight!" Abel pleaded, but none of the kinners heeded him. "We just had so much fun! Why ruin it?"

"Shred 'em all to ribbons!" Arvin's mom urged her goons, leaping down from her own dragon with a set of brass knuckles on. She was a boss, but she did her own dirty work.

Right away, Ally came charging toward Abel on foot, a nasty-looking knife drawn.

"HOW DARE YOU HUMILIATE ME AGAIN!" she bellowed.

"Stay on your dragon's back!" Abel warned her. Omi was so tuckered out, she didn't even open an eye, let alone blast Ally with her acid breath. None of the dragons were taking part in the human brawl.

"I don't care how young you are," Ally said. "I'm gonna slice you open from toe to top!"

"That is no way for a teacher to talk!" Roa objected.

"Good thing I'm not a teacher anymore!" she yelled back.

"You were never a good one anyway!" Topher snarled.

"She really kind of was, though?" Roa whispered.

"You're gonna defend her right now?!" Abel said.

"It's just the truth." Roa shrugged.

"Get down here and fight me!" Ally yelled up at Abel.

"You shouldn't walk here," Abel warned her again.

"Fine," she said. "I'll come up and get you!"

She charged for him, running across the open ground.

What she hadn't noticed, of course, were all the monitor lizard holes. Sprinting toward Abel in a white-hot rage, Ally suddenly vanished with a quick yelp.

She'd fallen in.

"Did she just—" Roa said.

A jet of flame burst out of the hole Ally had fallen into.

Abel shuddered. "That sounded like a burp," he said.

They all looked at the hole for a moment, where their former teacher and current attempted murderer had just been eaten. It was a complicated feeling Abel contended with, somewhere between grief and relief.

"Live by fire, die by fire." Topher shrugged. Apparently, he wasn't feeling so complicated about it.

"Mom!" Arvin tackled his mother out of the fight, just before she herself fell into one of the holes.

Suddenly, jets of fire burst from the ground all over, sending kinners scrambling onto the nearest dragons' backs. Not all of them made it. The monitor lizards ate well.

"What now?" Arvin called over from the back of his mother's Diamond Colossus, where they'd both taken shelter. The sun had fully set by now, and stars twinkled overhead. Every dragon was like an island over a dangerous ocean—and every kinner was stranded.

"Monitors are nocturnal," Roa said. "We can't get down until morning."

"We'll have to fly," said Abel. "The dragons are all asleep. It'd be a very big mistake to wake them."

The dragons weren't the least bit bothered by the flames below their bellies. If anything, they tickled.

"On whose back?" Topher wondered.

The sky answered with a roar. Everyone looked up as Karak swooped in for a starlit landing, followed by a hundred other dragons.

"On ours," said Brazza, landing among them. She looked over the strange scene and then back at Abel. "We are very proud of you. You ended a war without a single dragon killed."

Abel looked around at his friends and family. "I had a lot of help."

"I meant 'you' plural," Brazza deadpanned. "All of you." She then growled something and Omi perked up, huge tail swishing with happiness. "Especially this one," Brazza translated.

Abel's heart swelled with a feeling that was even cooler than victory, even better than imagining himself a hero like Dr. Drago. He felt like a part of something big, and he felt proud.

Already, teams of dragons from Karak's flock were hoisting slumbering dragons and their riders into the night sky to carry them to the dragon caves.

"When they wake up, we'll give them the choice to join us," Brazza said.

"And the humans?" Abel asked.

"They'll be given the same choice," Brazza told him. She didn't elaborate on what would happen to the ones who declined to join the Wind Breaker cause.

"Omi will take you and your friends back to your parents now," Brazza continued. "I will meet you there to discuss things."

"What things?" Topher wondered.

Brazza closed her eyes in thought, then leaned low so her head was level with Abel's. She spoke in as quiet a whisper as her dragon voice would allow. It rumbled in Abel's bones.

"Our plans for Drakopolis," she said. "We think it's time you return home to unite the kins and liberate the city's dragons."

"Us?"

"You," Brazza agreed.

Abel nodded solemnly. He wasn't sure he could do this, but he knew he *had* to do this. He reached into his pocket and pulled out the delicate glass flower Kayda had given him. It was unbroken, and it was beautiful.

"What's that?" Arvin asked.

"Humans can destroy a lot," he said. "But we can create a lot too."

"Just like dragons," Brazza said.

"Just like dragons," Abel agreed.

He grinned wide as a wyvern's wings as he looked at his friends, at his brother and sister, and at Arvin. They were a motley group, hardened by fire, and a lot tougher than they looked. He was glad to call them his kin.

"We're going home," he told them. "To create something beautiful . . . Though we might have to burn a few things down first."

"Savvy," said his friends.

"Ep ep!" said his brother.

Brazza tilted her head back and roared her assent—as loud as a neutron bomb, but as lovely as the opening chord of a symphony. Scary and beautiful at the same time. It was so loud they could probably hear it all the way in Drakopolis.

If they couldn't now, they would soon.

ABOUT THE AUTHOR

Alex London is the author of over twenty-five books for children, teens, and adults, with over two million copies sold. He's the author of the middle grade Dog Tags, Tides of War, Wild Ones, and Accidental Adventures series, as well as two titles in The 39 Clues. For young adults, he's the author of the acclaimed cyberpunk duology Proxy and the epic fantasy trilogy The Skybound Saga. A former journalist covering refugee camps and conflict zones, he can now be found somewhere in Philadelphia, where he lives with his husband and daughter, or online at calexanderlondon.com.